Virginia Dawning

John Davidson

Charlottesville, Virginia

Virginia Dawning

a novel

For my children, John, Georgia, and Luke.

You are the pleasure of my life.

Prologue

Overgrown shrubs are a good place to hide for a man who wants to slip behind a little girl with a house key in her hand.

It was broad daylight in one of those subdivisions that had spread throughout the South in the 1990s, subdivisions with perfect lawns and white-collar parents and cul-de-sacs that assure pockets of quiet with no traffic, even when kids are walking home from the neighborhood elementary school. The twin rows of gardenias and hydrangeas planted against the house's foundation had grown large in that fertile soil.

A drop of sweat rolled across the dirty pores of the nose of the man crouched behind them. When it dripped it made a dark splotch on his denim jeans, which he had worn for several days straight. His own rank stink buffered him against the sweet smells of the flowering bushes.

Have you ever squeezed a stick in the palm of your hand? A good-sized stick from a forest-grown tree, like one of those big white oaks that burst out of the red clay of the rolling Virginia countryside -- have you ever gripped it so hard that your knuckles went white and the bark started to crunch in your clenched fist?

That's how the little girl's arm felt to the man as he dragged her face-up across the front lawn. He'd rendered her painlessly unconscious on the front stoop with little effort. She would be fine when she came to. But for now, pulling her slack body across the lawn was surprisingly hard work. He was panting by the time he got her to his old Chevy.

At first he tried to heave her into the back seat, but her book bag was still strapped to her shoulders, and it got snagged on the door. Scowling, he dropped her to the curb and yanked off the book bag. Then he got into the back seat himself, reached back out, and hauled her in. Closing the door behind them, he quickly scrambled from the back seat to the front seat and got behind the steering wheel.

A few moments later, the screech of his car's tires silenced the yellow warblers perched in the flowering trees that lined the neighborhood road.

After the car was gone, the girl's book bag lay alone on the black asphalt, motionless and quiet. The pony pictured on the back of it smiled at the bright blue sky above her, standing atop a nametag with "Mrs. Spilman's Third Grade Class" and "Mary Beth Marshall" written in a mother's handwriting.

A minute later, the warblers started chirping again.

"Thus you will know them by their fruits."

The Gospel of Matthew, 7:20

"Everybody has a plan 'till they get punched in the face."

Mike Tyson, heavyweight boxing champion

Part One

Chapter 1

Luke J. Andrews, M.D.

I was driving home with the music turned up loud, playing air drums on the steering wheel because there was no one else on the road to see, when my phone buzzed.

Glancing down, I saw my phone didn't recognize the number. Probably a patient. Sighing, I muted the music and picked up the call just before it went to voicemail.

"Dr. Andrews? Judge Carter here," the thick Tidewater accent said in my ear.

Silver-haired and nearing age 70, Circuit Judge S. Dalton Carter had been raised down in southeastern Virginia, where peanuts and cotton grew on flat peninsulas between warm, slow-moving rivers, far from up here in the hills and mountains of the Blue Ridge. He still used a silver cigarette holder to smoke Richmond tobacco. I had given him my personal number a few years ago, after I finished my residency training after medical school and moved back home. He had asked if he could call me when he needed an evaluation of a defendant's competency.

In cities of any real size, I wouldn't be doing competency evaluations. A psychiatrist or high-end psychologist would be there on day one. But here in rural Jameston County, Virginia, with about 10,000 living in town and another 20,000 spread out in the county, a family doctor like me was good enough.

Judge Carter got right to the point. "I have this fellow coming to my courtroom tomorrow afternoon." *Ah have this fella comin' to mah coht-room tomorrow aftuh-noon.* "He was arrested today, and they brought him in for his initial appearance. He started acting up as soon as he got in the courtroom. He was hollering all kinds of bizarre things. Made a great big fuss. He even growled at me, like a dog. Mr. Reynolds thinks it's a big fake. So do I. But to be safe, I would like you to do a quick competency evaluation tomorrow morning, before his arraignment and bond hearing. Think you could handle it?"

I considered that for a moment as the woods rushed past on either side of the road. The gorgeous springtime weather had made the trees burst with leaves so green and fresh that a person had half a mind to pluck one and taste it.

Mr. Reynolds was Jimmy Wayne Reynolds, the prosecuting Commonwealth's Attorney in this area. I played softball with him in the church league. He was probably right about the crazy act being a fake. It was the usual way defendants would try to set up a claim of insanity or avoid prosecution altogether due to supposed mental incompetence to stand trial.

I could do the eval for Judge Carter. I'd been planning to go over some lab work and test results early in the morning before seeing patients, but I could save that until later.

"Sure," I said. "I'll take care of it. What's he charged with?"

"Kidnapping. Little girl named Mary Beth Marshall."

14

I sharply inhaled through my teeth, and the judge made a kind of noise in agreement. Reports of a missing child in our area had been in the news today. Ever since I became a father, I sat up and took notice of those missing-kid reports.

"They find her yet?" I asked.

"Not yet," Judge Carter answered. "Law enforcement is putting everything they have into this. They think she's alive, but they also think he's got her locked up somewhere. And if he's got her locked up without food or water . . . well, they just need to find her real soon."

After a long pause, I asked, "What's the guy's name? The defendant, I mean. What's his name?"

I heard the judge take a deep drag on his cigarette holder, hold it a moment, then let out his breath.

"Hiram Legrand."

Chapter 2

Mary Beth Marshall sat on the floor with her chin on her knees and considered the three peanut butter and jelly sandwiches stacked on a paper plate next to the door across the gloomy, windowless room. Thin streams of light from the early dawn outside squeezed through cracks in the walls and the door jamb, revealing lines of a floating haze of dust.

Mary Beth had not seen Hiram Legrand since he had dumped her here on Monday afternoon, though of course she did not know his name. After dropping her on the dirty floor, he simply walked out, locked the heavy door, and left. For hours, she had not made a peep, certain he was still around. She had forced herself to stay awake all of Monday night, sitting up in the dark and staring at the door. But by yesterday morning, when he had not come back and she was getting very hungry and thirsty, she'd started screaming for help as loudly as she could, crying out for hours until her throat hurt and her lungs felt spent, but no one came. Finally, by the time it got dark again last night, worn out and not having slept in over a day, she'd stretched out in the dust on the floor and closed her eyes.

She had just awakened and seen the PB&J sandwiches, plus a quart of milk, standing sentry next to the locked door. They had been placed there while she was asleep. The sandwiches still had their crusts on them, and they weren't cut in half. Mom always cut them neatly in half for her.

16

Actually, sometimes Mom forgot and still cut them in fours, even though Mary Beth had not wanted them that way since kindergarten.

Well, maybe first grade.

Mary Beth rested her forehead on her knees and scraped her feet along the floor, feeling the grit and occasional pebble through the thin soles of her sandals.

Chapter 3

Ten minutes before the alarm clock was set to wake me up on the day I met Hiram Legrand, our three-year old daughter, Emma, climbed up into our bed and onto my chest, then started bouncing on her knees.

I lifted my head and cracked open my eyes.

"Hey, sweetheart," I whispered tiredly, dropping my head back on the pillow.

Emma started patting her little hands on my face. "Time to wake up, Daddy," she said.

My wife was still sound asleep on the other side of the bed. She didn't budge. She never budged. Sarah Andrews was not a morning person. Now that both kids usually slept through the night, getting them breakfast in the morning was usually my job.

"Not yet, baby," I said.

"But I'm hungry," Emma said as Henry, our four-year-old, walked into our bedroom, hopped up on our bed, and perched himself behind his sister on my legs.

"Just a few more minutes, kids."

"We're really hungry, Dad," Henry advised.

"All right," I said. "Give me just another few minutes, and I'll give you some Saturday cereal when I get up."

In our house, Saturday cereal was sugary cereal made for kids. Peanut Butter Crunch, Cocoa Puffs, that kind of thing. We tried to limit it to Saturdays, but I sometimes let them have it on a weekday. Both kids took the bribe and scampered out.

After they left, I stretched in bed for a while, feeling soreness in one of my hamstrings. It was the same one I tore back when I played small-time college football at the College of William & Mary. I had tweaked it the other day working out in the gym I built for Sarah and me in our old barn outside.

I kept stretching until I was awake enough to shuffle down the hallway over the smooth heart-pine floorboards to the kitchen and get the kids situated with breakfast. Then I grabbed an apple for myself and looked out the window to watch the dawning sun gently warm the rolling pastures and patches of woods outside.

My parents had raised my brother, sister, and me right here on this farm. My father's side of the family had lived in a small cabin near the crest of the Blue Ridge until the Depression, when the government kicked out all of the mountain folks to make room for Skyline Drive and the Blue Ridge Parkway. So one day when my grandfather was a little boy, the family left the cabin, came down to the good red dirt at the base of the mountain, and made this farm and a new life.

Work beckoned. I had to examine this Hiram Legrand guy for Judge Carter, and then get over to my medical practice before the first patients started to fill up my waiting room. So I hustled through my shower, threw on the business-casual clothes I always wore under my white lab coat, kissed my pretty wife in bed until she hit me with a pillow, and gave the kids a big hug on the way out the door.

I was running late, but the sweet smell of honeysuckle growing thick against the nearby barn slowed me down outside. Breathing in its clean scent, I lingered for a few moments at my truck. I looked back toward our house, the lilacs and azaleas lining the front porch, the purplish rhododendrons growing wild in the mountain woods rising behind the house. Through the open window upstairs, I could hear Sarah was up and brushing her teeth.

Work. One more deep breath, and I slid behind the wheel and started rolling down our quarter-mile gravel driveway to the state highway that headed to town.

***

I pulled into the small parking lot behind creaky old Cent-West, the Central-Western Virginia Regional Jail, and walked in the visitors' door. When I showed my identification to the dour woman working at the front desk, she handed me Hiram Legrand's orange-and-black striped file, which Judge Carter had sent over the night before. I read through the file while I waited for a jail guard to come get me in the dingy waiting room and take me back to the jail's infirmary.

Hiram wasn't from Virginia. He was from the cotton country on the Arkansas side of the Mississippi River. His rap sheet from the Arkansas State Police had multiple violent crimes on it. His first lengthy stay in prison had happened at the age of 17, when

Hiram carved his initials on some guy's face with his pocket knife after knocking him out cold with a tire iron. "H" on one cheek, "L" on the other, with a ragged smiley face on the forehead. While in prison for that, he apparently stabbed another inmate in the groin with a shank, though they were never quite able to convict him for that.

Hiram's last and longest stay in prison was occasioned by his attempted rape of a 19-year-old girl on a farm in Tennessee. She was a tough country girl, but she might have lost the fight if her father had not heard her scream. Hiram spent a week handcuffed to a bed in a Tennessee hospital with a bad concussion – the father had brought a shovel with him – and then spent the next eight years in prison.

It was when Hiram was released that the kidnappings began. His part of Arkansas had a huge increase in missing children reports after he was released from jail. Hiram had been questioned several times, but they were just routine interrogations the cops did of all convicted felons in the area. He'd had a complete psychosexual workup done when he was in prison, and while he was a miserable human being and probably a menace to adult females, he did not have any indication of pedophilia, which was one of several possible motivations for kidnappings of children. And the cops weren't even sure that the disappearances were kidnappings at all. They just never could find the kids. They all simply vanished.

Then came a toddler named Owen last year. Owen was standing behind his mother as she picked through discount clothes at a sidewalk sale on an east Arkansas town's Main Street. A storefront video camera across the street captured what happened next. As Owen's mother's back was turned, a man walking casually down the street simply leaned down and picked up little Owen without breaking stride as he passed by. On the grainy video, the man had kept walking right off the screen.

Owen's mother went on shopping for exactly seven seconds, then the silent video showed her stiffen and whip her head around. Even at a distance, you could see her body convulse with the sudden rush of adrenaline. Then she caught sight of her little son captured in the arms of a strange man about 60 feet down the street and getting farther away. The camera captured her mouth open in a silent scream of fear and rage, then her sprinting down the street and off the camera after him. Witnesses said the man saw the mother lion charging and had immediately dropped little Owen and run off.

It took a day for the Arkansas State Police to improve screen shots from the video enough to see the would-be kidnapper's face. Hiram Legrand.

Hiram was long gone by then. He had disappeared into the countryside and wasn't seen for a year, until yesterday. Fingerprints had been left on the book bag of Mary Beth Marshall, the little girl who had disappeared Monday on her way home from school in one of those subdivisions they had built just outside of town. Those prints got a hit, and with the FBI's help, the sheriff's department had Hiram's mug shot on their computers less than 10 minutes later.

During the canvass yesterday by sheriff's deputies, the manager of a local car wash pointed out Hiram, who'd drifted into town and started working there a few weeks earlier. As the arresting officers wrestled Hiram to the ground and cuffed him, he angrily claimed that Mary Beth was alive but that he wasn't going to tell anyone where she was until he got immunity from the prosecutor. Upon hearing that, one of the deputies drove his knee into Hiram's back hard enough to make Hiram curse through gritted teeth, but he was been good to his word. He clammed up and, apart from demanding a lawyer, refused to say another word.

I carried the file under my arm as a jail guard finally came to the reception area to get me.

As usual, Cent-West smelled like an old sock someone had peed on yesterday. The glint of fluorescent lights left a sickly green patina on the walls. An inmate trustee sweeping the floor carefully made no eye contact with me as the guard led me back to the infirmary where Hiram Legrand was waiting for me.

I'd learned that big state prisons and smaller regional jails like Cent-West are very different. Cent-West did not employ the tough prison guards you see in movies. Cent-West guards were mostly softies who hoped to break into a job as a regular deputy in the sheriff's office. They wore white uniforms with black leather belts, which made them look like powdered jelly doughnuts with a black rubber band squeezing the middle.

I looked around as we burrowed deeper into the jail through a series of metal doors that the guard unlocked with one of his big brass keys. The jail was old and simple. No razor wire, no dogs patrolling the perimeter. Just some bars and locked doors and powdered jelly doughnuts with keys for the doors. Most of the inmates there were harmless knuckleheads who had pulled their second DUIs, or had taken a few hundred bucks that didn't belong to them, or were the winners of a drunken fistfight in some country bar. Just misdemeanors, for the most part, which earned them a week or two in the regional jail.

But sometimes the really bad guys, the ones charged with rape, murder, malicious wounding and other heavy stuff, were held here at Cent-West while they awaited trial. Soon enough, a jury would determine they were guilty beyond a reasonable doubt, and they would be sent off to the state prison system, the real hardcore lockups. Those prisons were always put way out in the middle of nowhere to create guard jobs for the tough young men in that area. They had plenty of razor wire and dogs and such.

The guard finally dropped me off at one of the windowless interior rooms that served as the infirmary. Hiram was already there waiting for me. The guard left us alone as soon as I walked in the door, locking it behind him.

Hiram was seated in a cheap plastic chair, across from a matching one for me, with a folding table between us. Even seated I could see Hiram was tall but with skinny shoulders and a small paunch. He had dark hair, a goatee, and deeply-set eyes. His nose was dotted with blackheads.

Hiram reeked. Most guys smell bad after some time in the can, even if they used all three of their allotted showers every week. You can't help getting that old-pee-and-sweat smell in your hair, skin and clothes. But even with five feet between us, this guy was something else. I sat down, breathed through my mouth, opened his folder on the table between us, and used my best professional voice.

"Mr. Legrand, hello. My name is Dr. Andrews," I told him. "I'm here at the request of the Court. I need to talk with you, if that's ok with you."

Legrand looked at me with an expressionless face. Then he slumped in his chair, looking down and scratching his leg under the table, like he had a mosquito bite or patch of poison ivy on it.

"I need to talk with you," I repeated.

Without stopping scratching, he looked up and said, "Well then talk, dumbass."

"You can call me Doctor. I'm here because Judge Carter asked me to tell him whether you are able to understand the charges against you and to participate in your own defense."

This was a minor ploy. Most of these people understood those magic words and leapt at them, eager to show me by some random behavior that they were nuts. If Mr. Legrand followed suit, I'd already be on the way to a conclusion that he was a malingering, lying, and mentally-competent piece of garbage.

"Yeah?" Legrand asked without much interest as he kept scratching away at his thigh or whatever was itching him. He had a high-pitched twang that sounded like an out of tune banjo. "I didn't do anything. I'm being set up." He paused for a second, then seemed to focus on me for the first time. "What you here for again?"

"Well," I continued, "we just need to make sure you're okay. Medically speaking."

"What for?" He scowled with half his face, the right side contorting up and the left staying flat. His scratching quickened, and he repeated, "What for?"

"You have had some serious charges leveled against you. If you did not do these things, it's important that you be able to help your lawyer defend you in court."

He flexed his cheek muscles in what passed for a smile. Then he ignored me as he bent his head to look at whatever he was scratching. When he did, I could see white skin in the greasy part in his almost-black hair.

Skin and hair is as good a place as any to start a medical history.

"Let me start by asking you a few questions about your physical health," I said. "Do you have any diseases of the skin? Melanoma, I mean skin cancer, anything like that?"

He was still ignoring me and grinding away at his itch. Something about the way he was scratching invited me to at least do a cursory job as a doctor and take a look at it. Given his apparent unfamiliarity with hygiene, I was sure I was going to see some angry dermatitis, maybe a jock itch earned more by dirty underwear than aerobic exercise. I half stood out of my chair and leaned over the table.

I sat back into my chair three times as fast as I had gotten out of it. The man was masturbating. He had been grinding away under the table this whole time. He laughed a breathy, wheezy laugh, then thrust his hips triumphantly upward, his face full of mirth at my surprise.

An impulse flashed through me to use the heavy file I had on Legrand to slam his thing flat for him. But I settled for giving him a nasty look.

He relaxed his legs, and his privates disappeared under the table again. "Oh, come on, it's all natural, ain't it? Besides, this," he gestured to the site of his recent masturbation, "ain't a bad way to pass the time while I'm locked up."

"Well, hold off on passing the time until later, after I'm gone. Then you can do whatever you want."

26

"Oh, you don't mean that, do you?" Legrand asked me, though he stopped touching himself. "Do whatever I want? No sir, you don't mean that at all."

He paused and peered at me for a few moments. Then he asked, "You got any kids?"

"No."

"Huh. But you're a churchie, ain't you? I bet you are. I can tell. You got that air about you."

I had nothing to say to that.

"So let's stop screwing around and get to it," Legrand said. "You're thinking maybe I hurt that little girl. Right? Well, I ain't."

"No?"

"No," he said. "At least, not yet." Then he smiled at me, brown tobacco stains filling the crevices between his teeth.

Ol' Hiram didn't know it, but the medical part of my exam was already over. This guy could play with himself all day if he wanted. He could even start eating it for lunch, for all I cared. I was going to opine from the depths of my medical education that he was plenty competent enough to have a trial, which would end with him rotting away in prison. If I wrote it up right, it'd be really hard for a psychologist or psychiatrist to come in later and convince Judge Carter to go the other way.

Legrand's small eyes bore into my face, trying to read my expression. Then he snorted and said, "That little girl's probably getting right hungry about now, I bet. Thirsty, too."

Son of a bitch. As disgusting as he was, he had been her caregiver until he was arrested last night. The little girl he had locked somewhere was probably scared out of her mind, and he was pleased with himself. I wanted to knock his teeth out for him.

27

"Well, where do you have her locked away?" I asked. "I'd be happy to go feed her for you."

He laughed his wheezy laugh at me.

"You ain't no cop. You ain't nobody. And I ain't telling you nuthin'. So you just get on with your exam. Doctor."

Chapter 4

Mary Beth kicked crusts of bread out of her way as she walked over to the ray of morning daylight streaming through the biggest crack in the wall. She squeezed her finger into the widest part of the crack, the edges crumbling a little as she pushed her finger to the outside air. Compared to the musty air inside, the warm breeze outside felt light and clean on her fingertip.

Pulling her finger back in the room, she looked at the crack for a long moment before sitting back down, facing the wall. Then she leaned back on her hands, lifted her bottom from the floor, and slammed her heel into the middle of the crack in the wall. Her sandal made only a muted thump against the wall, but little crumbles of material rolled into the room, and upon inspection the stream of light squeezing in from the outside through that crack was just a tiny bit brighter and bigger.

Mary Beth again leaned back on her hands and set her jaw. Then she jack-hammered her leg, slamming her foot over and over into the wall.

Chapter 5

My medical office was in an antebellum red-brick house with white trim in the heart of the historic downtown area. I was late after my early-morning session with Hiram Legrand at the jail. My full-time nurse, Jan McDaniel, was impatiently waiting for me in her yellow polo and white slacks when I arrived.

Soon I was in the groove and catching up, bouncing quickly among the exam rooms. I had handled an upset stomach, poison ivy, heavy allergies, an achy back, and an embarrassed birth control pill request by the time I had to walk a few blocks down the street to Rev. Crosley's house. Jan handed me a printout of his chart on the way out the door.

Rev. Crosley was my childhood pastor. He was past retirement age already when he stopped preaching at our church a year ago, and then only because the cancer had come back. I did everything I could for him, got him to the best oncologist in Richmond, and I thought we might be able to beat it again. But then I got the horrible news a month ago. I had waited until the end of the day, after work, to go to his house to tell him. I couldn't beckon the man who had baptized me come to my office so I could tell him that he probably would die before the year was out. When I

30

had choked out the words in his kitchen, he hadn't seemed surprised. No tears, no disbelief, no anger. Instead, he had simply touched my cheek with his hand, then put out a plate of peanut-butter cookies and two huge glasses of cold milk for us. He made me stuff myself while he told funny stories, until finally I laughed so hard that he was able to convince me it was ok to leave him for the night and go home.

With Jan guarding the fort, I made the five-minute walk to Rev. Crosley's house under flowering trees and past patches of periwinkle in front of the other old homes on High Street. I could hear the rubber soles of my Rockports padding on the sidewalk as the scent of an early-morning grass cutting wafted through the air.

After Rev. Crosley had retired and vacated the parsonage next to the church to make way for Rev. Rigsby, our church's new minister, he had stayed in town and rented a small bungalow with a deep porch filled with rocking chairs. I found him rocking away and humming to *I Second that Emotion* by Smokey Robinson on the little iPhone speakers plugged into the outside outlet on his front porch. I took the steps to his porch two at a time with a smile on my face.

"Pastor!" I called out with fake good cheer. "How are you feeling?"

"Good enough," he said. "And how about y'all? How's the Andrews gang?"

"Doing great," I said. "Henry's T-ball team won their game this past weekend. They're not supposed to keep score, but you know the kids all do. And Emma has been talking up a storm this week."

"That's great," he said. "I know y'all were worried about her a few months ago, but as I recall it, you were speech-delayed too when you were a little tyke. Though we didn't call it speech-delayed back then. We just called it being quiet. How's Eli doing?"

"Good," I answered reflexively, and Rev. Crosley nodded. He knew my younger brother was living in the Wytheville State Prison for selling marijuana out of the back door of the tavern where he had tended bar down in Richmond. The cops should have seen that he wasn't a serious dealer; he just sold to local potheads to make some extra money on the side. But it didn't help that Eli's supplier, a Budweiser truck driver who occasionally dropped off more than cases of beer along his route of taverns and convenience stores, had already been caught and, in an effort to get a good deal from the prosecutor, exaggerated about how much stuff he delivered to Eli and others. The Richmond judge had nailed Eli with a stupidly long prison sentence.

"Seen much of him lately?" Rev. Crosley asked.

"Not as much as I'd like to," I said. At first I had kept up with Eli after he was sentenced, getting down there for visits and sending him letters with updates of the kids' latest milestones and stuff going on at the farm, and an occasional clipping from our hometown newspaper. Just some things to keep him connected. But I had really slacked off in the past year. If it wasn't for Eli's getting email privileges at the prison last year, we probably wouldn't have touched base for months. What with the kids and building the medical practice, I just kept running short on time.

It hadn't always been so. We'd been close when I was a teenager and he was a little kid, especially after our folks died. I'd pretty much raised him myself after that.

I took a closer look at Rev. Crosley. His color wasn't so good, and he looked tired. Probably just a little short on sleep, but I made a mental note to have one of the nurses stop by tomorrow to double check on him.

On the iPhone speakers, Otis Redding's *Sittin' on the Dock of the Bay* accompanied us as I got down to the business of showing Rev. Crosley his most recent lab results.

Chapter 6

Mary Beth's sandal was wrecked. Its heel had popped off after the first few times she had slammed her foot against the wall. But the small gap in the wall had grown a tiny bit bigger each time she kicked it, so she had kept going until the sole of the sandal had completely separated from the straps and simply fallen off her foot, which felt hot and raw. She lowered her leg down to the floor, letting the fine dust coolly soothe her hurt foot.

The gap in the wall was now maybe two inches, letting a strong stream of light into the room.

Mary Beth scooted over to her right, took a deep breath, held it, and started slamming the wall with her other foot.

Chapter 7

"And so, your Honor, I believe that Hiram Legrand is competent to understand what's happening in court and to assist his own counsel," I told Judge Carter as he peered down at me on the witness stand, his silver hair complementing the rich mahogany of the judicial bench. "My professional opinion is that he is perfectly capable of understanding, and facing, the consequences of what he has done and to assist his counsel in his own defense. I hold that opinion to a reasonable degree of medical certainty."

Out of the corner of my eye, I could see Legrand's scowling and angry face on the closed-circuit monitor they used here and at the jail to do bond hearings so the sheriff didn't have to transport prisoners to court for pretrial hearings. Legrand was sitting in a windowless, cinderblock room in the jail at this very moment, watching me ruin his effort at short-circuiting a trial.

I had made up my mind about exactly how I was going to nail Legrand a few minutes before I walked into the courthouse, as I sat on one of the benches outside in Court Square. Jimmy Wayne Reynolds had long ago taught me how to testify in court, the things judges and lawyers needed to hear, the kind of words I had to use. And I wanted to be extra sure that no defense lawyer could pick it apart. So I had sat there on the bench in the shade of the gigantic pin oak tree at the corner of Court Square and quietly worked on the tone and facial expressions I was going to use to make sure Legrand went down in flames.

Legrand's defense lawyer, a northern transplant working in the regional public defender's office, had looked increasingly glum as I sliced through his client's potential future claim of insanity. Hiram wasn't crazy. He was just evil. Judge Carter had no problem finding him competent to have the proceedings go forward. I watched from the gallery as the judge immediately switched over to a perfunctory hearing on whether Legrand would be released on bail pending trial.

"This man has been charged with a heinous crime, Your Honor," Jimmy Wayne was saying on behalf of the prosecution. He was a bulky guy, but for some reason he wasn't a real strong hitter in our softball games.

"And while the evidence is not yet as complete as it will be by the time of trial, he is a danger to the community," Jimmy Wayne continued, displaying his habit of stabbing the table in front of him with his index finger while making his points. "He should be held without bond."

Northern transplant had a given name – Eric Wajda – and he actually was a good guy. Wajda was lean and had perpetually tanned skin set off by thinning blond hair. He had grown up near the ocean somewhere in southern New Jersey in the 1980s, and even now in middle age, he still had a laid-back, surfer-dude way of talking. The only time I ever saw him get animated was when I started to equate people from the Jersey Shore with people from New York, the way they did on television. I thought he was going to have a coronary event. He proceeded to lecture me about how Hollywood had gravely defamed his home by doing the same.

Wajda was putting on his game face. "Your Honor, we do not have proof that a crime occurred at all, let alone that Mr. Legrand committed it," he said. "The girl is missing. But that does not mean she has been kidnapped. She could be a runaway. Or maybe she took a shortcut through the woods and got lost. Kids get lost sometimes, judge, and they're found in a day or two, with nothing worse than a few tick bites and some scratches from a briar patch after getting turned around in the woods."

And sometimes the stories end badly and involve a body stuffed in a culvert or an abandoned well, I thought to myself. Especially after more than a few days had passed. Mary Beth had been missing almost 48 hours already.

Wajda pressed on. "Even leaving that aside, defending Mr. Legrand will be much easier if he is free and readily able to meet with me, to examine the prosecution's evidence and to find witnesses," but Judge Carter was already shaking his head. No dice.

Judge Carter sometimes went easy on defendants in non-violent drug cases, but he richly deserved his reputation for being rough on violent criminals. This animal had a little girl locked up somewhere, and there was no way any judge would release him from custody before trial. Hiram Legrand was staying put, and I was glad.

Chapter 8

Mary Beth put her face right up against the 3-inch gap in the wall that she had kicked open. Compared to the dark, dusty smell inside this place, the outside air smelled clean and fresh, as fresh as her mother's bathrobe coming out of the dryer. The song of a bird outside came as a welcome friend into the room.

Mary Beth stood up to her full height and surveyed the dark room, looking again in vain for any kind of tool she could use to scrape at the edges of the gap and make it wider. She was barefoot now; her ruined left sandal was on the floor aside the ruined right one.

A few minutes later, if any people had walked up from the outside, they would have seen a curious sight. They would have seen a lively little hand growing out of a gap in the wall, pawing and pulling and yanking at the edges. Again and again, they would have seen the hand's delicate fingers growing white with pressure before the edge crumbled a little and the hand lost its purchase. Then it would start pawing again to find a new grip.

Chapter 9

Richard Byram and Jeanne Healey were waiting in my reception area when I got back to the office after the hearing in Judge Carter's courtroom. They handed me their Federal Bureau of Investigation cards as we walked past waiting patients to my little office in the back. The cards identified them as members of the FBI's Crimes Against Children Unit – Southeast Region. They got right to the point.

"Dr. Andrews, we need your help," Byram said. "We need you to go back to the jail and meet with Hiram Legrand again."

"What? Why?" I asked.

"Because we think you might be able to get him to give us more information," he explained. "The most important thing is to find Mary Beth Marshall. Every hour that goes by makes it harder to find her. We've got to find her as fast as humanly possible. It's a CANR, but now we've found the kidnapper."

"What's a CANR?" I asked.

"Child Abduction-No Ransom," Ms. Healey answered for him. She was a lean woman with watchful eyes and a severely short haircut that accentuated her long neck. She somehow looked both intense and weary at the same time, like one of those overtrained Russian gymnasts in the Olympics who desperately want to win but will be enormously relieved when it's all over.

"Dr. Andrews, let me tell you about us," she continued. "We're both members of the CARD team assigned to this abduction. 'CARD team' stands for Child Abduction Rapid Deployment team. In every suspected kidnapping of a child, a CARD team establishes an on-site command post to lead the investigation. Because we're some distance from any FBI office, we've set up shop in the sheriff's office.

"For a CARD team, getting the child back safely is the most important thing. Here, we don't have the kidnapped child yet, but we do have the kidnapper. We need someone to gather info from him that we can use to find Mary Beth. We think that someone should be you."

"Wait. Why me? I mean, are you positive Legrand is your man?"

"Absolutely," she said. "He left some fingerprints on her book bag. When it turned out those fingerprints belonged to a convicted felon, obviously that caught our attention. Then the special agent in charge of our Little Rock field office in Arkansas let us know Legrand was a person of interest in several old abductions there. Plus Legrand blurted out that the little girl was still alive when he got arrested. He's our guy. He's probably a snatcher."

"A what?"

"A snatcher. That's a kind of guy for whom the rush is in the snatching. He just likes to take kids. He doesn't ask for ransom. The good news is we don't think Legrand molests them. The bad news is that he's got a history of violence. He might hurt them or kill them. Or he might simply stash them away until they . . . well, until who knows what."

Agent Byram took back over. "He's the only one who knows where Mary Beth is. We think he might have hinted at where she is in your exam. And we're acting on that. But we need more information."

"He hinted at where she is during my exam? How do you know what he said to me?" I asked.

"Because we planted a recording device in the Cent-West jail's infirmary first thing this morning, and we listened to your examination of him," he said matter-of-factly.

"Really?" I asked. "You can do that? I mean, I personally don't care about doctor-patient privilege here, but won't he sue you?"

Byram made a face. "Doctor-patient doesn't apply here. You're not his doctor. You're doing a job for the court; you're paid by the state."

"Well, what'd he say that was so important?" I asked, but Ms. Healey was already tapping on her tablet. She scrolled ahead on the audio file to the point she wanted, and hit play.

The quality of their equipment must have been very good. The recording of Legrand's voice and my own voice during my examination in the jail that morning was crisp and clear:

> "I see you got a big file on me there. What's in it?" Hiram asked in his twangy voice.
>
> "A lot," I said. "But most of it doesn't have anything to do with my examination today."
>
> "Did you read it?" he asked.
>
> "Yeah."
>
> "Like it?"
>
> "What?"
>
> "Didja like it? What you read. Didja like it?"

41

"Except for medical issues, I'm not interested in it," I answered.

"Yeah, right."

"Believe what you want."

"I will," Legrand said. "Now you best not lose that file. I don't want it getting in the wrong hands around here. That's private stuff, and there's some real bad guys in this place. You keep it under lock and key, somewhere close by. You lose it, you gotta answer to me."

"Is that some kind of threat?" I asked, trying to sound mildly amused and relaxed.

"I'm just telling you. You need to lock it up wherever you lock up all your own valuable things, and you keep the key yourself. You know the ad. You lock it, you keep the key."

Byram gestured at Ms. Healey to stop the recording, and he leaned forward in his chair to rest his forearms on my desk. He was a late middle-aged man with mild blue eyes and gray hair swept back from a reddish, furrowed forehead.

"Midsouth Storage is the only storage facility in this town," Byram said. "And it's only a quarter of a mile from the carwash where Legrand worked these past few months. You probably never paid attention to it, but that's the exact sign they have out front – 'U lock, U keep key.' So we immediately had the sheriff's deputies open every single storage unit at Midsouth while you were testifying in court earlier today, and she's not in any of them."

He looked at me for a few moments with his mild blue eyes, which were a little bloodshot, before continuing.

42

"A storage facility, a quiet one, isn't a bad place to hide a kid. We've had it happen before. Most people who use them are strangers to each other, they're all locked tight, and there's usually no one around to ask questions. There must be a hundred or more storage facilities within a three hour drive of here, and we need to search each one, at least until we get a better lead than this. We have local law enforcement in each county going to each one, just as fast as we can get them moving. They all have a picture of this."

He flipped over a 5 x 7 photo of Mary Beth, obviously a school picture. She was a pretty little girl with a freckled nose and pink ribbons in her hair. Her mother had put her in a light green dress that day, surely her best for picture day.

"The truth is that local law enforcement, especially in the rural counties, just don't have the manpower to do this for us quickly," Byram said. "They'll get who they can, when they can. We don't even know Legrand has her in one of them. It's just a guess, based on what he said to you. That's why we need to know more. We figured you could go back in there and talk to him some more. You could claim that Judge Carter had second thoughts about your testimony and ordered you to do a more thorough examination and report back."

"That would never happen," I said.

"Yeah," Byram said, "but Legrand doesn't know that. He's never been in this situation. Plus if you acted a little annoyed with Judge Carter, maybe hinted that he's a flip-flopper and often changes his mind, it'd give you an excuse to spend extra time there and him a reason to talk more."

I looked at Ms. Healey's tablet on my desk. She had placed it next to a framed picture of Sarah and the kids sitting in the sand with their backs to the ocean in Virginia Beach last summer. A wave had unexpectedly rolled up the beach to where they were building sand castles. The wave reached Sarah just as I had snapped the picture. Behind our smiling children, frozen for posterity in the picture, Sarah's back was arched and her mouth was wide open in shock as the cool seawater suddenly splashed her sun-warmed skin. I knew as soon as I took the picture that it was a classic.

"Wouldn't it be better to get one of your agents in there, I mean someone undercover, and make him Legrand's cellmate or something?" I asked.

Agent Byram shook his head at that. "Negative. Everyone who's been in the system, like Legrand, knows that inmates are always looking to trade information to a prosecutor in exchange for getting a good plea deal. There's no way he'll spill his guts to a new cellmate on day one, even if we could install an undercover there right away without arousing suspicion. We need information from this guy, and right now. You gotta go back in there."

I started to respond, but Ms. Healey gently talked over me.

"Dr. Andrews, we know it's not easy to do this. But it would be such an enormous help to us. We can't send you back right away; we at least need him to think that maybe Judge Carter had second thoughts and called you later this afternoon – but if you would go back today, it would be a huge help to us. To her. To her mother."

Chapter 10

Mary Beth's fingers were raw, but she didn't notice. The gap in the wall was nearly 6 inches now. Sweet outside air gushed into the room.

Her head cocked sideways, she pushed her face into the gap until her temples touched the top and bottom of the gap. She could see the outside, the wisps of grass, and the wild flowers at the edge of nearby woods. She stubbornly pushed her head harder and harder into that gap, until the skin on her face was stretched and the pressure of wood on bone hurt and her head would go no further. Making the gap wider by another inch, maybe two, was all it would take to make it big enough to slip through. But there was no crumbly stuff left to rip at. Just hard wood.

With some effort, Mary Beth tugged her head back into the room, scraping a little strawberry on the skin of each temple.

Chapter 11

2:00 p.m.
Wednesday afternoon

My old college roommate, Arthur Turner Dixon, Jr., Esq., made
partner at the Huntington & Powell law firm in record time. His
office in a high-rise building in downtown Richmond had a spectacular view of the James River as it rushed down from the mountains to the west, then slowed, warmed and grew wider as it me-
andered east, down to the Tidewater plantations growing lushly
on its fertile banks.

"A.T." in the office, Arthur to his parents, and Stumps to his
friends, he was already the best commercial litigator in Richmond
and one of the best known African-American lawyers in Virginia.
I'd known Stumps was a brilliant guy back when we were room-
mates at William & Mary, which didn't give athletic scholarships
for wrestling back then. Rather, it was an academic scholarship
that had taken him from a rundown high school to the oldest operating college in the South.

Because college football is a fall sport and wrestling is later in
the winter, Stumps and I were able to watch each other compete.
Our senior year, Sarah and I drove 900 miles to St. Louis to watch
him in the NCAA championships. He was fantastic. Barely 5'6",
he plowed through his weight class at the tournament and won in

the finals by pin. I watched talented wrestlers shoot in at his legs to take him down, only to stop shudderingly short, as if they had slammed into a pair of oak-tree stumps. I bellowed "Stumps!" in the stands every time it happened.

"A.T. Dixon here," he answered when I hit his office number on my speed dial. His soft Richmond accent offered a faint to vanishing pronunciation of his R's.

"Stumps! How's it going? Still representing The Man and sticking it to the little guy?"

"Hey, Luke, what's up? Did the Board of Medicine finally find out that you got your medical degree from a classified ad in the back of Rolling Stone magazine?"

"Ha. Good one. So how's everybody? How's Turner?" Turner was Arthur Turner Dixon, III, his five year-old son with his ex-wife, Lydia.

"Growing up too fast," Stumps said. "I'm coaching his soccer team this spring, which mostly means I'm in charge of handing out Goldfish crackers and juice boxes after the game."

Lydia had walked out on Stumps two years ago, and the ensuing divorce had been brutal. Here, Stumps's partnership in the vaunted Huntington & Powell law firm was a negative. The high-end world of Big Law was not well liked in the gritty Richmond divorce courts. Losing primary custody of Turner to Lydia and getting him only on the weekends was one of the few losses Stumps ever had experienced in a courtroom. Though Richmond was almost 100 miles away from Jameston, he had brought Turner to our farm on several of those weekends to play with Henry. It gave the two of us time to shoot the breeze and throw down a beer or two.

47

"Well," I said, my voice lowering to get down to business, "I've got a problem. You know how I do those competency evaluations once in a while for the judge up here?"

"Yes."

"I did one this morning," I said. "The cops think the guy kidnapped a little girl up here. The FBI thinks he's a 'snatcher.' I gather that means that he gets his jollies out of snatching the kid, and he's not looking to give her back."

"Oh, the poor kid," he said.

"Yeah, no kidding," I said. "I examined the bad guy this morning and then testified just an hour ago that he's completely competent. That's not the problem. The problem is that the FBI wants me to try to get information from him. When I met him this morning, they had bugged the prison infirmary, and he said a few things that they thought were . . . well, I guess you'd call them clues. They think if I go back in there, he might say more about where she is."

"Then what are you waiting for?" he asked. "Get back in there and try to get any info you can that can help."

"Really? What about patient privacy and all that? Can't I get in legal trouble if I let them record a conversation with a patient?"

"Who's going to complain?" Stumps asked. "That kid needs help. The FBI says you can help. You should help. As your legal counsel, I hereby advise you to get your tail back in there before I drive up there and kick you around that little hick town of yours."

Stumps and I used to have semi-serious sparring contests in the W&M wrestling room. I was a linebacker on the football team, 8 inches taller than him and maybe 50 pounds heavier. But he was my equal in strength, and we had some real brawls back then. When Eli and I were kids, my father had taught us the martial arts

48

he had learned when he was in the service and stationed in Army bases in Southeast Asia. As long as I kept Stumps at a distance I could tag him with some hard knocks. But if he could get close to me, he would take me down in a flash before I could even react and then just bulldoze me around the mats and make me look silly.

"All right, all right," I said. "You just put a memo in my file that you told me that. I want to be able to sue you for legal malpractice if the Board of Medicine comes calling on me. And by the way, this conversation took 15 minutes, tops. Don't be sending me a bill for four hours of legal work, counselor."

"No worries there," he replied. "You're a deadbeat anyway, so it doesn't matter what I put on the timesheet. Now stop talking to me and call the FBI back and let them know you'll do it. Call me if you need me."

Chapter 12

Mary Beth plunged her arm though the gap in the wall up to her shoulder. The sun felt warm on her bare skin and the sore fingertips of her hand. She waved her arm around, opening and closing her fist and reveling in the freedom of her arm and hand.

Outside, two squirrels chased each other, making a real racket in the dry leaves. Mary Beth managed a smile as the two squirrels furiously chirped and squeaked at each other next to the big white oak, fighting over what remained of last fall's acorns.

The hard wood above and below the gap in the wall was a little splintered. Mary Beth had started plucking at it with her fingernails, and she soon learned that the wood was dry and old. Toothpick-sized pieces could be ripped out one by one, if she was careful and didn't rush it. The walls were frustratingly thick, but she had doggedly picked away for several hours and added another half inch to the width of the gap. No more than another inch, and she should be able to squeeze through and escape from this place.

Chapter 13

I couldn't believe I was back in the jail's parking lot a second time in one day.

Sitting in my truck for a few moments after I turned it off, the windows magnified the bright spring sun, rapidly warming the air inside. It was right then Rev. Rigsby's knock at my window made me jump.

"Hey, Luke, what brings you here to the nice side of town?" Rev. Rigsby asked me as I got out of the truck.

"I got called to do a competency evaluation for Judge Carter over at the courthouse. Some guy who was arrested for kidnapping. Are you here for the prison ministry?"

Rev. Rigsby, the new pastor at our church, had started a program at the jail a month ago. When asked about it after church one Sunday, he explained that people whose souls most needed saving weren't necessarily in church. Amos Hudson, the jail warden, had helped him set the program up.

"Yep, it's that time of the week," he told me. "Got to try to straighten out a few of these fellas now, while there's still time. But a kidnapper? Really?"

51

Preachers must not watch a lot of television. The kidnapping of Mary Beth Marshall had led the local news last night. "Yeah, that's right," I said. "This guy named Hiram Legrand snatched a little girl. He's a real nasty son of a gun."

"You've met him already?"

"Yeah, earlier today," I said. "But they asked me to come back."

"Who asked you to come back? The judge?"

"No, the cops did," I said. "To be honest with you, I don't want to be here at all. But they want me to talk to him again to see if he'll give me any info they can use. They've actually bugged the medical infirmary. They just want me to talk to him so they can listen in."

"Luke, is that really the kind of thing you ought to be doing?"

His question stopped me short. The answer was that I didn't want to be involved at all. But I couldn't walk away and not help that little girl.

"I don't know," I answered.

"You're right to be uneasy," Rev. Rigsby said. "You'd be bearing false witness."

"What do you mean?" I asked. "I already told the truth in court this morning."

Rev. Rigsby smiled. "That's not all the Ninth Commandment means. You'd be talking to this man in jail in a way designed to make him believe that your conversation with him is private, when in truth it's not and you're working against him."

I was just standing there, nodding but not really sure what to say next, when the phone buzzing at my hip caught my attention. I took a glance and saw that it was Sarah.

"Go on, you take the call," Rev. Rigsby said. "I need to get in there now. I'm late for the prayer group."

"All right," I told him. "And I understand what you're saying."

I watched him walk across the parking lot and into the Cent-West Jail as I picked up Sarah's call.

"Hey, sweetheart," she said. "I'm sorry to bug you in the middle of the day, but did you go back to the jail yet to help the FBI find Mary Beth Marshall?"

"How the heck did you hear about that?"

"The little girl's mother called me on the phone. That poor woman. She said she heard from the FBI that you didn't want to go back to the jail, and she asked me to talk you into it."

"Old news. I decided to do it. I'm actually here in the jail parking lot right now. I'm about to walk in."

"Good. Why were you so hesitant, anyway?"

"I don't know," I said. "I guess the man unnerves me a little."

"Luke, you're 6'2" and weigh 210 pounds. And he's locked up. Exactly how does he intimidate you? I thought you were tough."

"I didn't say he intimidates me," I said sharply. "He's just a really bad guy. I don't want him knowing me."

"I was just kidding, honey."

"I know," I said. "I'm sorry, I didn't mean to bark at you. Look, I better get going in there. It's getting late, and I have to get this done and pick up Henry by five."

"Ok, sweetheart," Sarah said. "You're doing the right thing. Call me if you're running late and I'll come back to town to get Henry."

We hung up after an exchange of I love you's, and I opened my truck door to lock my phone inside. I pulled my wedding ring off and locked it up with the phone in the glove compartment. As I headed into the jail, I rubbed the white skin on my finger where the ring usually rested to make it flush a little and blend in.

***

For the second time that day, a guard led me down various hallways and deposited me in the jail infirmary. I had to wait alone for another 10 minutes or so until another guard led Hiram Legrand into the room.

Legrand's eyes blazed and his nose flared when he saw me. As soon as the door closed and it was just Legrand and me alone in the infirmary, he started talking before I said a word.

"What're you back here for? To screw me over again?" he demanded.

"I didn't do anything to hurt you," I said. "I told the judge that you are healthy. What's wrong with that?"

"Go to hell. You screwed me over. You know you did."

"Well, believe what you want," I said. "I just call them as I see them. I have no idea if you're guilty or not. That's not my concern. My job is only to check you out medically. Legal stuff is someone else's game."

"It ain't a game. This is my life. So answer the question. What're you doing back here again?"

"Judge Carter thought he needed more information about your medical condition," I said. "He's reconsidering whether you

54

really are suffering from medical issues that make it unfair to put you on trial for this. He asked me to come back to see if I can find evidence of that to give to him."

Hiram abruptly stood up from his chair, so quickly that the back of his knees knocked the chair over backwards and made it clatter noisily on the floor.

"Bullshit!" he said furiously. "I ain't stupid. That's just some bullshit story the cops gave you for an excuse to come back in here."

For whatever reason, I hadn't noticed until then that the guard had left the handcuffs on Hiram rather than take them off. Still, even with his hands cuffed in front of him, I didn't like him standing over me, even with a table between us. So I stood up, too, but I tried to be casual to balance it out.

"That's ridiculous," I lied. "I'm not a cop. And believe me, I'm too busy to play cops and robbers with you. I have a busy medical practice. I need to get this examination over with and get back to work. Are you going to cooperate or not?"

Hiram's face grew even more furious as I was talking, and he leaned forward at the waist toward me. Even though his eyes were dark, I could see his pupils clearly enough to see that they were constricted, tightening with his anger.

"I ain't cooperating with you. You're helping them to put me in some hellhole for the rest of my life, not some little pissant baby jail like this one. Maybe I should let your kids know what a punk their daddy is."

A jolt went through me. I said, "What makes you think I have a family?"

"Because you just told me with your face," he said. "You just showed me with your face that you got a family."

"No, I don't."

"Yes, you do. Bullshit again. How would your kids like to know that Daddy is trying to screw me over?"

"I don't have kids."

"Sure you do. Maybe I'll tell them all about it when I hogtie 'em and let them rot in a cellar somewhere for a while, until I get around to strangling them with my own bare hands," he said venomously, holding up his handcuffs and flexing his hands in front of my face.

Rage instantly roared through my veins, and my hands fired out from my sides and grabbed fistfuls of Legrand's orange jail jumpsuit. I yanked his upper body across the table between us until his nose was just inches away from mine and his jail-issued slip-on shoes were off the floor behind him.

"Don't you ever threaten my family again! Not ever!" I shouted into his face. An almost irresistible urge bellowed deep in my gut to slam my forehead into the middle of his shocked expression. "Don't you even *think* about my family again! You got that?" I hauled him in even tighter and repeated, "You got that?" over and over as I shook him bodily.

The room suddenly filled with white uniforms as jail guards poured in, grabbing him and me. I let them pull me off him, my anger dissipating nearly as quickly as it had come. Out of the corner of my eye, I saw Amos Hudson, the warden, directing his men as they hustled Legrand out of the room, his face still full of shock at my explosion.

After the door closed behind them and brought sudden quiet to the jail infirmary, Amos stayed behind to talk to me. Surprised at what I had just done, I exhaled hard and sat back heavily in the plastic chair. The post-adrenaline fatigue was already starting to seep into me.

"Hey, Luke, we heard what he said to you," Amos said. "That's a lot for any man to take. So we're just going to forget about this. He isn't hurt. But you have to understand, he's our prisoner. If he gets hurt on our watch, that's on us."

"I know. Jeez, I'm sorry," I said, running my hand over the cool dampness that had popped on my forehead. "I don't know what got into me, Amos. It's just that when he threatened my kids . . ."

"Yeah, I know," Amos said. "The sergeant who escorted him down to you radioed me and said Legrand was really fired up on the walk over from C-pod. So I had the sergeant and some others stay outside the door. I got there just as Legrand mouthed off to you. I'm sure glad you didn't hit him. You're a pretty big guy, and you would've broken him somehow for sure. I don't think I could've squared that. I'd have to tell the sheriff about that, you know, if you had marked him up."

"I understand." After a few moments of quiet, I took another deep breath, exhaled hard again and said, "I just want to get out of here. Whatever else he is, he's sane. A real bastard, but sane enough to stand trial."

Amos patted me on the back as he walked me out of the room. "Glad you think so."

***

The two FBI agents called me right away; my phone was ringing as I got back to the truck in the jail parking lot. After I explained to them what had happened -- they could hear it but not see it on their audio bug -- Agent Byram had the guts to suggest I go back in there a *third* time tomorrow. I let them know what I thought of that request before hanging up.

I calmed down by the time I rolled my truck back into town and pulled into the parking lot for Henry's 5 o'clock pickup. His preschool was on the second floor of our church. On many a Sunday he had dragged us into the empty preschool classrooms to look at some of his finger-paint art on the walls.

A few minutes after situating my truck amidst the brigade of minivans, the kids emerged, holding their little preschool tote bags. Claire Michaels, the lead preschool teacher, was busily directing traffic as I swept Henry up in my arms and gave him a kiss on the cheek. Then I buckled him into a front-facing car seat that I had anchored crushingly tight in the extended cab of my truck and tossed his tote bag on the passenger seat. Henry loved to have the wind in his face when we drove together, so I put the windows down and started to roll towards home.

"Daddy, me and Jake played on the swings today," Henry yelled from the gusty backseat. "And I jumped farther than he did."

I glanced back at him in my rear view mirror. He was in the center of the back seat. I had read that was the safest part of a vehicle in the event of an accident.

"Oh, well, who went further doesn't matter," I said. "So long as you both had fun, that's what counts. What did you pick to read during reading time today?"

"*Goodnight, Moon*," Henry answered.

"Again?" I asked.

"Yes."

"Are you ever gonna get a new favorite book?"

"Maybe. Daddy, do you wanna hear a silly song?"

Miss Claire had a book called "101 Silly Songs," and she'd been teaching a couple of those nonsensical songs every day to her gang of a dozen giggling kids. Henry loved them.

"How about we wait until we get home, and then you can sing it for Mom and me at the same time," I answered.

He nodded agreeably and then hummed to himself. Soon after we got outside of town on the road heading home, the rich, earthy smell of a hay field's first cutting of the year filled the truck. We were passing by old Earl Brown's place. He had been one of my father's friends. Tomorrow or the next day, Earl would rake the cuttings into long lines to dry in the sun for a few days before he ran his hay baler over them.

"Daddy, when people die inside their house, does the ceiling stop them from going to heaven?" Henry asked.

I took that one right between the eyes.

"Um, I don't think so, buddy. Why do you ask?"

"Well, wouldn't the ceiling get in the way?"

"That's a real good question, Henry. Good for you to be thinking about that. I think God knows how to get you to heaven when it's time."

"How does God know?"

"Hmm. Well, I think God knows everything."

A few moments of easy quiet passed as he thought that over. Then he asked, "Daddy, are you sure you don't wanna hear a silly song?"

"Of course I want to hear a silly song," I said. "Make sure you sing some good ones."

I lowered the driver-side window the rest of the way down so I could rest my elbow on the door and listen to my boy sing as we headed home.

Chapter 14

Mary Beth swallowed a huge gulp of air when her ears picked up the sound of a car approaching.

The sound of the engine came closer and louder, then stopped as the driver put the car in park, then cut it off. It couldn't have been more than 100 feet away. Mary Beth walked backwards on suddenly weak legs until her back was against the rough wall.

She held her breath and listened.

The car door slammed shut, and big steps, strong steps, a man's steps, crunched through last fall's dry leaves. The crunch, crunch, crunch grew louder as he moved in a straight line directly toward her. Trembling, Mary Beth sat down and hurriedly tried in vain to put her ruined sandals back on her feet.

The thick ray of setting sun, beaming into the dark room through the gap in the wall she had kicked and ripped open until it was nearly wide enough for her to squeeze through, was so welcome just a few minutes ago. But now it was a dead giveaway to what she'd been doing. If he had only come back an hour later, the sun would have been down, and maybe he wouldn't have noticed.

Her chest heaved with gulped breaths and her pulse pounded in her ears as his heavy footsteps got to the door. But when the metal of the door's lock clinked as he worked the key, she stood barefoot to face him.

Clenching her hands into small fists, she raised them in a completely unconscious pantomime of a prizefighter.

A few moments later, her confusion almost matched her fear. The face of the man filling the doorway was covered by a ski mask the color of brown and gray camouflage, but even so, she could see that he was not Hiram Legrand.

Mary Beth followed Ski Mask's gaze from the thick ray of light, to the gap in the wall she had kicked open, to the incriminating little pile of crumbly material beneath it. She cringed as she waited for his reaction, but she did not lower her fists.

"I'm taking you out of here tomorrow morning," Ski Mask said to her, his deep voice cutting through the quiet in the room.

"I don't want you up here anymore."

Chapter 15

<u>Sarah Andrews</u>

I first started to like Luke because he wasn't looking at himself in the mirror.

Four weeks into my first year at the College of William & Mary down in Williamsburg, and I was in my aerobics class at the college athletic center. In one huge gymnasium, they had aerobics in one corner, free weights in another corner, and a collection of treadmills and stair climbers in the third corner. I was there with some girls from the same floor of our freshman residence hall.

A bunch of football players were there that day. They were pumping enormous weights, showing off, strutting around and admiring their own muscles in the mirror. I rolled my eyes and was about to shift my gaze to the guys on the treadmills when I noticed Luke.

He looked good, that's for sure. Big, definitely one of the football players, but in great shape, with broad, muscled shoulders atop a lean midsection and long legs. His hair was dark brown, and that September he was still tanned from the summer. Even at a distance, I could see his eyes were handsome and bright. He was

63

ignoring his peacock teammates and their mirrors and instead was working out hard with a short, muscular guy with a tightly-trimmed afro, who I later learned was Luke's roommate and on the college's wrestling team.

Afterwards, when I found out that Luke and I lived in neighboring dorms, I kept my eye out for him. I hadn't had any real boyfriends before, mostly because I had been heavy growing up. The teasing finally died down after middle school, but the romance sure hadn't picked up in high school. So, my entire senior year, I pounded my way through the Atkins diet and aerobics. "A&A," I called it in my diary as the weight fell off me. By then some of the boys in my high school started to notice me, but I blew them off with an emotion that felt suspiciously like joy. Then came that blessed day just before high school graduation when clothes in the petites section fit me. I had called my mom from the dressing room.

So one warm evening in that first September in college, not long after I first noticed Luke in the gym, I spent longer than usual on my hair and face. I put on my white sandals and my newest little sundress and finished it off with the white seashell necklace I bought in the Outer Banks that past summer. Then I grabbed my violin and out the dorm I went, 15 minutes before Luke usually came back after football practice.

Parking myself in front of the dorm, I started playing on the violin every song I knew by heart and generally tried to look as pretty as I could. A bunch of other kids were tossing balls, throwing Frisbees, and flirting. Right on cue, Luke passed by with a small group of his teammates after practice, tired and walking slowly, and heading to the showers in the dorms. I pretended to ignore him as he made a pathetic effort not to be obvious in checking me out as he passed by. Just before he went into his dorm, as he was barely still within earshot, I heard him ask one of the other guys, "Do you know that girl with the fiddle?"

I almost blew my cover by giggling when the other guy had cracked up and called him a redneck for calling my violin a fiddle.

A week later we hit on all those first-date conversation topics as we shared nachos ordered from the TGI Friday appetizer menu. I told him of my quiet childhood in Lexington, Virginia, a little college town where my father had been a professor at Washington & Lee. I learned between Luke's bites of bacon cheeseburger that I had lived in a more genteel part of Virginia than the rugged farm where he had grown up. Later, after we'd been in one of those nonstop college romances for months, and Luke had taken a creative writing course and I had smoothed over a few of his rougher edges, he said my people were more apt to drink tea while his drank raw milk.

It was during dessert on that first date, as he was wolfing down his carrot cake, that he laid claim to my heart. He swallowed after a thought palpably crossed his mind, then asked nonchalantly, "How long have you been playing your violin?"

He had just the slightest emphasis on that last word, like a foreign exchange student who had to translate a word in his mind before saying it in English. He did not want me to know that the word was fiddle in his mind.

Looking back now, I started to fall in love with him then.

I was in the homestretch of my run on the treadmill in the gym Luke had made for us out here in the old barn, on his family farm, where we'd moved to raise our own family after he finished his medical residency. I pushed a button to make the treadmill go a little faster. The TV remote jiggled in the cup holder. I had the television on with the sound muted, and my music coming through my earbuds was on full blast. There was just enough reflection on the TV screen to catch Luke standing in the barn door and enjoying a look at my backside. He was probably close enough to hear the snick-snick of my running tights.

Even being completely aware of his presence, his smack on my behind just as I was slowing the treadmill speed to a cooldown walk caught me by surprise. It always did. He was an expert at slipping up behind me and giving me a fresh little smack.

"Hey," I said. "Hands to yourself."

"I respectfully decline to obey," Luke said, then did a little hop up on the side of the treadmill with one foot, gave me a smooch on the cheek, and jumped back off.

"Kids go down ok?" I asked him. He was wearing old gray sweats and a nice T-shirt I bought him because it set off the color of his eyes.

"Yep. Both are already asleep. How was your day?" he asked as he plopped himself down on a mat to stretch out.

"It was fine," I said, still huffing between deep breaths as I cooled down. "Kind of busy, though. I probably got only an hour of work done on your books while Emma was down for her nap. You're caught up through March, but that's it."

I had majored in music and accounting at William & Mary, an oddball double-major. Luke had called it the "Soul for Nerds Double-Major" back in college one day as he stretched out on a student-lounge couch and rested his head on my lap. We had been dating long enough that he felt safe making wise-guy comments, but those words had floated in the air for only about two seconds before I had reached down and tweaked his nose hard enough to make his eyes water.

I still played my violin whenever I had the time, but that was never going to earn a paycheck for me, so I had been telecommuting for an accounting firm up in Manassas before Henry was born. Since then, helping with the books in Luke's office at least gave me a little contact with the adult world. Plus I got to keep an eye on the various part-time nurses who worked for him, two of whom were a touch too pretty, though they dressed professionally at work, so I couldn't say anything.

After I cooled down and he finished warming up, I asked him, "Were the FBI people happy with your second meeting with that kidnapper guy?"

"I don't know," Luke said. He was working out with his weights now, his back to me. I could hear clink of metal on metal as I stepped off the treadmill.

"Well, did you talk to them?"

"Yeah, I talked to them on the phone right afterwards, while I was on the way to get Henry," he said. "But they were recording and listening to my whole meeting with Legrand anyway, so I didn't really have much to add."

"No hint on where he might be hiding that little girl?"

"Not really. He was pretty mad at me for nailing him in court. At one point he actually threatened me, something about locking me up in a basement and throwing away the key, or something like that. I laughed at him. Big words for a guy in handcuffs and behind bars."

Luke stopped talking for a minute as he got into a set of bench presses. Even after having been with him since college, seeing the amount of weight he could move was still arresting. I gave a light tap to the boxer's heavy bag he had hung from one of the rafters and asked, "So, from that, do they think maybe he has her locked in a basement somewhere?"

"I guess," he said through gritted teeth as he pushed out his reps.

"It sure sounds like they're grasping at straws now," I said.

He racked the bar, the flush of exertion in his face quickly draining as he sat up. "I know," he said. "It's really a shame. I just don't think they have any idea where that girl is. Too bad we're not allowed to just break his legs and make him tell us."

"And you're the guy who's going to break his legs and make him talk, Mr. Tough Guy?" I said affectionately, then walked over and changed the channel to ESPN and turned up the sound so he could listen to Sports Center in the background.

"Thanks, sweetie," he called over his shoulder to me as he stood there curling a barbell.

I did a quick skip back over to him, gave him a kiss on the cheek and smacked his bottom hard.

"No problem," I said as I slipped out the door to head to my shower back inside the house.

***

Early the next morning as the sun rose outside, I stretched in bed for a few minutes after Luke left for work and worried about him.

He had been preoccupied and quiet last night, even after his workout. Knowing that he wouldn't talk about what was on his mind until he was ready, I had stifled the urge to ask him about it. It could have been any number of things. For all of his tough-guy exterior, I'd learned a long time ago that Luke has a tender heart. Sometimes he lost sleep at night thinking of a particularly sick patient, and I knew he had seen sweet old Rev. Crosley earlier in the day.

So when he had come back in the house after his workout last night, and taken his shower, I had clicked off the lights in our bedroom and made him lay face down in bed so I could rub his back. My fingers kneaded between his shoulder blades and down along the hard muscles of his lower back, then into his neck and shoulders. Then I leaned across his back, letting my chest brush against him as I took one of his big arms in my hands and rubbed it, inch by inch, from his shoulder down to his hand. Then I switched and did the same to his other arm. When I was done, I gently pawed at one of his shoulders so he would roll over onto his back. Then I put the palms of my hands on his chest and made love to him.

Later, snuggling up to him and feeling very much in love with him, he had held me a little more tightly than he usually does. So I waited in the dark until I felt his arms relax and heard his breathing deepen before I picked my head up from his shoulder to look at him. The moon had been bright outside, the kind he would have called a harvest moon if it had been in the fall. It let enough light in our bedroom for me to gaze at his sleeping face for long, quiet minutes. Finally I had gently brushed his hair off his forehead so I could kiss it, softly so as not to awaken him, before I nestled back down into his warmth for the night.

My morning daydream of the previous night was broken by the unexpected rumble of a car rolling up our gravel driveway. I looked to see if Luke maybe had forgotten something on his way to work and came back in his truck to get it, but it was a white

Honda Accord coming up to the house. As I watched from our bedroom window, a woman a little older than me parked and got out of the car. I quickly got dressed and hurried down the stairs.

She was already rapping her knuckles on the door by the time I got down there. I could hear the kids were playing in Henry's bedroom upstairs as I opened the door.

The woman standing in the doorway looked exhausted. Her face was drawn, and the dark circles under her bloodshot eyes were threatening to become bags. But she was breathing rapidly, and she radiated a desperate kind of energy. I knew who she was before she said a word.

"I'm Allison Marshall," she said. "Mary Beth's mom. We talked on the phone yesterday."

"Oh, my goodness," I said. "Please come in. Let me get you some coffee."

"No thank you. There's no time for that. Mrs. Andrews, I need your help."

Chapter 16

Ski Mask was driving into the morning sun while Mary Beth squirmed in the back seat.

Last night, Mary Beth had been nearly as afraid of Ski Mask as she had been of Hiram Legrand. Right off, he had pointed at the gap in the wall and said, "I'm going to be up here all night. Don't even think about it." After that, he had hardly said a word to her.

Sharply clapping his hands together and barking out at her, he had awakened Mary Beth in the earliest part of this morning, when it was still dark. He led her to the car, where he duct-taped her legs tightly together until her knees were crunched against each other. He pinned her upper arms to her sides by taping around her body from elbows to shoulders. He made many passes with the silver duct tape, and Mary Beth could hardly budge. He finished up by tying a red handkerchief around her eyes before he drove them off in the car.

After about a half hour of driving, Mary Beth worked up the courage to tell him that the handkerchief was too tight and hurting her eyes. He was quiet for a few moments before he offered a laconic, "All right," then reached back and pulled the handkerchief off of her. It was still dark out, though the eastern sky was lightening a bit. Mary Beth didn't recognize where she was.

They drove for a while longer before he killed the headlights. Then he slowly crept up the road for another quarter mile or so, and pulled in front of a farmhouse that was about 200 yards from the road.

There was just enough light in the pre-dawn by then to see. Ski Mask pulled out binoculars and stared at the house for maybe 10 minutes or so. Then one light, then a second light, came on in the house. Somebody was getting up for the morning.

After a few minutes, Ski Mask put the binoculars back down on the passenger seat and got driving again.

Chapter 17

"What do you mean, he threatened my kids?" I asked Allison Marshall.

"Sarah, I heard it on the FBI's recording myself," she answered me. "Hiram Legrand told your husband he'd hogtie your kids and let them rot in a cellar. I'm sure that's why your husband doesn't want to go back in there. I thought he'd told you. But please, he has to go back."

I sat back in one of the chairs at our kitchen table. My head was spinning. I had coaxed Allison to come into the house and poured us both a cup of coffee. Without taking a sip from her cup, she immediately started telling me how the FBI called Luke on his phone yesterday afternoon, right after the second meeting, to go back to visit Legrand a third time, today. But Luke had refused.

"Every time your husband talks to him, that evil bastard pops out with a little more information, like maybe he's hiding her in a storage facility, or maybe he has her tied up in a cellar," Allison said, her eyes welling up with tears. "The FBI agents think that if your husband goes back in there today, he could tell Legrand that Judge Carter ordered him to go back and finish his exam. Then, even if they have an argument, and maybe *especially* if they have an argument, Legrand might say some more things that can help us find Mary Beth."

Allison stopped talking for a minute and looked at me as she put both of her hands on mine. Then with one blink she sent a tear spilling down each cheek, and she slid from her chair and onto her knees in front of me. Mortified, I tried to pull her back up but she refused, sticking stubbornly to her knees as she spoke.

"Please, Sarah. Please, please, please, I'm begging you, get your husband to go back in there. I'm doing everything I can to find my daughter. Please, she's just 9 years old. I'm going all-out, 24 hours a day nonstop. But I don't know where to look. Neither does the FBI. For Christ's sake, please, get your husband to go back in there."

I burst into tears as I stood out of my chair and hauled Allison up to her feet and embraced her.

"Of course I will," I said.

Chapter 18

Luke Andrews

The day was already going downhill. Sarah had just stormed out of my office after I held my ground and told her I wasn't ready to commit to seeing Legrand a third time. She had come in here seriously fired up at me, and I felt awful for Mary Beth's mother, but I just wasn't convinced yet that I should go back in there. I knew the FBI wanted me to do it this afternoon. I told Sarah I was going to have to think about it a little longer this morning.

I was about to get back to my patients when I got another interruption, this one from Paige, one of my part-time nurses, calling from Rev. Crosley's house. I had sent her down to check on him.

"He doesn't look so good, Dr. Andrews," Paige said on the phone. "I think he has pneumonia again."

Listening to her descriptions of Rev. Crosley's symptoms, it sounded like she was right. He'd had pneumonia before. It was common among chemo patients who weren't very mobile. The cancer had spread into his spine, which made walking around tough for him. He was a sitting duck for pneumonia. I told Paige to run over to the drugstore to pick up amoxicillin right away. I would call in the prescription myself. She could get him started with that, and later this afternoon, I'd set him up with some intravenous antibiotics at home.

I hung up and Jan immediately buzzed me at my desk. She said, "It's the FBI calling again. The woman this time. Ms. Healey. She said she really needs to talk to you."

I shook my head.

"I already talked yesterday to her buddy, what's his name. Byram. Tell her I'll call her back after lunch," I told Jan. "Tell her I'm busy with patients."

Chapter 19

Mary Beth heard a buzzing sound, and Ski Mask quickly answered his phone.

"Yeah," he said.

A voice said something back to him, though Mary Beth couldn't hear what it was.

"Where?" he asked.

The voice responded with something or other.

"Yeah, I know where it is. Listen to me. You need to stay in the woods until I get there. Then hustle in the car when I pull up. I have some clothes for you."

Although very few cars passed them on the road, Ski Mask made sure Mary Beth was still lying down on the back seat, out of sight, and he kept the sun visor way down. Eventually, he turned down a little side road. He crept along quietly, then stopped and let the car idle near a patch of woods that rose up on a hillside away from the road. Mary Beth could feel the vibrating drone of the engine through the upholstery of the back seat.

Mary Beth froze as Hiram Legrand emerged from that patch of woods and sprinted down the hill. He dipped below her line of sight for a moment and then abruptly reappeared, flinging himself into the front passenger seat of Ski Mask's car. He was wearing a blaze orange jumpsuit that had "Cent-West Regional Jail" stenciled on the front and back.

"Why are you wearing that mask?" Legrand asked as he caught his breath and Ski Mask sped off.

"Good to see you, too, Hiram. I'm wearing this because I don't want her to see what I look like," Ski Mask answered, gesturing his head in the direction of the backseat.

Legrand did a double-take when he saw Mary Beth trussed with duct tape in the back.

"What is she doing here?" Legrand demanded.

"We're not keeping her," Ski Mask answered.

"We aren't? Why not?"

"Because you weren't supposed to take her in the first place. Because you gave law enforcement a jump on this before we've even gotten started, got yourself caught, and your father and I had to make arrangements to get you out. Because you're of no help to me, Hiram, if you can't control yourself."

"Fine. Just seems like a waste, is all."

They drove in silence for a few moments. Then Ski Mask asked, "Have any trouble?"

Legrand smirked as he held up a big brass-colored key in his hand. "Piece of cake. Nothin' beats the warden's own master key to open the doors to the jail."

Legrand's unpleasant smile faded as he gave a troubled glance back at Mary Beth in the back seat.

"I'm still good to go on taking the other kid, right?"

"You're still good," Ski Mask said. "I know where he's going to be. Get changed. Clothes are in the bag right there. I'll get you close to him. Then you take it from there."

Chapter 20

Rev. Crosley was sitting on his front porch again when I stopped by to visit, but he looked a fair bit worse than he had just 24 hours earlier. Pneumonia was like that. It snuck up on people. His lungs crackled like Rice Krispies when I listened to them through my stethoscope, and I didn't need a chest X-ray to be sure that he had pneumonia.

"How's it going, Luke?" he asked between coughs. "Are they any closer to finding that poor little girl?"

"Maybe," I said. "Legrand hinted --"

My phone buzzed, interrupting me, and I glanced down at it. It was the office. Someone probably just needed a prescription refill or something, so I ignored it. I'd deal with it later.

"He kind of said a few things to me that the FBI agents think they can use," I said.

"Like what?"

I started to explain but stopped when Rev. Crosley started coughing hard, leaning his body over. After a few seconds, he took a relieved breath and sat back, his face red from exertion.

"You all right?" I asked with concern.

"I've had enough of the coughing, but the cup is half full, because the old man is still breathing," he said with a tired smile. Then he gestured to his iPod and speakers next to him and asked, "Can you turn that on, please? Something smooth. Maybe some Marvin Gaye."

Chapter 21

Mary Beth recognized where she was. Her mother had often brought her downtown for the farmer's market in the VFW parking lot on Saturday mornings. The buildings looked achingly familiar to her, even from her vantage point lying down on the backseat of the car with Ski Mask and Hiram Legrand in the front seat.

They slowly cruised past a downtown playground, which occupied an entire block of the town. A big metal play set with a slide, a fort, a fireman's pole, and swings anchored the park, and an assortment of tee-ter-totters, bouncy horses resting on heavy springs and other outdoor toys were scattered about.

"This is it," Ski Mask said as he made right turns to circle the park.

"I'll have you drop me off near there," Legrand said, gesturing to a big forsythia bush that was near the edge of the park. "That way I can get close."

"Ok," Ski Mask said. He handed a picture to Legrand. "Here's the kid. This is from this past fall. Make sure you get the right one."

"No problem," Legrand said, his eyes greedily boring into the picture. Then, after looking up and surveying the playground one more time, he jerked his head back at Mary Beth.

"So when do we get rid of her?"

Chapter 22

"I think you're right," Rev. Crosley said as I sat in the other rocking chair across from him. "You should do whatever will help that little girl."

"Yeah, I'm calling the FBI lady when I get back to the office and telling her I'll do it this afternoon," I said. "I hope they have a halfway decent fib for me to give to him to explain why I'm back again. That man is unnerving."

"What do you mean?"

"I don't know," I said. "Being in the same room with him is like being in the same room as a writhing pile of snakes. His presence just sets off every alarm bell. And look at what he does. What kind of man goes after little kids? What kind of man laughs at the prospect of one of them starving to death wherever he has her locked up? It just makes you wonder how the Hiram Legrands of the world get away with doing the awful things they do."

Rev. Crosley smiled at that and asked, "You mean, why does God allow it to go on?"

"Yeah, something like that."

"I first had to study that question back in seminary," he said. "If God is all good and all powerful, then how could He let a guy like Hiram Legrand do what he does? I'm not sure anyone really has a perfect answer to that. Some say that God has given us the gift of free will, and it wouldn't be free will if God intervened every time someone chose to do something wrong or bad or evil. There's probably some truth to that. But I think there's a little more to --"

He stopped and looked past me. Then he said, "Looks like we have company."

I turned around and saw Jan, my head nurse, running full speed down the street to us. She was getting up there in years, and I had never seen her run in my life. From the bright red flush on her face, it looked like she had run the whole distance from my office, more than a quarter of a mile away.

She started yelling as soon as she caught sight of me at a distance of 75 yards or more, but at first I couldn't make out what she was saying.

Chapter 23

The playground rested on a little knoll, so that even lying down in the backseat, Mary Beth was able to look through the car window and see Legrand snatch the little boy.

Just before it happened, Ski Mask checked the time on his phone, then parked the car in a leafy, quiet section of the street, about half a block down the hill from the playground. Legrand got out of the car and walked nonchalantly up the street to the park. Although Mary Beth's eyes never left Legrand, she saw that he was terrifyingly inconspicuous as he slipped up to the park. It was as if he had the ability to simply choose not to be noticed by others.

Once he got to the corner of the playground and hunkered down into that big forsythia bush, she couldn't see him anymore.

A few minutes later, a small blonde-haired woman coming from the other direction led a line of preschoolers to the park, each of them having a small hand on a rope she was holding at the head of the line. Bringing up the rear was another woman, a gray-haired lady who looked like somebody's grandmother.

Once the kids got to the park, the blonde-haired lady allowed them to let go of the rope, and the kids scattered to their favorite toys. Most went right to the swings and slide of the play set, with the gray-haired

84

lady following them. The rest chased each other around on the other side of the playground, near the bush where Legrand was hiding and waiting.

When it happened, Legrand struck as fast as a snake.

Two little boys were kicking a ball back and forth. They got closer and closer to the bush and the corner of the park. The blonde-haired lady was nearby, and she kept glancing at them to make sure they didn't go too far. Then Mary Beth heard a little girl, on the swing across the park, call out to the blonde-haired lady.

"Hey, Miss Claire, look at me! Look at how far I can jump!"

The blonde-haired lady named Miss Claire turned to look, a concerned expression on her face and a caution right on the tip of her tongue that the swing was too high to jump, but it was too late. The little girl leapt off the swing in a big arc. Miss Claire kept her eyes on the little girl as she landed to be sure she was okay.

Legrand grew tall out of that bush as the little girl was in the air. In less than a second, he seized one of the two little boys and started carrying him right out of the park. Even at the distance, Mary Beth could see that the little boy was more perplexed than alarmed by what was going on and hadn't yet made a sound.

Legrand made it to the edge of the playground when Miss Claire's head swiveled around. She blinked twice, and then her eyes widened as she saw this strange man saunter off with one of her kids. Her shriek pierced the air as she charged.

Legrand turned contemptuously to face her, and so unprepared was he for her ferocity that she almost knocked him off his feet. She yanked as hard as she could on one of his arms holding the boy, and with her other hand she had raked at his face with her nails as she screamed at the top of her lungs.

Legrand dropped the boy to the ground to cover his face from this little wolverine of a woman. He struggled with her for a moment, towering above her. Then, pulling his fist back as far as it would go, he swung *hard and punched Miss Claire squarely in the face. She fell to the ground, and Legrand snatched up the boy again and sprinted to their car. He held the little boy firmly as Ski Mask sped them off in the car.*

As Ski Mask accelerated down the street, Mary Beth could see the gray-haired lady chugging through the group of wide-eyed children and across the playground to where Miss Claire lay bleeding.

Chapter 24

Jan was still yelling as she ran, so I stood up and trotted down the steps of Rev. Crosley's porch to hear what she was saying. Out of the corner of my eye, he was fumbling with his iPhone to turn the music off.

"Luke! Luke!" Jan panted as she ran as fast as her legs could carry her. I opened my arms and she ran right into them, her panicked eyes wide.

"Luke, Hiram Legrand escaped!" she blurted before sucking in another breath and crying out, "And he's got Henry. Your son. My God, Luke, he's got Henry. Henry's gone!"

Chapter 25

Speeding down a dirt road about five miles outside of town, Ski Mask abruptly pulled over, sliding the car to a stop at the edge of a field. The heads of all of his passengers – Mary Beth, Legrand, and the little boy Legrand had just snatched – bounced as he stomped on the brakes and turned the steering wheel over. The car was still rocking from the hard stop when Ski Mask quickly hauled Mary Beth out of the back seat and dumped her on the ground next to the car. He drew a hunting knife out of the leather sheath on his belt and knelt by her side as she lay on her back. Gripping her shoulder with one hand, he brought the edge of the blade to her side.

The knife's silvery-gray blade was scraped and abraded where he had recently sharpened it.

"About a mile down this dirt road, it connects with a paved highway," Ski Mask said as he slashed at the duct tape pinning her upper arms at her sides. To avoid cutting her, he sliced in the small gap between each of her arms and her sides, then he gripped each wrist and jerked at her arms until they were free of the cut tape.

"It's gonna take you awhile to get your legs free," he said, gesturing to the duct tape that covered her from her ankles to her hips. He had used a full roll when he had taped them together in the darkness of the morning. "When you do, start walking down this road until you get to the

paved one. Make a right, and there'll be an old gas station a few hundred yards down the road."

Ski Mask thought for a moment, then looked Mary Beth in the eyes again. He gestured near her face with his knife as he spoke, moving it up and down to enunciate his words.

"One other thing. They'll be asking you to help. To describe what you saw and heard. But don't do it. Don't help them," he said. Then, jerking his head back at the car where Legrand was, "If you do, I'll find out, and I'll have him come back and get you again."

As the car drove off and left Mary Beth behind, the last thing she saw was the little boy looking at her through the passenger side window. She watched the car until it disappeared behind some woods. She kept looking in that direction until she could no longer hear it.

The air grew quiet again. Cattle grazed on a distant rounded hilltop, and a red-tailed hawk cruised just above a fallow field before pulling up and settling into an old tree. The hawk blinked twice as it watched the young girl sitting on the side of the road. Then it took to the air again, searching for a mouse or mole slipping through the broom sedge and pine seedlings covering the unplanted field.

Alone, Mary Beth started to pick at the duct tape at the top of her thighs. When she made a big enough flap to pinch with her thumb and index finger, she peeled away at the tape, slowly at first, and just with her hands. Then the effort spread to her arms, then her shoulders, picking up speed and effort until finally her unraveling became frantic, and she cried out and used the force of her whole body with each yank and rip.

Part Two

Chapter 26

<u>Sarah Andrews</u>

Clutching the steering wheel until my knuckles were white, I pushed our minivan to 90 miles per hour on the road to town. Emma was quiet in the back, her eyes wide and never leaving me. The minivan's tires squealed in protest at every curve in the road.

Ten minutes earlier, Luke had gasped words into the phone after I picked it up at home. Between heaving breaths he managed to get out that he was sprinting on foot to the preschool because Hiram Legrand had stolen Henry from us after somehow escaping from the jail.

I somehow didn't understand what he was saying for a beat or two. Then sudden comprehension slammed into my lower belly, its razor-sharp serrations slicing through my core. Even as I had snatched up Emma with one arm and ran out the door, my other hand was pressed flat on my stomach above the button on my jeans as if I really had been stabbed there.

I was five minutes outside of town when I punched the redial button. Luke answered on the first ring. His voice drilled through the earpiece of my phone.

"I just got here. Nothing! Sarah, I don't see him anywhere!"

"Are the police there yet?" I asked, forcing the words through the clenched muscles in my throat.

"They're pulling into the parking lot now," he said. "Let me run to them."

"Go," I said and hung up and crushed the gas pedal against the floorboard.

A few minutes later, people scattered as I screeched into the church parking lot. Henry's preschool teacher, Claire Michaels, was off to one side, holding an ice pack on her face. Parents of kids who had heard the news were already there, picking up their kids and staring at me as I hurtled out of the minivan and ran to my husband, who was talking to a middle-aged man wearing a blue blazer and tie.

"I'm Agent Richard Byram with the FBI Crimes Against Children Unit," the man in the blazer said to me. "The kidnapping unit. My partner, Agent Healey, spoke to you about Mary Beth Marshall yesterday."

"Where's Henry?" I almost screamed at him. "What are you doing to find my son?"

Byram spoke calmly to me. "Hiram Legrand escaped from the regional jail less than two hours ago. We attempted to notify your husband as a precaution but couldn't reach him. Still, we thought it was virtually certain Legrand would flee, so we set up roadblocks ten miles outside of town in all directions. Obviously, he didn't flee."

He looked at me for a moment before he continued.

"Based on her description," he said, nodding in the direction of Claire Michaels, "and everything else we know, there's no doubt this was Legrand. What Legrand almost certainly did this

94

morning was stay within the roadblock perimeter, come right back into town and find your son."

"How did he even know we have a son?" Luke barked out.

"I don't know," Byram answered.

"How did he know which kid was our boy?"

"I don't know that, either."

Byram explained that Agent Healey was at the sheriff's office, overseeing and directing communications to the roadblocks on all the roads leading out of town. As he spoke, more parents filed into the parking lot, finding and clutching their children. All of them were staring at us, thinking their genuine compassion hid their overpowering relief that it was not their child who had been stolen away.

Jan, Luke's nurse, pulled Claire aside to look at her face while Agent Byram was talking to us, and I heard her tell Claire that her nose likely was broken. When I looked in that direction and made eye contact with Claire, she shrugged Jan off and came to me, crying. Her delicate nose looked bent and her upper lip was badly swollen.

"Sarah, I'm so sorry. I just didn't see him until it was too late. I tried to get Henry back but that man hit me so hard." After a quick inhale she tried to continue, but a braying sound escaped from her as her sobs stole away her ability to talk.

Luke was still wild-eyed and barking at Byram. "Do you know who was driving the car?"

"No," Byram said. "We have sheriff's deputies doing a canvass in the neighborhood to see who saw anything. Ms. Michaels saw that he got into a gray sedan and that someone else was driving, but that's all."

"How did Legrand escape?"

"I don't know," Byram said. "Agent Healey already has interviewed the warden of the jail, a Capt. Amos Hudson. It turns out his master key is missing from his own keychain. He realized it after the escape; he rarely uses it because he mostly works in his office during the day and doesn't transport inmates around the jail himself. Maybe an inmate swiped it from him this morning and somehow got it to Legrand. No idea how or when an inmate would get a chance to do that, unless the captain was sloppy as heck, and the sheriff says he's not. Even if he was, we have no idea why an inmate would help Legrand, unless Legrand paid him enough."

Luke's neck was splotchy red as he demanded, "Well, what *do* you know?"

Byram's voice remained calm and professional. In some distant recess of my racing mind I registered that he probably had a lot of experience with hysterical parents.

"Dr. Andrews, we don't know much of anything yet. All of your questions are good ones. We're going to push as hard as we can to get answers, because they can lead us to your son. But our most important goal is immediate. It's been less than 30 minutes since Henry was taken. Our best chance to get him back is right now, while the kidnappers – Legrand and whoever his driver is – are running away with him. That's where all our energies are right now. With any luck they'll be snagged up in one of the roadblocks."

Luke stalked off across the parking lot to the street, looking up and down it, as if he might see Henry. More people were packing into the parking lot – the church members who lived in town and had walked over, the deputies pulling up with their flashing lights going on their cruisers, the various neighbors coming by to see what was going on. Rev. Rigsby had come out of the church and was talking with several of them.

Agent Byram was only a few steps away from me when his phone went off in a default ring tone. He jumped and answered it right away as Luke dashed over to us to hear Byram's side of the call.

Byram listened to the caller, then asked, "Where?"

I blurted out, "Did they find him? Did they find Henry?"

Byram asked the caller, "She is? Is she ok?"

Luke seized him by the shoulder and repeated my question, but Agent Byram held up a hand and kept listening on his phone, then said into it, "Ok, go notify the mother. Have her take the kid to her pediatrician for a precautionary exam. Congratulations, Jeanne."

He clicked his phone off and looked up at Luke and me.

"Mary Beth Marshall just walked up to a gas station a few miles south of here. She doesn't appear to be harmed. She'll get checked out by a doctor, then we'll try to talk to her."

Agent Byram looked at Luke, then me, before he continued.

"But no sign of Henry," he said. "Not yet."

Chapter 27

Hiram Legrand smirked as Ski Mask lowered Henry down on the dusty floor, situating the boy so he was seated with his back against the wall. Without another word, the two men left him there, locking the heavy old door behind them.

Henry sat calmly in silence for a few minutes as he looked about the room. A pair of girls' sandals looking all beat up rested unevenly in one corner of the room.

Otherwise, it was completely empty.

Chapter 28

Luke pulled our minivan into the parking lot of the county sheriff's office fast enough to make the tires squeal. Emma was in the backseat. Luke had said she would never leave his presence until Hiram Legrand was recaptured.

The sheriff's office was practically empty as Agent Byram led us back to the conference room the two FBI agents had borrowed from the sheriff. Almost all of the deputies and the sheriff himself were out on roadblocks, hoping some old gray sedan carrying our son would come into view. The few clerks and dispatchers left behind in the office gave us pitying looks as we swept past. Luke clenched his jaw and I fought to control my breathing as we hurried down the hallway.

Agent Byram introduced me to Jeanne Healey in the conference room where she had been working. Laptops and papers were strewn on the conference room table, and a large paper map of Jameston County was tacked up to the wall. Little yellow post-its with notes scribbled on them dotted the map.

"Mrs. Andrews, Dr. Andrews, I'm so sorry for what has happened," Agent Healey said. "Please know that we are going to do everything we possibly can to get Henry back." Then, following my eyes to the map of the county, she continued, "We have road-blocks on every paved road leading out of town, and we're calling in deputies from neighboring counties to help us with the un-marked dirt ones. Hiram Legrand isn't a local, so he probably only knows the main roads. Chances are very good he's still contained within the perimeter."

Luke kept his eyes on Emma through the window in the con-ference room to the adjacent hallway, where she was playing with a few dolls I had in the minivan. Emma was too little to under-stand what was going on, but we still didn't want her to hear what we were saying. One of the secretaries in the sheriff's office was on her hands and knees, keeping Emma occupied.

I asked Agent Healey, "Did you get the pictures of Henry we texted to you?"

"Yes, I did. Even before then, we already had put out Henry's preschool photo, because we were able to get that right away from his preschool teacher. But these pictures you sent are extremely helpful. As part of the Amber Alert, I've sent them out to the tele-vision network affiliates in Richmond, Roanoke, Virginia Beach, Danville, and northern Virginia. So even if Legrand does slip past our roadblocks, there's going to be thousands of pairs of eyes out there looking for Henry. See?"

Agent Healey turned around her laptop. The lead story on the website of the NBC affiliate in Richmond was the kidnapping of Henry. They had set up a slide show with the half dozen pictures I had emailed to Agent Healey. The first picture was one I had snapped myself last fall, catching the happy look on Henry's face as he slid into a pile of leaves. That bright October afternoon, Luke and I had raked a huge heap of leaves at the bottom of the slide on the kids' play set in our yard.

"I've heard Amber Alerts on the radio before," Luke said to Agent Healey as I gazed at the photos flipping by on the television station's website. "Is that all there is to them? A radio alert?"

"No, it's more extensive than that," Agent Healey said. "An Amber Alert is a child-abduction alert bulletin in use throughout most of the United States when a child is abducted. Basically, it's a fast mass-communication device to let people know a child has been taken, what the child's physical description is, and if possible a description of the kidnapper as well."

As she spoke, the slideshow on the television network's website moved along to a picture of Henry, Luke, and me last Christmas. We were cheek to cheek, all of us wearing red and white Santa hats and giving big smiles to the camera.

Agent Healey continued, "Amber Alerts are sent over radio stations, but they're also spread on television, email, and even traffic-condition and weather-condition signs on highways. Some people have an app so that their phones buzz when an Amber Alert goes out. On radio, we use the Emergency Alert System. You know the loud noise that comes up on radio sometimes, followed by the official-sounding voice, usually saying it's just a test? That's the Emergency Alert System. It was designed for weather and other national emergencies. Amber Alerts were grafted upon that as the best, most widespread manner in which to communicate with the public quickly."

The Christmas photo faded on the network's website and was replaced by one of Henry blowing out the candles on his 4th birthday cake. Luke had taken that picture. My hands had been on Henry's shoulders as he blew.

Agent Healey was still talking. "We were able to get a good Amber Alert out for Henry right away. Fortunately, we have Hiram Legrand's mug shot from just a few days ago. While our description of his vehicle could be better --"

I cut in on her.

"What does the 'Amber' in Amber Alert stand for?"

"The Amber in Amber alert is an acronym," she said. "It stands for America's Missing: Broadcasting Emergency Response. Amber."

There was quiet in the room. Then I asked her in a softer voice, "Is that all 'Amber' means?"

Agent Healey hesitated, her eyes dropping to her paperwork.

"Who was she?" I asked.

"We shouldn't focus on that now," she said.

"It matters. Tell me what happened to her."

"I don't think it'd help."

"Please."

It was Agent Byram who answered me. When he did, his voice sounded completely different from the smoothly efficient agent that I had heard up until then. Now, it had a muted tremble in it.

"Mrs. Andrews, Agent Healey does not want to answer you because the story is tragic," he said. "But you have the right to know, so I'll tell you.

"On January 13, 1996, a young girl named Amber Hagerman was abducted while riding her bicycle in Arlington, Texas. A neighbor who witnessed the abduction called the police. But it took a few hours to really get rolling. Then we -- the FBI, I mean, and untold numbers of volunteers -- went all out and put on the hardest search we could."

102

He took a big inhale of breath before continuing.

"Four days after Amber's abduction, a man walking his dog found her body in a storm drainage ditch."

Though his eyes didn't drop, they lost their focus, and I knew he was remembering. Then he blinked and came back to the present, and he said, "Back then I was still working in our Chicago field office, serving warrants and crashing down doors and living the life of a grunt agent trying to angle for promotion. Then came Amber. The day her body was found was the day I put in to transfer to our Child Abduction Rapid Deployment teams. I've been doing it ever since."

He kept looking at me, the expression on his face rising from sadness to compassion to hope.

"Amber was a wonderful little girl, an absolutely beautiful child," he said. "Because of what she inspired, thousands of other little kids like your Henry will be found."

Agent Healey's phone went off then. She gave an update on how the search was going and then thanked the caller several times in response to whatever he was saying. Then she hung up and looked back up at us.

"That was Judge Carter. He just said he would sign whatever search warrant we need and will give us any help his judicial offices can provide to us. We can call him anytime day or night. That's really nice; often we don't have a proactive local judge like that. That'll be handy going forward," she said.

"He just feels guilty for getting me involved," Luke said bitterly.

"Stop it," I said to Luke, then turning to Agent Healey, I continued, "What can we do to help you find Henry?"

"I understand that you've been calling friends and family to help with search parties and such," Healey said.

"Yes," I said. "We've already called a lot of people. As soon as we're done here, we're heading back to the church, where Henry's preschool is, to organize them."

"That's good," Healey said. "That preschool looks to be a good staging point for the volunteers. Go back there now and get to work. You'll feel better if you do."

***

After we were done with the two FBI agents at the sheriff's office, Luke insisted that we drive to Keith Watson's pediatrics practice, where Mary Beth Marshall was with her mother at that very moment getting checked out.

"Luke, when we get to Dr. Watson's office, you need to let me talk with Allison Marshall." I said from the passenger seat. "Agent Healey just told us Mary Beth said she couldn't remember anything about where she was. The girl is scared. If you go in there and push too hard, she'll just clam up and not talk at all."

"I know," Luke said, his voice tight as he sped the minivan through one of the three traffic lights in town.

"I'm serious, Luke," I said, my voice screechy from my barely-contained panic. "We can't go barreling in there, or she won't say a word."

"I said I know. But Mary Beth may know something about where Legrand was hiding her, something that can lead us to Henry. We have to try talking to her. I just hope her mother doesn't stop us."

104

"No mother would refuse to help parents in our position, especially Allison Marshall, of all people."

"I hope you're right," Luke said, "because otherwise --"

Luke's phone buzzed, interrupting him in mid-sentence. We both looked at his screen. It was Agent Byram. Luke stabbed the speaker button so both of us could hear at the same time, then he answered the phone with a barked question.

"Did you find Henry?"

"No," Byram's voice said. "But we found his preschool tote bag."

"*Where?*"

"Your medical office. In your waiting room."

The minivan's tires shrieked as Luke made a flying U-turn and crushed the gas pedal to the floorboards.

Chapter 29

Henry could hear Hiram Legrand and Ski Mask talking outside, but he couldn't make out what they were saying.

Thinking about his mother, Henry absently ran his hands along the worn-smooth wood of the walls. A three-foot length of a new board had been nailed into place over a gap in the wall, near where the pair of girl's sandals lay in the dust. The board was freshly-cut and still lightly weeping sap at its cut edges, the yellowish-white color of milled pine much out of place in the gray-brown walls of this old place. The silver nail heads someone had hammered into the fresh piece of lumber gathered what little light there was in the dimness of the room.

Henry sat back down on the floor and drew a tic-tac-toe board with his finger in the dust. He idly wondered how big a trouble Legrand and Ski Mask would be in when his mother came by to pick him up.

Pondering, he put an X in the middle square. Daddy had said that was the best first move.

Chapter 30

Luke Andrews

Jan turned from Agent Byram to me as soon as Sarah and I burst into the waiting room of my medical office.

"Luke, it was just sitting there when I came back," Jan said. "I stayed at the preschool with Claire Michaels after you left, to patch her up a little. Then I came back to check the voicemail. I'm the only nurse on the schedule today, and I just locked the office and ran to you when I heard about Henry. When I got here, the door was wide open, and there it was." She gestured with her hand.

Henry's navy-blue tote bag was resting right there on one of the chairs in my waiting room. Sarah darted over to it, but Byram stopped her.

"Wait," he said. "We need to do forensics on this. If you touch it, it could destroy evidence we need. Now, can you confirm this was Henry's?"

"Yes," Sarah said, "it's his." Her eyes welled and she put both her hands over her mouth and nose. Then she repeated in a hoarse whisper, "It's his."

Of course she was right. Henry's name was written in white atop the church-preschool design on the side of the tote bag. Henry diligently carried it to and from preschool every day, carrying snacks on the way in and the day's artwork on the way out.

I gradually became aware that Sarah's breathing was getting ragged. Her eyes were growing wider as she stared at Henry's tote bag. When her lips and chin started quivering, I reached out to her, but before I could get to her, she abruptly shrieked aloud Henry's name and sprinted out of the waiting room to the hallway, calling Henry's name again and again, running from room to room as if he might be hiding just out of sight in one of them. Her running shoes made a tearing noise along the low-pile carpeting in the hallway.

Emma bounced in my arms as I went after Sarah. Byram called out to us that he had already looked through the whole building, but Sarah was frantically searching, throwing open every closet and yelling Henry's name at the top of her lungs. It was at least a full minute before I could calm her enough to get her to stop near a supply closet. Even then, she was still breathing hard and her eyes were still darting around the room. Finally, I put Emma down by my side and gently placed my hands on the soft skin of Sarah's cheeks and jaw, cradling her head. I waited until she finally focused on me, our faces barely a foot apart.

"Sweetheart, we're going to get him back," I said. "I promise we're going to get him back. Legrand let Mary Beth go free. He's going to let Henry go, too." Then I gently rested my forehead on her forehead.

Sarah was crying hard then, tears streaming down her cheeks and forming tiny puddles against the sides of my hands. I shifted and put my cheek against her cheek, my warm skin soaking in the moisture from her tears.

When her breathing calmed, I reared back just far enough to kiss her on the forehead. "We'll get him back," I said to her again. "I promise."

We stood there for a while, Emma hugging herself to my leg, Sarah squeezing me tightly with her face buried in my shoulder. Eventually we shuffled back out to the waiting room, where Byram and Jan were both waiting for us. We were too badly hurt, too overwrought, to feel embarrassed in front of them. As if nothing had happened, Byram picked up where he left off.

"Legrand, or maybe his driver, or both, probably did this right after Henry was snatched," he said. "The preschool was empty while the kids were at the playground. One of them must have slipped in to grab Henry's bag out of his cubby at the preschool.

"After the snatch, they probably watched your office until it was empty, when your nurse here ran out to get the message to you about Henry. Then he kicked your door in – it's just an old lock, see?"

He gestured to the door jamb. A small hunk of wood had been ripped out of it, where the lock had broken free under the weight of a heavy kick.

"Then he dropped off this tote bag inside the office."

He paused long enough to use a special kind of tongs to slip Henry's tote bag into what looked to be a giant-sized manila envelope. It had the word, "evidence" in block letters on it with a series of black diagonal slashes all around the edges of it. He kept talking as he sealed and put his initials on the evidence bag.

My mind was spinning, and I asked, "Why would he do all of this?"

"I don't know," Byram answered crisply. "It's very personal. Maybe that's the goal; to be very personal with you. But he sure wasted time to do this. Your medical office is less than a mile from the church preschool. Your nurse here didn't get the call from Claire Michaels until maybe three to five minutes had passed from the snatch. He almost certainly waited at least a few minutes – more wasted time – to drop this tote bag off in your office."

"What happens now?" Sarah asked.

"We'll check it for fingerprints," he said. "We couldn't have done it years ago. This tote bag is made out of fabric. Very hard to lift a print off any kind of cloth. But now we have a new technique called vacuum metal deposition, where we use gold and zinc to recover the fingerprint mark on fabric. It might work here, if we get lucky. Obviously, finding Legrand's fingerprints on this bag would be expected.

"But if we find another set, we might get a hit on it and find out who that driver helping Legrand is. And that'd be big. Finding Legrand or his driver is the best way to find Henry."

***

The crowd in front of me in the church preschool's parking lot was comforting, at least a little bit, because I was finally about to do something tangible to help find my son. The majority of the group were friends and neighbors and people who lived around Jameston, but another large group was led by Stumps, who had pulled a remarkable number of his extended family members out

110

of their jobs and homes and led them in a caravan up Route 64 from Richmond. All of them waited patiently in the warm late-afternoon sun as I tried to cobble together words to say.

Standing on the sidewalk next to the church, a modest six-inch rise over the parking lot, I said, "Thank you all for coming. For those of you who don't know Henry on sight, his picture is on these."

I held up thick sheaves of paper in each of my hands. Jan and Sarah had used my office computer and photocopier to make over a thousand flyers. Each flyer had a big picture of Henry, with his height, weight, and hair and eye color as well as the phone numbers for the FBI and me written underneath. They also had an equally large picture from Hiram Legrand's mug shot from just a few days before. Stomach acid burned in my throat watching them cut-and-paste Legrand's picture next to Henry's picture.

"Please, start by going to every business you can," I said. "That means every country store, gas station, restaurant, whatever. Post as many of these as you can. Put it on their windows. While you're there, ask the owner of each of those businesses if they've seen him. Our boy. Henry."

I felt myself in danger of choking up as I said Henry's name aloud, so I gritted my teeth and swallowed hard. At the back of the crowd, Sarah was standing with Emma on a tidy bed of mulch in the parking lot's island, in the shade of a flowering cherry tree that had been planted there when I was a child. I faked a small coughing bout before continuing.

"You all should split up somehow," I said. "You know, so you don't -- so you don't all go to the same places. The more you spread out, the better the chances are that we'll find Henry. Maybe you could -- well, I'm gonna have to figure this out."

111

My throat was constricting hard, and I knew I was going to lose it if I said another word. So I fumbled with the flyers and tried to cover my pause by pretending to be working out logistics. Finally Stumps stepped forward authoritatively, turned to face the crowd, and began to speak to them in his strong courtroom voice.

"I'm going to have you break into groups of three or four people in just a minute," he said as he pulled a roadmap of Jameston County out of his back pocket and held it up high. "This is going to be the master map. I'm going to have some groups each take a piece of the county and post flyers at every rural business out there. You'll have a lot of driving to do, so we'll get you started in just a minute. The other groups will go to every business here in town, walking around on foot. We'll start putting flyers on every telephone pole and stop sign we can find, both in town and out in the country. At every intersection, too. Understood?"

All eyes were on Stumps as he spoke, and a wave of gratitude for my friend rushed over me. He looked out at the nodding heads answering him.

"Good," he said. "All right, everyone form your groups. Now."

Stumps kept his eyes on the crowd, watching people separate themselves into small groups. Satisfied that they were doing what he directed, he then turned to face me, moving his hand from my shoulder to the back of my neck.

"Luke, let me handle this," he said. "You're in no condition to think straight. This is really a job for the sheriff's department, but they're already stretched thin trying to keep up with the roadblocks. I saw on the way in that they're even using the county game warden to help man one of the roadblocks."

112

I nodded. Over his shoulder, Sarah was taking Emma inside the church preschool, probably to use the bathroom. As soon as she was out of view, my eyes starting welling, and I clamped my mouth shut.

"All these people, they're here to help," Stumps said. "I brought as many people as I could find on short notice, and there will be more and more coming until we find Henry. Let me get this organized for you."

He looked at me for a long moment. His warm brown eyes were soft as he watched me fight for all I was worth against the tears. Then I felt his hand tighten on the back of my neck as he spoke again.

"There isn't anything I wouldn't do to make this better for you," he said.

With that he roughly pulled me by the neck down to his shoulder, but I was already crying before I got there.

Chapter 31

6:00 p.m.
Thursday evening

<u>Sarah Andrews</u>

I left Emma with Luke to go to Allison Marshall's house alone.

After two efforts at well-mannered knocking at Allison's front door without any response, I pounded the heel of my hand on it, hard enough to make the door shudder in its frame.

Out of the corner of my eye, a blue French-country curtain fluttered in a nearby window. After an interval, a tall, well-dressed man with a manicured beard finally opened the door. The scent of Polo cologne breezed over me as the cool air-conditioning from the house escaped into the warm spring evening air. The man was lanky and had a very large Adam's apple that sat oddly low on his neck, well below where his beard stopped.

"Can I help you?" he asked in a deep bass voice.

"My name is Sarah Andrews. I met Allison earlier this morning. I need to talk to her."

"I'm Todd, her brother. She's resting now."

"I understand that, but I really need to talk to her," I said. "Could you please let her know it's me out here?"

"She and Mary Beth have just gone through a lot. She can't have visitors right now. I'll let her know you stopped by," he said.

"But this is very, very important. I wouldn't be here otherwise."

"I can't help you," he said, and he abruptly started to swing the door closed. Without thinking, I smacked the palm of my hand on the door and stepped forward to stop the door from latching closed. The bottom edge of that heavy door hurt my foot when he banged it.

I swallowed back some bile that burned my throat.

"Sir, my son is missing. He's been kidnapped by the same man who took Mary Beth. Your niece is safe now, but my son isn't. I need to talk to Allison right now. Please."

"Todd?" I heard Allison's voice call from inside the house. "I'll come out."

Allison herself walked out the door. She had changed her clothes from this morning. She was wearing gray sweatpants, a T-shirt, and white socks that contrasted with the gray slate of her front stoop. Todd kept the door open and stood there looking at us with his arms folded in front of him.

I took a deep breath and said, "Allison, thank you so much for coming out. I need your help."

She looked at me with unreadable eyes.

"You know that my son is missing now, too," I said.

"I know," she said tonelessly.

An unwelcome wave of uncertainty rolled over me. "We're looking everywhere we can for Henry. My husband is organizing volunteers to help with the search right now. And we need help. The FBI has no real leads, except of course that it's Hiram Legrand who did it --"

115

"Don't use that bastard's name here ever again," Allison hissed. "Todd is here because that evil son of a bitch is on the loose. He's going to stay here with us until they find him again and lock him up in a real prison, instead of that joke of a jail we have here. He brought his shotgun with him."

"I know how you feel," I said, "but now the man who snatched your daughter has our son. And I know Mary Beth probably doesn't feel like talking about it, but if she could give us any description of where she was held --"

"No."

"Please, it would take just a few minutes. Anything she saw, anything at all, could help us find Henry."

"No."

"Please, Allison," I begged, one octave higher.

"No."

"But I helped you this morning. You know what it's like to be a mother missing a child. How could you not help me?"

"You and your husband didn't help me today," she said venomously, her eyes narrowing to angry slits. "I talked to the FBI this morning before they found my little girl. They said your husband still wasn't going back in that jail. He wasn't going to lift a finger to help me or my daughter. So now you and your husband can go to hell. I got mine. You go find your own." And with that, she wheeled around and stomped down the hallway back inside her house.

Todd looked at me levelly, and his Adam's apple bobbed from the hairline of his beard almost all the way back down to the base of his neck as he said, "You heard her. She's done. Mary Beth doesn't have anything to say to you."

With that pronouncement at first hanging and then drifting slowly down into the bushes and shrubs lining the front of the house, he closed the door firmly. The deadbolt twisted home with a decisive click.

Stunned, I walked on unsteady legs back to the minivan and slowly slid behind the wheel.

Chapter 32

When we had done everything that could be done that evening, when every flyer had been posted everywhere anyone could think of, Luke and I went home for the night.

The surreal absence of Henry in our house lay heavy on us all. Even Emma was sluggish as we went through her bedtime routine. After we clicked off her bedroom lights, leaving the bedroom door open a crack so she could see the hallway light, Luke asked me if I wanted to pray with him. I said no. He nodded and went by himself down the hallway to our bedroom. Through the open door I saw him flop on his back on the bed and throw an arm loosely across his eyes.

I stayed there in the hallway with my head down, just standing and not moving, vacantly gazing at the baseboard molding, listening to the quiet of the house.

Then, somehow, I was outside Henry's bedroom. Taped to his door was a construction-paper sign proclaiming his name, brush-painted in watercolors and dotted with stickers. Fingerprint grunge from dozens of play dates graced the white-painted wood around his doorknob.

118

Blowing all the air out of my lungs, I held my breath and twisted the doorknob. I walked right to the center of his little bedroom, still holding my breath. Then I closed my eyes and waited ten seconds, then 20 seconds, then 30 seconds, until my body started to ache for oxygen. Then, with an anticipation that was two parts welcome and one part dread, I inhaled deeply, filling my lungs with the bedroom air.

Henry's scent exploded in me, and my eyes popped open from the impact. His scent was tactile. It poured into my nose, my mouth, even my throat. I could smell him everywhere, in everything. I smelled his clean pajamas in his dresser, his stuffed animals strewn about his bed, the box of pull-ups hidden away in his closet, the children's shampoo lingering on his pillowcase. They combined with his own little-boy scent to make a fresh-smelling posy that was uniquely and unmistakably Henry. I stood there breathing in that scent, as delicious and unsatisfying as any withheld food has ever smelled to the starving.

The last time I had been alone in Henry's empty bedroom at night was over four years ago, when I was eight and a half months pregnant with him. Luke and I had been getting ready to put up a wallpaper border we had picked up that day at the Babies R' Us on West Broad Street in Richmond. Luke was downstairs at the kitchen sink, filling a dipping bin with water, and I was upstairs in this very bedroom, leaning against the stepladder he had just opened up. It was July, and the evening songs of the katydids and whippoorwills outside the open windows were the background music to that first cramp in my belly. A midnight drive in my old car and one epidural later, and all eight pounds, three ounces of Henry had been swaddled in my arms, a couple of weeks ahead of schedule.

Without him here now, I was desperate to cuddle with something. Emma was asleep in her own room. I already knew from holding her all afternoon that I could never put on her shoulders the duty of being a surrogate Henry. It wasn't fair to her. And even if it was, she couldn't do it. She was Emma, and he was Henry. I had two children, and each of them independently owned all of me. Somehow she could fill all of my heart at the very same time he could empty all of it.

So I left Emma where she was and picked up Monkey off Henry's bed. Monkey was Henry's favorite stuffed animal. We'd had whole emergencies at bedtime if Monkey couldn't be found. Once when Monkey's arm had been torn off and I was out for a rare night with my girlfriends, Luke had achieved rock star status in Henry's eyes by doing a hasty repair with the sewing kit I kept in a drawer in our home office.

I lay down on my belly on Henry's bed with one arm under the pillow. I put Monkey high up on my shoulder so that the side of my face rested on Monkey, just as Henry did every night.

In Henry's bed, with Monkey kissing my face, Henry's scent grew stronger, heavier. It almost brought him right here to me, right where I could stroke his little-boy hair, feel his little-boy squirming, and hear his little-boy stories. At that moment, Henry filled my senses in every way, except by his presence.

Breathing in my little boy, I fell asleep in Henry's bed.

Chapter 33

11:30 p.m.
Thursday night

Henry was asleep on his belly on the dingy floor, his right arm tucked under his head as a pillow, his left knee bent to the side. The two men standing outside the door talked quietly, as people do when it is dark and no light can be seen outside.

"If we bring him to town, he could call out or make noise. Someone could hear," Hiram Legrand said.

"I doubt it," Ski Mask said. "No one will be awake. Believe me, the town rolls up the sidewalks at night."

"Yeah, but if someone happens to walk by the church just as we're doing it, we're going to have to kill them both fast," Legrand said. "No guns. Has to be quiet. I'm bringing my knife."

"Ok."

"You need to bring yours, too."

"I know."

"All right, then."

Chapter 34

4:25 a.m.
Friday morning

Luke Andrews

At first, the ringing of the phone slipped into my dream and became part of it. It was a dream like those the feverish experience in their sleep -- writhing and hot, unclear in outline but certain in the shape of its malice. Then the ringing ripped me awake, and I was up on my elbows, sweat on my forehead. The sound of Sarah's feet running down the hallway from Henry's bedroom got me moving. I rolled across her empty side of the bed and plucked the phone.

"Dr. Andrews? This is Agent Healey. I'm sorry to wake you, but please clear your head. I have something important to tell you."

Sarah bolted into the room and skidded on her knees across the bed sheets until she came to a stop against me.

"I'm awake. Tell me what's going on," I said tightly.

"Ok, I want you to prepare yourself," Healey said, waiting a beat and taking a breath before continuing, "Rockbridge County deputies have found a body in the Maury River. It is the body of an unknown male child, estimated age four or five years old. We have no other information. I need to emphasize that we are not, repeat not, sure the unknown male child is Henry. It could be another child. But you need to know the body was found only an hour away from the abduction here in Jameston, and the basic description fits."

I couldn't help letting a choked "Oh my God" slip from me, and Sarah's hand turned into a talon on my arm.

Agent Healey was still talking on the phone. "Again, I have to be clear, it might not be Henry. But we need you to start heading to the hospital in Lexington to view the body and make a positive or negative identification. Do you know where the hospital is?"

"Yes," I answered thickly, my lips feeling sluggish and numb. "I'll be on the road in a few minutes."

"Good, I'll meet you down there. I'm already on the way."

I hung up the phone and turned to Sarah so that we both were on our knees on the bed facing each other. I would have felt unmanned if I did not have to take care of my wife at that moment. I put my hands on her shoulders.

"Sweetheart, they don't think it's Henry," I said to her. "But they found the body of a child down in Lexington. They need us to confirm that it's not Henry. So we're gonna have to get in the car and start driving there. They just need us to confirm that it's not Henry."

Sarah's breathing was uneven while I was speaking, and she pulled away from me to get off the bed and stand on the floor. Her face tensed, then trembled, the way land looks at the start of an earthquake just before the earth rips open into jagged edges and gaping chasms. I had the feeling of a man looking down at the shaking earth underneath his feet with dawning awareness that he is standing right on top of where one of those chasms is about to open.

Then, so quickly as to be almost abrupt, the earthquake ended. A look of unhealthy composure paralyzed Sarah's features into place. It was through a slight smile that she replied to me.

"It's not Henry," she said confidently.

"That's right, it's probably not Henry," I said.

"No, not probably. Definitely. It's not Henry. I'd know. I'm his mother. I know he's still alive. Ok?"

Sarah's last word was more challenge than question, and I nodded. She gave me a look that lived somewhere between defiance and triumph, and she was breathing a little heavily like she had just won a short race.

"Let's get moving," Sarah said. "I want to confirm for them right away that it's not Henry, so they get back to work on finding him for us. Let's go."

And with that she turned away and pulled her T-shirt over her shoulders in one motion and walked briskly over to her dresser to rummage through the top drawer for a bra, a woman on the move. She finished dressing and hustled out the bedroom door and downstairs well before me.

After I pulled on my sweats and tied on my running shoes, I slipped into the darkness of Emma's room and gently lifted her up, blanket and all. With my precious bundle cradled in my arms, I went downstairs into the eye-squinting brightness of our kitchen. There I found Sarah bustling about, her hair swept into an efficient ponytail, packing a breakfast to go for Emma.

***

How does a man feel as he drives the family minivan toward a hospital that may hold the body of his first-born child? When he prays to God in the green glow of dashboard lights, does he think about his own sins? Does he fear the awful penance he may be about to pay for taking the good times for granted? Does he try to hide his anticipation of rage at God if God chooses not to help him? Does he do those things, does he, does he, on the interstate as the red eyes of tractor-trailer taillights watch him in the dark?

We arrived in Lexington just as the sun was beginning to dawn over the Blue Ridge and awaken the valley below. When I pulled into the hospital parking lot and turned off the van, Sarah and I looked wordlessly at each other for a few moments. Then Emma was awake, and she held both our hands and walked between us as we made our way through the parking lot. We were nearly at the front automatic doors of the hospital when my phone started buzzing. It was Ms. Healey's number.

"This is Luke," I said. "We're just getting here now. Are you inside?"

"Yes," Ms. Healey said. "Are you still on the road or literally outside in the parking lot?"

"We're walking in the building right now."

"Ok, good. I'm in the business office of the hospital administrator. I'll meet you in the lobby."

We waited in the lobby for just a minute before Ms. Healey came to greet us. Her expression was full but unreadable, and she ushered us into a side conference room belonging to the hospital administrator. We all sat.

"I am so glad I can tell you that the body we found is *not* Henry," Ms. Healey said. "The body that was found in the Maury River overnight has been positively identified. He was not, repeat not, your son."

Sarah yelped and leaned over at the waist, hugging her own legs and whispering "Thank you," over and over. I felt as if I had instantly lost 100 pounds. Only Emma's weight in my lap kept me from oozing out of the chair onto the floor.

Sarah reached over to hold my hand. "I told you it wasn't him," she said. I nodded, and we both threw our heads back on the chairs, the classic breathing of our extreme relief the only noise in the room. Emma felt the change in mood and wriggled comfortably against my chest.

I would have kept basking there for a long time, but then Sarah stiffened and sat up in her chair. She had recognized the obvious first.

"Who was he?" she asked Ms. Healey.

Ms. Healey's countenance sagged, and she lowered her head. "He was a local kindergartener who was missing since last weekend," she said. "He tagged along with his older brother and the brother's friends as they snuck in the Boy Scout camp in Goshen, just west of here. He apparently had been playing by himself a little apart from the older boys, near one of the trout streams that feed the Maury River. Very likely, he fell into the water and was swept downstream. The water rushing off the mountains is still cold this time of year, and at his age, he probably lost consciousness quickly. We called his parents at the same time we called you. They live closer, so they got here first and made the identification."

Our elation dissipated nearly as quickly as it had arrived. We were thinking of that other mother and father, and their crushing loss. They were probably still in the building right now. Maybe we could --

"I know your minds must be completely blown by now, and I apologize for pouring it on, but there's more I have to tell you," Agent Healey said, pulling something out of a manila folder she had with her.

"About 20 minutes ago, just as I was getting here, I got a call from Rick. Agent Byram. Someone just called it in. We have . . . we found a photo of Henry. And we believe it was taken within the last few hours."

Sarah and I gasped in tandem as Ms. Healey handed us a copy of what she was holding. It was a picture of Henry at night, dressed in the clothes he had worn to preschool yesterday. He was standing in front of our church, in the very same parking lot where Stumps and I had addressed the crowds of searchers yesterday. Henry was looking quizzically at the camera. Standing behind him, where he couldn't see, was Hiram Legrand himself. Legrand had a wolfish grin on his face, and he was waving at the camera, his fingers folded at the knuckles in a mockingly childlike wave.

I could feel the pulse pounding in my head and taste the metallic bitterness in my mouth, and distantly I knew my adrenal glands had just dumped an enormous load of adrenaline into my bloodstream. Even so, I found my speech again before Sarah did.

"Henry was taken yesterday at lunchtime," I said, my voice shaking. "This must have been taken last night, just in the last few hours. Right?"

"Yes," Ms. Healey said. "You're right. We'll reach out to one of our consultants – an astronomy professor at the University of North Carolina in Chapel Hill – to see if we can pinpoint the time any better. We might be able to improve the quality of the photo enough to identify the position of stars, and that might let us identify the time, maybe within an hour or less. For now, what we know is that sometime between maybe eight last night and six this morning, when your minister found it and called it in, someone took this picture of Henry and Hiram Legrand. My personal guess would be sometime between one and four in the morning, when it's quietest in town."

"Rev. Rigsby found this picture? Where?" Sarah asked.

"It was found taped to the front door of your church," Ms. Healey said. "Rev. Rigsby saw it when he got to the church this morning, pulled it down, walked into the church office and immediately called Agent Byram."

Sarah said, "So someone took this picture, then somehow printed it, came back and took the time to tape it to our church, so that it would be found first thing in the morning. Why?"

"We don't know," Ms. Healey said. "But I have to be honest with you. I think Hiram Legrand is trying to inflict as much emotional pain on you as he can. As far as the person who took this picture, maybe there wasn't anyone at all. Hiram could have been alone, using a camera with a timer, the way people do at family reunions. But yes, if someone was on the other end of this camera, then that person is helping Hiram. For reasons we do not know."

Chapter 35

Friday was a haze. Our morning had started before dawn with the heart-ripping drive to the hospital in Lexington, followed by the trip back home in stunned silence. At midday, we had a meeting with the two FBI agents and learned the photo of Henry had been printed on plain paper that could be purchased at any office supply store, using standard ink from a standard printer. An FBI child psychologist studied the photo and opined that Henry looked unsure but not forced or coerced, which Sarah and I could have told him ourselves.

Sarah and I medicated ourselves with work. I helped Stumps organize search workers, whose numbers had swelled since yesterday. True to his word, Stumps seemed to bring half of Richmond with him, and they joined in with our neighbors, parents of preschoolers, friends, mothers from Sarah's playgroups from when Henry was a baby, and others. Once that was launched, Sarah and several of her girlfriends busied themselves with social media. They had laptops open on a folding table upstairs from the preschool in the church's fellowship hall, spreading the word and creating a website dedicated to finding Henry.

For my part, I spent the rest of the day driving back and forth across Jameston County with a stack of flyers and a staple gun. Emma was with me in her toddler car-seat in the back of my truck. I told her various white lies when she got restless and asked what we were doing and where Henry was.

The updates from the FBI kept rolling in through the afternoon. The deputies' canvass of the neighborhood had not improved the description of the car Legrand and his driver used yesterday. No one had a license plate, no one got a good look at the driver, and no one had any idea who the driver could be. FBI criminologists were debating among themselves, without consensus, about why Legrand would risk so much to come back to the scene of the crime and take a photo, let alone go to the trouble of printing it somewhere and posting it at our church. Amos Hudson was distraught over his missing master key and the escape of Hiram Legrand from his jail. Agent Byram had questioned Amos himself, and he believed Amos's anguish was genuine.

All of these updates and a dozen others buzzed in through the phone on my hip.

As it got past dinnertime for Emma, I picked up Sarah and headed home. We all needed a break. The frantic initial part of the search for Henry was over. There might be days, not hours, ahead of us. Both Sarah and I knew it.

When we got home, Sarah wanted Mom-and-Emma time, so I went up to our bedroom as Emma cuddled with Sarah on the couch in our living room. Closing the door behind me, I sat on the side of the unmade bed we had left in a rush 14 hours earlier, and stared at my Bible on the nightstand. The faux-leather cover had lost the shine it had when it was new, back when I was in third grade, and the car wreck that took my parents and sister was still years in the future. The date of my Bible was inscribed on the inside cover by a much younger Rev. Crosley, the graying of middle age just starting to nip at his temples back then.

I turned the Bible over in my hands before resting it on my lap and struggling my way through a prayer.

> *God, please bring Henry back to Sarah and me. We love him so much. God, I'm so sorry for all the things I've done wrong in my life. I don't read my Bible enough. I should visit Eli more; I know I should help him more than I have. I should spend more time seeing charity patients at the free clinic, give away more for free. I promise, promise, promise, if you can just bring Henry back to us, I'll do those things and more. I promise. Please --*

I couldn't finish. It felt all wrong. The sense of well-being and reassurance that usually came with prayer was absent. So I put the Bible back on the nightstand and walked heavily back down the stairs, finding Emma at the dining table waiting for Sarah to finish making her a grilled cheese sandwich. Then I went out the back door to take in some outside air. Out behind our house, my feet crunched along gravel paths my father had built years earlier.

When I was young, my parents took our family to Mount Vernon, the historic home of George Washington, up in northern Virginia. The neoclassical Georgian mansion stood on a commanding bluff high over the Potomac River. Hundreds of years earlier, people would walk down that bluff and throw huge nets into the Potomac to catch herring and shad, thereby creating a commercial fishery at the working plantation, which also had a blacksmith shop, gristmill and distillery to go with the gardens, fields and orchards.

But none of that impressed my father. He never wanted other men to do his work for him. What he liked most were the well-manicured gravel paths that crossed through the plantation's green lawns. He commented on the pleasant-looking tan paths as we crunched across them while the tour guide pointed out huge old trees that she claimed Washington himself may have planted. By that weekend back home, he was laying out similar paths around our house, leading to our barn, driveway, garden and wood shed.

These were the paths on which my feet scuffed and sent tiny pebbles flying into the grass as I thought about Henry. He couldn't be far. And just last night he had been tantalizingly close, right in front of our church. If only a sleepless night-owl type had passed by while walking his dog, or if only Rev. Rigsby had been working late, or even if Henry had abruptly yelled at the top of his lungs and awakened the closest neighbors, a quick 911 call could have ended this nightmare.

I walked to the end of the farthest path behind our house, down to where our woodshed was filled with firewood of oak, hickory, and poplar. The mountain rising behind it had an official name on the maps, but we always called it Andrews Mountain, as if it were entirely ours. I looked up the mountain, my skin cooled by the slight breeze wafting down off of it. Breathing in the distant scent of pine and cedar up on the mountain, I welcomed the calm it gave me.

I was about to take a second shot at prayer when my phone buzzed, pulling my eyes off the mountain and back down to my hip. I didn't recognize the number, but that had been happening all day. It was probably from one of the searchers keeping me posted about where they had distributed flyers of Henry. They had started to venture into neighboring counties as we ran out of places to post in Jameston County. I picked it up on the fourth ring, just before it went into voicemail.

"This is Luke," I said.

A pause. Then a breathy snicker.

"How do you like me now?" Hiram Legrand said in my ear.

Chapter 36

7:05 p.m.
Friday evening

Henry was alone with the man who always wore a ski mask. Hiram Legrand had left awhile earlier. Henry had heard Hiram and Ski Mask talking about Hiram's going back into town after it got dark.

Ski Mask rustled outside the room in which Henry was locked, then came back in and handed Henry a Yoo-Hoo chocolate drink and a candy bar. Henry put them both down without opening them.

"What's wrong with you?" Ski Mask asked.

Henry kept looking at the floor said, "I want to go home."

"You can't," Ski Mask said.

"Daddy is gonna come here to get me," Henry said stubbornly.

Ski Mask nodded gravely.

"I hope he does. I truly do."

Chapter 37

Sarah Andrews

Through the window over the deep-basin porcelain sink in our kitchen, I watched Luke meander outside. I thought he might go inside the barn, to our gym, and pound away at the boxer's heavy bag he has in there. But he only looked in the barn briefly and then slowly walked away, over toward the woodshed. He leaned up against it and stared up at the mountain for a while.

My handwritten list rested on the kitchen counter as Emma munched on her grilled-cheese sandwich behind me. I had jotted down about 30 phone calls I wanted to make tonight. Most would be to college friends who lived within a few hours of driving distance. By tomorrow I wanted as many as possible here to help with the search. Allison Marshall was on the list of people to call, too. I was saving her for last.

I glanced outside the kitchen window again. Luke hadn't moved. He was still just staring up at the mountain.

Just as I was about to look away, Luke plucked his phone off his hip and put it up to his ear. His back was to me and I couldn't see his expression. But then he visibly shuddered, and a moment later he abruptly threw his phone down on the grass, furiously shouting so loudly that I could hear him inside the house. My heart leapt into my throat, and I dashed outside, the screen door slamming against the side of the house from the force of my shove.

"Is it Henry? Is it Henry?" I screamed as I ran up to him.

He wheeled around and saw my fear that he had just heard the unspeakable.

"No, Sarah, no, that wasn't any news about Henry," he said, his face churning. "But for God's sake. That was Hiram Legrand!"

"Hiram Legrand! What did he say? Did you hear Henry?"

Luke shook his head angrily and said, "Just Legrand. He called just to mock me. No information at all. It just lasted a few seconds. I'm going to kill that --"

Just then, Luke's phone started buzzing again in the grass, and we both looked at it like it was a bomb. At the second buzz, he started over to it, but I said "No," and waved him away and snatched it up off the grass myself. I closed my eyes and took a deep breath before answering it curtly.

"Hello."

"Sarah? Agent Richard Byram here. I thought I had called Luke's phone."

I expelled the air in my lungs in a big whoosh and hunched over. I waved Luke off and mouthed "FBI" to him.

"You did call Luke's phone," I said. "I just --"

"We've found another picture of Henry," Byram interrupted me. "He's alive and unhurt in the picture. We think it was taken today. We found it on the telephone pole closest to the park where he was kidnapped. It was stapled right on top of the posters that the searchers put up."

136

"What!"

"Yeah, I know," Byram said. "Listen, do you have anything at all that might have Henry's fingerprint on it? The tote bag was a zero, but our field tech says we may have a partial print on the photo we just found. Just in case, it makes sense to exclude Henry as the source of the print, if we're able to get anything."

"I'll find something. We're on the way."

"No, no. You sit tight. I'll come to you and Luke. If you have anything at home with Henry's fingerprint on it, I'll want to bag it myself."

"Ok, but Luke just got a phone call I need to tell you about."

***

Agent Byram inspected Henry's handprint art from preschool on the wall upstairs in our bedroom hallway. Henry's two small handprints in paint on thick paper flanked either side of the little poem:

> *This is the hand*
> *You used to hold*
> *When I was only*
> *4 years old.*

He looked at it for a good long while before he shook his head.

"I'm not a techie, but I don't think this would work. The paint filled in too much of the lines and swirls of his hand. What else do you have?"

I let him look around Henry's room for something that might have his fingerprint on it. He spotted the University of Virginia plastic tumbler, the souvenir kind you get in a football stadium when you buy a big soda. One of Luke's patients had given us tickets for the home game against Clemson last season, and our family had spent a glorious fall day at Scott Stadium in Charlottesville.

"Did Henry handle this cup himself?"

He had. I'd seen Henry any number of times take the tumbler off the shelf and study the football players pictured on the side.

"Yes."

"Good," Byram said. "A surface like this holds a fingerprint really well. I'll bag it."

He'd already received a preliminary report from FBI techs tracing Hiram Legrand's call to Luke. It had come from an unknown number, he said, which almost certainly meant a prepaid mobile phone. He explained that prepaid phones were used by smarter, more sophisticated gang leaders and drug dealers because they weren't registered to any particular user and could not be traced to a service subscriber. The FBI techs had tried to trace the phone to a cell tower. Sometimes, he said, a cell user's location could be approximated based on the phone's signals to the nearest cell tower. But when they tried, the signal was dead. It probably meant that someone had yanked the battery out of the phone, he said. It was a dead end.

Once he was done bagging the cup, we went back downstairs to find Luke still staring at the piece of paper Byram had placed on our kitchen table.

It was a poor photocopy of the picture of Henry. Agent Byram had said that he couldn't bring the original photo for fear of smudging any prints, but we still could make out from the photocopy what the original looked like. Henry was standing by himself outside, in what seemed to be a clearing in some woods. His expression again was more quizzical than scared or upset.

It was what was written underneath his picture, in block letters, that captured the attention.

"SAY GOODBYE, DADDY."

Luke's fists were clenched so tightly that his forearms trembled as he stared at the picture.

"It'd be easy to set up a remote campsite in Shenandoah National Park or maybe Washington and Jefferson National Forest," Byram said. "That's where we think this most likely is. And none of it is far from here. Unfortunately, the Forest Service tells us there are over 1.6 million acres in the National Forest alone. Add in Shenandoah National Park, and we're talking several thousand square miles of woods. Together, the national forest and national park represents the largest block of undeveloped wilderness in the eastern United States. According to my guy at the Department of the Interior."

Luke was tuned out. All he could do was stare at that picture.

"Did you learn anything else from the picture?" I asked.

"We've already had someone from the Virginia Department of Forestry take a look at the original photo. He says those trees are all Virginia natives. They could be anywhere in the upland of Virginia. They're all common. Nothing that can help us pinpoint where the photo was taken.

"Also, you can't see it in this photocopy, but in the original, it looks like Henry's feet are wet. His sneakers have a glisten to them. Given the light in this picture and the possibility of dew, we think this photo was taken this morning."

"And the writing? What does it mean?" I asked.

"I've never seen anything like this before," Byram said. "So I'm checking with our criminal profilers to get their thoughts. But I agree with Jeanne Healey's take on this. It's obvious."

"What's obvious?"

"Legrand, and maybe whoever is helping him, they just want to inflict pain. On both of you. Especially on Luke."

Chapter 38

12:05 a.m.
Saturday morning

Luke Andrews

Sitting at the kitchen table just after midnight with an untouched sandwich in front of me, I scrolled through some texts. Stumps was bringing an even larger group tomorrow to help search camp sites near the Appalachian Trail, at the crest of the Blue Ridge in the northern part of the national park, for signs of Henry. Jan and Rev. Crosley, working the phones together, had arranged for dozens of more volunteers to join in with Stumps's group tomorrow for the search. News directors of the television stations in media markets all around Virginia had run at least a 30-second story about Henry in their 6 p.m. and 11 p.m. slots earlier tonight, as well as placed prominent stories on their websites.

Sarah was upstairs, sound asleep. At 10 p.m., I'd given her something to knock her out. Her body was exhausted, but she was so torqued up that she would have had no chance of resting otherwise. Starting again at dawn, we both were going to work like hell. For that she needed a good night's sleep tonight. She had been reluctant at first, but then gave in and took the pills with a swallow of water before lying down in bed.

My phone buzzed in my hands. Agent Healey's number. I answered quickly.

"This is Luke."

"Luke. I apologize for calling so late. Am I waking you?" she asked.

"No. What's going on?"

"Well, there's been a big development. We don't have Henry yet, but we've recaptured Hiram Legrand."

"You've got him!"

"Yes, sir, we've got him," she said, the pleasure in her voice palpable, having finally delivered good news to us. A raw joy coursed through my veins, and I pumped my fist as she explained how it had gone down.

"We picked him up about a half hour ago," she said. "A deputy sheriff, a young guy named Riggs, caught Legrand sneaking around that small brick house next to your church. Legrand was alone. He did not have Henry with him. Or the driver who helped him yesterday."

"Did he tell you where Henry is?"

"No, he hasn't been talking yet," she said. "But Rick Byram and I are about to question him."

"No hint, no nothing?"

"No, but again, we're getting ready to question him now. We just picked him up, within the last 30 minutes."

I thought that over for a bit, then asked, "You found him outside the small brick house next to the church? You must mean the parsonage, where Rev. Crosley used to live. Where Rev. Rigsby stays now."

"Yes, that's the one. We think Legrand may have been planning to post another picture of Henry right around there. That would be the third one either at the church or within a block or two of it. So we have a couple of other deputies on foot with flashlights looking around to see if he maybe got rid of it just before he was arrested. Nothing yet. Anyway, we got lucky. Deputy Riggs happened to swing by at just the right time, spotted Legrand, and then did everything right. Legrand saw him and started to run, but Riggs caught up to him with a Taser in hand, and zapped him. By the time backup got there, Riggs had Legrand face down on the ground and handcuffed."

"Where is he?"

"Who, Riggs?"

"No. Legrand. Where is he?"

"He's with us. Here in the sheriff's office. Until we know for sure how he escaped from Cent-West Jail, we're going to keep him in custody here. The sheriff doesn't have a cage here, but he does have a handcuff bar in an interrogation room. That's a thick metal bar drilled into the wall that you can attach handcuffs to, so that the prisoner can't go after you as he's being questioned. Plus there's several deputies babysitting him right now. Legrand's not going anywhere this time."

"What now?"

"Agent Byram and I will start questioning him shortly," she said.

"All right, I'll be there in maybe 25 minutes, a half hour tops."

"No. No need," she said. "These sessions can take hours, and we can't have you in there during questioning, anyway."

"Why not?"

"It's not protocol," she said. "We can't have a victim in the room during questioning."

"Protocol. You sure I shouldn't come up there?"

143

"Yes," she said. "Believe me, we'll be questioning him hard."

"All right. But *please* keep me posted, ok? Anytime. I don't care if it's three in the morning."

"Absolutely."

"One more thing, Ms. Healey. Jeanne. Do anything and everything you can to get Henry back. Promise Legrand money if he wants money. Lie to him and tell him you'll set him free if he tells us where Henry is. Whatever it takes. Get him to give Henry back to us."

"I know," she said. "We're on it. No one's better than Rick Byram at talking to guys like this."

After we said our goodbyes, I sat in silence in the kitchen, thinking about my son.

Henry had been a colicky baby. Sometimes in the wee hours of the night, I'd take him out of his crib and walk downstairs to my recliner. Laying him on my chest so he could feel the vibrations of my vocal cords, I would hum gentle songs to him, over and over, to comfort him. "Amazing Grace" was a favorite. The quiet humming would take a while, but eventually he would fall asleep, and then eventually I'd fall asleep too. One of my favorite pictures of Henry and me together was one Sarah took when she slipped downstairs and found us both conked out in the recliner.

And that made my decision for me. The hell with protocol. I was going to town to see Legrand face to face, and he was giving Henry back to us. Period. If need be, I would break his arms and legs to make him tell us where Henry was.

I cast a look up the stairs. Sarah would be dead to the world by now. I'd given her a pretty strong benzodiazepine. I tip-toed upstairs and looked in on her in our bedroom. Her breathing was deep and slow. Then I said her name in a low voice. No move. So

144

I walked up to her, brushed her long hair off her cheek and gave her a soft kiss there. Still no move. She was deeply asleep.

I decided to let her sleep. "I'm going to get our boy tonight, sweetheart," I whispered to her. "I'm going to bring him home to you by morning."

Quietly closing the door behind me, I went down to check on Emma. Her little face scrunched up as the light from the hallway spilled across her when I slowly pushed open her door.

"Daddy?" she said in her sleepy, sweet little-girl voice.

"Yeah, baby. It's Daddy."

"Where are we going?"

"Nowhere, baby. Go back to sleep."

"'K. I love you, Daddy."

"I love you, too, baby," I said back to her, but she was already falling back asleep, nestling so deeply under her blanket that I could only see the waves of her honey-blond hair peeking out and resting loosely on her pillow.

Emma was at a stage where she often got scared in the middle of the night, and sometimes she needed help with the potty by two or three in the morning. One of us then would have to come retrieve her from the safety of her bed. If I left her at home, the chances were good that she would call out for us at some point, and Sarah might not wake up from just the sound. True, Emma physically could get Sarah up if she went into our bedroom and gave Sarah a shake. The meds had just made Sarah fall fast asleep. They hadn't put her in a coma. Still, if Emma woke up Sarah like that, at first Sarah would be a little dazed and disoriented, and then she would probably freak out about my absence. Plus it would ruin the good chance I had of delivering a wonderful surprise of waking her up in the morning by having Henry leap out of my arms and into bed with her.

Better to take Emma with me.

I stepped quietly into Emma's room and swept her up, her sleep-warm body soft and small against me. She stirred briefly but settled right down again, her head resting on my shoulder.

On the way out of the house I double-checked the deadbolts on the doors and the locks on the windows and flicked on every outside light we had. Putting Emma in her car seat in Sarah's minivan, I left my own truck parked prominently in the spotlight nearest our barn. Anyone passing by would believe that I was home.

Sarah was locked in tight, and Emma was safe with me in the minivan and already dozing again in her car seat. Popping the parking brake, I rolled quietly at idle speed down our long gravel driveway.

***

Emma was a sleepy lump in my arms when I got to the sheriff's office. I wanted to thank Deputy Riggs, but he was debriefing at the home of his boss, the sheriff, who'd been in bed when he heard one of his deputies had recaptured Legrand. One of the other deputies, a heavyset man named Smith, greeted me with a strong handshake.

"Dr. Andrews, we're really glad for y'all that we found that sum'bitch," Deputy Smith said, his comfortable country-boy

146

drawl dropping to a whisper on that last word out of deference to Emma dozing on my shoulder.

"Thank you very much," I said. "Sarah and I are incredibly grateful to all of you."

"Hey, that's what we're here for. And don't you worry. We ain't resting. At dawn we'll have another gang of guys out there looking for your boy. We'll be joining in with the volunteer fire department guys and looking in the national forest tomorrow. Even our deputies with days off will come in to do it. Ain't none of us taking off until we find your boy."

"I can't thank you enough," I said, and meant it.

"Don't you worry about that. Besides, now that they got that sum'bitch in custody," he shrugged his head back towards the hall that led to interview room, "it won't be long before we know where your boy is."

"Well, that's why I'm here. I need to get in there where they're questioning him."

Deputy Smith's forehead rumpled into thick folds.

"You do?"

"Yeah. Agent Healey called me at home and told me to get on up here."

"Oh. Well, ok then. Guess the feds do things a little bit differently. What about your little girl?"

I looked over at a youngish female deputy who had been watching us from her desk. I recognized her from my medical practice, and I could even remember why I had last seen her – sprained knee from a fall on a snowy sidewalk last winter – but I couldn't place her name. She gave me a shy smile as she saw that I recognized her. I walked over to her.

147

"Hey there," I said. "How's that bum knee doing?" Her badge had the name Shawe written in blue block-letters.

"Oh, so much better," she said, pleased that I remembered her. "The swelling was pretty much all gone within two weeks, just like you said it would. Next time I'll find my snow boots instead of trying to shovel in my old tennis shoes."

"That's great. Hey, I could use a favor. See my little pumpkin here? I need someone to watch her for a few minutes while I go back there," I said, throwing my head back toward the hallway that led to the interview room. "It'd be a big help." Then, without waiting for her response, I turned to Emma, jiggling her slightly to get her awake.

"Sweetie, can you play with Deputy Shawe for a few minutes?"

"Susan," the deputy said. "Call me Susan."

"Miss Susan, then," I said to Emma. "Can you stay with Miss Susan for a few minutes?"

"'K, Daddy."

I quickly rested Emma with her Dora the Explorer blanket on Deputy Shawe's lap, who hurriedly adjusted her badge and thick leather cop-belt to make Emma more comfortable. I mouthed "thank you" to her as I started to stride toward the hall to the interview room without an escort, like I owned the place.

Just as I was getting to the door of the interview room, I ran into Agent Byram himself. He was coming back to the room from the other direction, holding a cup of water in each hand.

"Dr. Andrews," he said with a note of surprise in his voice. "What are you doing here?"

"I'm here to see Hiram Legrand."

"Oh, no. No, no. We can't let you do that," he said.

"Why not? Two days ago you had me talk to him twice and wanted me to go back and talk to him a third time yesterday."

"Yeah, but this is different. This is a law enforcement interrogation."

"He tell you anything about where my boy is?"

"Not yet."

"Then I'm going in," I said, and I brushed right past Byram and went to the door. He made a little motion as if to stop me, but my move was sudden and his hands were full with the two cups of water. My throwing open the door to the interview room silenced whatever he was about to say by way of protest.

And there Legrand was. He and Ms. Healey were sitting on opposite sides of the table in the interview room. Out of the corner of my eye I saw the surprised look on her face at my abrupt appearance, but I kept my focus on Legrand.

The room was small. Legrand was sitting at the table but still could rest his back against the wall. One of his arms was nearly horizontal and slightly behind him, handcuffed at the wrist to a bar on the wall that looked like one of those handicapped bars in a public restroom. It was the handcuff bar Ms. Healey had mentioned to me on the phone.

"Dr. Andrews decided to pay us a quick visit," Agent Byram explained to Ms. Healey.

"Where's my boy?" I asked Legrand without preamble, my voice low and tight. I stood at the corner of the table, about six feet away from him, with nothing but the open little alley created by the table and the wall between us.

He smirked at me and said nothing. I took half a step closer. I could see in my peripheral vision that Byram and Healey were

149

starting to move, as if readying themselves to escort me out the door.

"I said, where's my boy?"

Legrand looked at me, his smirk growing until I could see a narrow slice of his yellowish-gray teeth.

"You ain't never gettin' him back."

"Where is he?" I demanded, my voice loud in the small room.

He turned to face me directly and spoke in a sweetly informative tone.

"Maybe I already sliced him up the gut with my knife. Maybe I filleted him, just like a fish."

From your toes to your fist, my father had said. A punch doesn't come from your arm, your shoulder, or even your hip, he had said as I stood as a kid in front of the heavy bag in our barn and little Eli was off to the side watching us. A punch starts at your toes. Then you push off with your foot to load your leg, and you drive through your hips, twisting your shoulder and firing out your arm until the first two knuckles of your fist crack like a whip one inch behind your target, with every ounce of the full weight of your body behind those two knuckles.

I lashed out so quickly that Legrand was still smirking when the first two knuckles of my fist smashed into him just below his cheekbone and nose. My blasting yell covered the gross thumping sound of hard flesh-on-flesh contact, and through his cheek I felt the tooth roots of his upper bicuspids break under my knuckles. I knocked him clean out of his chair, and he sagged nearly to the floor, utterly unconscious, dangling by the arm still handcuffed to the bar on the wall. Then I felt Agent Byram's weight on my back, and I shrugged him off me, too hard, and he slid across the table

150

and off the other side. He was scrambling to his feet and holding up his hands and I was blurting sorry to him and then it was over.

Silence.

In the sudden quiet of the room, Healey, Byram and I looked at each other and then at Legrand, eyes closed and dangling by the arm. A red splotch flushed hard on his cheek and mouth, right where I had hit him. It was going to swell up, real big. And he was going to need dental work.

Byram broke the quiet spell first. He went over to the audio recorder on the table, hit the rewind button and listened to the sound on it. Then he clicked it off again and looked at me.

"I can't tell on this who went after who," he said. Then he picked up one of the cups of water he had put on the table, walked over to Legrand, crouched next to him, and tossed the water in his face. Legrand started to sputter. His eyes opened, but they were unfocused, and he was obviously dazed. He probably wouldn't be clearheaded for another five or ten minutes.

"Stay with Legrand," Byram said to Ms. Healey. "I'll be back in just a minute."

He pulled me back out to the hallway and closed the door behind me. Taking a furtive glance down the hall to the big open area where the various deputies were working at their desks, he whispered to me.

"You weren't supposed to be in there," he said, looking at me meaningfully. "Like a stupid civilian, you got too close to him. Before I could warn you, he lunged at you, and you hit him in self-defense. You understand?"

I nodded my head, uncertainly at first, then gradually more briskly as understanding dawned on me that he was covering my backside.

151

"Good. That's how it'll go on the report. He lunged at you, and you hit him in self-defense. Can you keep that straight, if anyone asks?"

"Yes."

"All right. Now get out of here. Go home. I'll call you right away if we get any good info out of him. Don't worry. We're going to find your boy."

"Thanks," I said. "For everything."

He patted me on the shoulder and said, "Don't mention it. Now go home and take care of your wife and daughter."

I walked down the hallway, straightening up just as I got to the open area. Emma was still sitting in Deputy Shawe's lap, drawing pictures on blank sheets of printer paper on her desk, and I went over to them.

"Come on, baby, it's time to go home," I said to Emma. Then I looked at Deputy Shawe and said, "Thank you for watching her. I hope it wasn't too much trouble."

"Oh, it was no problem at all. We had fun together, didn't we, sweetheart?" she asked. Emma nodded and smiled.

After saying our goodbyes, Emma and I walked outside, going down the concrete steps slowly because she jumped with both feet on each step, one at a time.

With Emma taking three steps for every one of mine, we slowly made our way through the dark parking lot, first past a few empty police cruisers, then past the deputies' private cars and pickup trucks, and finally to our minivan near the back. By 2 a.m., I'd have Emma back in bed at home.

I was thinking about how I would explain this to Sarah when she woke up in the morning. Maybe my punch to Legrand's face would soften him up, and Byram or Healey would get him to spill the beans about where he was holding Henry. I probably wouldn't be able to surprise Sarah with Henry in my arms at dawn, but hopefully by tomorrow night both our kids would be sound asleep in their own beds at home.

I got to Sarah's minivan and pulled her keys out of my jeans pocket with one hand as Emma held my other hand. I jingled the keys around, looking for the little fob button that would pop the locks. Then Emma's little hand tightened on mine.

"What, honey?" I asked her distractedly as I fumbled with the keys. Finding the fob, I glanced down at her to see what she wanted, but she was looking behind me.

Just before it happened, her eyes suddenly widened.

For a split second I felt the heavy blow on the side of my neck, right where my carotid artery and vagus nerve pass close to one another. One carries crucial oxygenated blood from the heart up to the brain. The other carries signals regulating heart rhythm from the brain back down to the heart. For the briefest of instants before I was knocked unconscious, an intense jolt fired like lightning above and below the impact of the blow.

Then everything went dark.

Chapter 39

1:55 a.m.
Saturday morning

A nameless midnight-shift deputy had nearly run me over in the parking lot as I laid face down and unconscious in the dark and he came back to headquarters for a meal break. My wail had filled the parking lot when he roused me and I instantly realized that Emma was gone.

Byram and Healey had come racing out of the building, and then gave each other flabbergasted looks that left me nauseated. They didn't have to tell me. I knew they had never seen anything like this.

For the next half hour I stood just feet away from where our little girl had been stolen from my very hands, a bag of ice on my neck, watching law enforcement officers descend on the sheriff department's own parking lot and search each square inch for a hair, a dropped item, or any other kind of evidence. I had no answers to any questions. I hadn't seen or heard a thing.

Then my own truck came bouncing into view, Sarah behind the wheel. It rolled to a stop next to the yellow police tape the deputies had set up on cones. Someone had awakened her with a phone call and told her the news.

Sarah's eyes were a little glassy but focused when she stepped out of my truck. Everyone in the parking lot looked up to see the mother who had suffered the awful fate of having had both of her children stolen from her. So I, the father, let the bag of ice drop from my neck and jogged over to her, my arms reaching out to hold her. But when I got to her, she stopped me with one light hand on my chest. She cocked her head slightly to look at the bruise swelling on the right side of my neck.

Then, locking her eyes on mine, Sarah smacked me hard across the face.

The slapping sound cracked in the night. All the deputies and the two FBI agents looked down and away, busying themselves with the tasks at hand of processing the crime scene. Sarah stood there glowering at me. As I held my hand to my cheek, I thought her wordless facial expression of mute betrayal was what hurt the most. Then, in a low voice, she said things that hurt worse.

When she finally strode off to go talk to the FBI agents, I stood facing the same direction I had been looking when she slapped me, my hand still covering the part of my face she had smacked.

Part Three

Chapter 40

3:00 a.m.

Saturday morning

Henry was awakened by the light clank of the door lock, and he rubbed his eyes as the door swung open.

In the darkness of night, Ski Mask's outline quietly appeared in the doorway. He had something sizable in his arms. Then he put down whatever it was, walked back out, and closed the door again. The lock clanked again as Ski Mask secured the door and walked silently back into the night outside.

A few moments later, Emma Grace Andrews hesitantly stepped forward into a ray of moonlight slipping into the room. When the two children saw each other, they ran into the comfort of each other's hugs.

Henry asked, "Are you hungry?"

"A little," Emma said, and he handed her an open box of Pop-tarts. She pulled a package out, and Henry opened it for her, giving her one of the rectangular toaster pastries inside and keeping the other for himself. Looking at each other, they silently ate their Pop-tarts, swirling their tongues over the sweet frosting that stuck to the back of their teeth. When they finished eating, they lay down together on the floor and looked up at the cobwebbed ceiling of this place, her head resting on his outstretched arm.

For all that they were confused and out of their routines, they were still very young children, and it was still the middle of the night. With

few words between them, their eyes got heavier, and within five minutes
they both were sound asleep.

Chapter 41

Sarah Andrews

I had an intense morning of work, updating the website and social media to fill them with information about Emma, creating new flyers for Emma and Henry together, and making sure the nearby search parties had everything they needed.

It had been 11 hours since some strange man had stolen my daughter away from my husband. She had been wearing only her pajamas. Thin, light, vulnerable pajamas. It was warm outside, but I would have given anything for her to have been wearing her thick denim jumper, sturdy shoes, and a coat zipped up to her chin.

In the overnight hours at the sheriff's station after Emma had been taken, and the FBI didn't need anything more from us, Luke had wordlessly handed me the keys to the minivan, his cheek still lightly pink from where I had hit him for the first time ever in our marriage. Then he sat heavily in his truck and drove slowly away, heading towards home. I had stayed behind and listened to Agent Healey and Agent Byram map out their search strategies. As I sat in the sheriff's office during those quietest moments of night when it was too late to be today and too early to be tomorrow, I heard the Amber Alert for Emma on the radio and confirmed with overnight news producers that their regional television stations would play stories about Henry and Emma for their 6 a.m. morning shows.

Finally, when my watch read 3:40 a.m., with nothing more to do for several hours until the search parties planning to look for Henry would congregate at the church after dawn and learn that they had added Emma to their workload, I had gone home.

Luke hadn't been in the house. I found him in the barn, shirtless and shoeless, asleep on the floor of our gym right next to the boxers' heavy bag. I knew he had come home and started pounding away at the heavy bag, kicking and punching and working himself to exhaustion. Then, not wanting to face me in the house when I got home, he had simply lain down and fallen asleep. I left him sleeping there, going back inside and crawling into our bed as slowly and gingerly as I would if I had a bad case of the flu.

Luke was gone when I woke up at dawn. I tried him on his phone first thing, but he didn't pick up. Before I left our house to meet with the searchers, I texted a quick "where r u?", but it'd taken him a half hour to give me only an "out looking" in response. All morning since then, he'd gone silent.

After a morning of online and social media work to get as many people looking for my kids as humanly possible, I headed over to the sheriff's office to ask Agent Healey for an update in person.

She was visibly animated when I walked into the conference room, which was cluttered with laptops and papers and maps. She ripped her eyes away from her phone and looked at me with an excited smile as I came through the door.

162

"Mrs. Andrews, you have great timing. We think we've had a sighting of your kids," Agent Healey said.

Every muscle in my body instantaneously locked up, and I yelped out a single word.

"*Where?*"

"On I-81, heading southwest, roughly 90 minutes south of here," she said, striding over to a small piece of electronic equipment that I took to be a police scanner. "Five minutes ago, an off-duty state trooper spotted a gray sedan leaving a McDonald's at a rest stop. A white man, estimated age 50 to 60, not Legrand but maybe his driver, is driving. Two kids in the back. One boy, one girl. Estimated ages 4 or 5 for the boy and 3 or 4 for the girl. The boy has medium brown hair; the girl has honey-blond hair. She was wearing pink pajamas. The off-duty trooper couldn't see what the boy was wearing."

My heart pounded uncomfortably as I listened to Agent Healey describe my children to me.

"Is the trooper chasing them?"

"No," Agent Healey said. "He was off-duty and in his private vehicle. He actually was stuck in line at the drive-thru with his own kids when he spotted them driving off. He had seen the pictures of Henry and Emma come across his cruiser computer during his shift, so it was on his mind. He got the license plate of the gray sedan and immediately called in to dispatch on his private phone. They're trying to locate the sedan now, and –".

She was cut off by the buzz of her phone, which she picked up immediately.

"Agent Jeanne Healey, FBI. Go."

I could hear a voice talking in her earpiece but couldn't tell what he was saying, so I was left with just her side of the conversation.

"Yes, captain," Agent Healey said. "Please put all available units on it. This is highest priority. Child abduction."

A pause as Agent Healey listened to her earpiece.

"Yes, I'll hold," she said. "No, wait. Better idea. Give me the channel that trooper is on, and we'll listen in."

Another pause.

"Got it," she said. "Listen, captain, tell your trooper. No firearms. If he pulls the perp over and approaches the car, I want his hands on his Taser, not his sidearm. There are kids in that car. Make sure you tell him."

The voice in her earpiece rose, though I still couldn't make out the words.

"Apologies, sir," Healey said. "I just didn't know if he's a 22-year old rookie or what, so I was spelling it out for him, not for you, sir. I know you know what you are doing. We'll listen in. Thank you, sir. I'm out now."

She called him a jackass a fraction of a second after she stabbed the off button on her phone. Then she hustled over to the police scanner, and she said to me, "That was the state police captain in charge of the Appomattox barracks. He says one of his troopers on highway patrol has spotted the car on I-81 and is following, a few miles south of where the off-duty guy first saw him."

My breathing was coming fast as Agent Healey found the right channel on the scanner. Then a disembodied male voice filled our conference room.

"Sir, he's 50 yards ahead of me. Do I pull him over, sir?"

My heart flailed as I realized I was listening to the trooper who was at that very moment following the car that had my kids in it. The trooper's southwestern Virginia twang sounded very young.

"No, not yet," said an older-sounding, heavier male voice. "I've got another unit from Radford in route." Agent Healey mouthed to me that the older voice belonged to the captain she just had on the phone, who was back in the barracks directing his young trooper.

"Say again, sir?"

"Trooper Daniels, you keep them in view but you do not engage your lights and you do not pull them over," the captain said. "Do you roger that?"

"Yes sir," Trooper Daniels said. "Do not pull over, do not activate lights, keep them in view. Roger that."

A static-y silence came over the radio. I gripped the edge of the conference room table and looked at Agent Healey.

"What's happening?" I asked her.

"The captain is making a good call here," she said. "He's got a trooper on the perp's tail. But with your kids in the back, it makes no sense to pull the perp over by himself. Better to have a lot of backup so the perp feels overwhelmed and gives up without running. Or a fight."

We kept listening to the radio static. She saw me look down at my phone.

"You probably can't reach your husband," she said to me. "Rick Byram told me this morning that Dr. Andrews had joined in with several groups searching campgrounds way up in the National Forest. No cell phone coverage up there unless they're near a ranger station."

165

Young Trooper Daniels came over the radio again.

"Sir! The perp is reaching to the backseat where the kids are!"

I gasped loudly.

"Say again, trooper," the captain said.

"The perp is reaching in the backseat. Where the kids are. Wait, now he's facing forward again. No, wait, now he's reaching backwards again. Swerve! He's just swerved in the road! Ok, he's ok now. He's looking forward again and holding the car steady in his lane."

"Tell me what you're seeing," the captain commanded.

"Sir, he's just put on his directional, and he's heading to an exit."

"GPS has you near Exit 105," the captain said. "That's Route 232. Confirm that."

"Yes sir, roger that, that's where I am."

"Follow him if he exits off the interstate."

"Roger that. And there he goes -- he's exiting. I'm following, captain. Over."

A long pause. Agent Healey looked up at me from the scanner and said, "It's possible that Legrand's driver is taking the kids to their hideout, and leading the trooper right to it. It's farther from Jameston than I would have expected, but it's still close enough from here to be the place."

"Won't the driver spot the trooper?"

"Probably not, if the trooper is keeping his distance well," she said. "It's amazing how often people are oblivious to cop cars when the lights aren't activated. In that dark blue and gray paint the Virginia State Police use, those new Fords they drive aren't eye catching if the trooper doesn't activate his lights."

Trooper Daniels came across the radio again.

166

"Sir, he's pulling into a shopping center parking lot. Wait, now he's parking. Sir, what do I do?"

"Is he reaching into the back seat again?"

"Say again, sir? I didn't copy that."

"I said, is he reaching into the back seat again where the children are?"

"No. Wait. Wait -- yes sir! He is, sir!"

"Activate lights and apprehend immediately!"

Agent Healey winced. "Taser, you forgot to remind him to use the Taser," she said under her breath to the deaf scanner.

Both my hands covered my mouth as we listened to Trooper Daniels opening his car door and then barking out commands.

"Turn off the car! Now!"

Agent Healey nodded and whispered at me, "He's got his shoulder radio – "

Trooper Daniels's voice burst out again on the scanner. "Hands! Hands on the wheel where I can see them!"

"Oh, Jesus," Agent Healey said. "It sounds like his gun is drawn. Come on, trooper, please be smart. Don't risk gunfire."

Trooper Daniels's voice boomed on the scanner, "Tell the children to exit the vehicle! Do it! Do it now!" He still sounded young, but his voice was strong and authoritative.

Agent Healey said, "He's got his shoulder mike open. That's why we can hear him. But he won't be able to hear his captain unless he toggles it."

Trooper Daniels called out, "Kids! It's ok! I'm here to help you. Walk over behind me. Over here."

A pause.

Then he continued, "Son, take your sister by the hand and walk her over here. That's it. That's it. No, not right next to me.

Walk her behind my cruiser. Where the trunk is. What? The trunk
. . . the back of my car, behind the car. That's it. Thataboy."

Agent Healey did a fist pump. "He's got your kids out of the
driver's car. And he's got them not right next to him but instead
behind his cruiser, which is the safest place to be."

Trooper Daniels's voice interrupted her again. "Get out of the
car slowly. Slowly! Keep your hands where I can see them at all
times!"

A distant siren could be heard coming over the radio.

"That'll be his backup coming," Agent Healey announced,
sounding relieved. "Thank God."

"Face away from me, get on your knees and place your hands
behind your head," Trooper Daniels's voice commanded over the
radio. Then we heard the sounds of jostling for a few moments,
then a radio click, before he came back on.

"Captain, this is Trooper J.A. Daniels. I have the suspect
cuffed and in my control. A Radford City cruiser is pulling into
the parking lot now. Two city officers are coming up to me right
now. Request instructions, sir."

"Have the two locals guard the perp," the captain said. "You
go secure the children."

"Roger that."

"And confirm their identities."

"10-4."

There was a silence for five seconds, then ten. Agent Healey
said, "He didn't leave his radio mike open this time."

Another impossibly long minute passed, then Trooper Daniels's voice came on again.

"Captain, the kids look ok to me, but they won't tell me their
names. They won't talk to me at all."

I burst out, "That's because they're terrified!"

Interminable seconds passed as static was the only company to Agent Healey and me in the conference room. Just as I was about to tell her to call the captain on the phone, Trooper Daniels came on the radio again.

"Captain, one of the city uniform officers is telling me the suspect is claiming these kids are his grandchildren. He says he was just getting a tissue for his granddaughter in the backseat because she's sick and was sneezing and needed to blow her nose."

"Liar!" I screamed at the deaf scanner.

The captain's voice came on the line again.

"Trooper, do you have your personal phone with you?"

"Yes, sir."

"Then take a picture of the kids and text it to me."

"Yes, sir."

Agent Healey was on her phone in a flash.

"Captain, this is Agent Jeanne Healey, FBI. As soon as you get the photo of the kids from Trooper Daniels, please send it up to me. I have the mother with me now. We can make an immediate identification."

As she ended her call, I was hugging my own arms, remembering exactly what it felt like to hold both Emma and Henry together. They were too big for me now to pick up together at the same time. But I could still hold them both when I was sitting on the couch at home and they scrambled into my lap. Intense hunger for those touches swept over me -- the soft warmth of their skin against me, the tickle of their bones poking into me, the feel of their fine hair against my face.

Trooper Daniels said on the radio to his captain, "Sir, the photo is on the way to you, but you need to know, sir. The kids are saying the suspect is their grandfather."

Agent Healey held up her hand and shook her head at me.

"Doesn't mean anything. Lots of times kids get scared and say what they've been told to say. It's very common in these cases."

A few more seconds passed, then Agent Healey's phone started buzzing. She hit a button and stared. Then her head dropped, and she handed the phone to me.

Her eyes were closed when she said to me, "Not them. Right?"

I looked at the 3 inch screen. On it was a handsome brown-haired boy and a smaller blond girl who shared his eyes and mouth. The bitter taste of disappointment flooded my mouth, and I couldn't speak. I could only shake my head.

These weren't my children.

Chapter 42

A couple of hours later I was still drained when Agent Healey heard from Agent Byram. The National Forest search crews were taking a break near a ranger station and planning their searches for the rest of the day. I knew Luke was with them and had a signal for his phone. So I called him.

"Hey," I said. "How's it going up there?"

"Fine," he said.

"What are you doing?"

"A lot of walking," he said. "We're going on foot along trails, from campsite to campsite. Byram said that whenever someone hides out in the woods for a number of days, they usually choose to be near a stream or a lake, because they need water. So we're walking those first. Stumps got U.S. Forest Service maps for everyone and set up the plan. Byram is overseeing it. There's a couple hundred people climbing around these mountains and looking now."

"Are you okay?" I asked.

"Hang on a sec," he said. He was talking to someone off the phone about driving back to town to get food for the volunteers.

That conversation went on for a while before he got back on the phone.

"So what were you saying?" he asked.

"I was just asking if you were –"

"Hang on again," he said. Then he started to talk with someone else about breaking all the search parties into smaller groups. That exchange went on for much longer than I would have expected.

"So Agent Byram told me you had some kind of false alarm," he said when he finally got back on.

"You could call it that."

"Oh," he said.

After a pause, I continued, "I was calling to find out if you're going to Hiram Legrand's arraignment later this afternoon at the courthouse."

"What does he need to be arraigned again for?" Luke asked irritably. "He was just arraigned a few days ago. That's how I got into this whole mess."

"That was for the kidnapping of Mary Beth Marshall," I said. "Agent Healey told me this is for the escape and for the kidnapping of Henry."

"Well, there's no reason for me to be there," Luke said. "I'm going to stay up here searching until dark."

"I'm going to head over to the courthouse and watch."

"Why? He's just going to be on that closed-circuit television for a few seconds. There won't be a bond hearing. Not in a million years would Judge Carter release him on bond."

I said, "Agent Healey said it's going to be in person, because the sheriff's office has no closed-circuit television the way the jail does."

"Don't go. You should be helping with the search."

"I'm going," I said. "I need to see this man. You've seen him. I haven't."

"That's stupid. You know what he looks like."

"I don't think it's stupid. I want to see the man who stole my son from his preschool playground. I want to see the man who got some other animal to steal my daughter, while my husband was supposed to be watching her."

After a few beats, he said, "Fine." Then he hung up the phone.

Chapter 43

3:55 p.m.
Saturday afternoon

Emma and Henry were alone and passing time blowing on the dust that floated in the thin lines of daylight slipping into the dim room through cracks in the wall. Henry took a deep breath and blew hard, making the lazy dust particles rapidly scatter before gradually settling back down again in the ray of light.

"Do you think Mama and Daddy are going to come get us soon?" Emma asked.

"Yes, they'll be here soon," Henry said. "And don't say 'fink.' It's 'think.'" Then he put his tongue under his front two teeth and exaggerated a demonstration of the "th" sound.

"Why aren't they here yet?" Emma asked.

"I don't know," Henry said.

"I don't think they're coming," Emma said.

"Stop saying 'fink.'"

"I'm not saying 'fink.' I'm saying think."

Chapter 44

Because it was Saturday, the courthouse was nearly empty. Judge Carter was well within his rights to wait until Monday to conduct the arraignment. But he thought that a quick and unannounced Saturday arraignment made sense. He didn't want the usual extra lawyers and litigants hanging around, not to mention the news media that was rapidly growing in town, all getting a voyeuristic glimpse at our family's tragedy.

The judge had been as nice as he could be when he heard I was in the almost-empty courthouse. He had one of the bailiffs bring me back to his chambers. The bailiff escorted me through the chambers' anteroom, where the judge's secretary and law clerks worked during the week, and then we went down a short hallway until we entered the judge's own huge, high-ceilinged office.

Rich wood paneling, softly-glowing sconces, and prints of equestrian and fox-hunt paintings adorned the walls. The office was enormous; it had to be at least 30 feet by 40 feet. Judge Carter himself was sitting at a large wooden desk built well before computers were standard office equipment. As soon as the judge saw me come in, he put down the papers he was reading and hurried over to me.

"Mrs. Andrews, I am so terribly sorry for what has happened to your family. If Mrs. Carter were still alive, I know she would be here to comfort you," he said kindly, shaking my hand in that courtly way that gentlemen of his generation were taught to do with ladies.

"Thank you," I said.

"Please let me know if there is anything I can do to help. I have told the federal agents this already, but I can sign search warrants any time of day. And at night, even if the agents cannot get to me in person, I can authorize warrants over the phone and do the paperwork in the morning."

"Thank you again. We very much appreciate it."

"It's the least I can do," he said. "I heard they have taken to the mountains to search. If I was ten years younger, I would pull on my boots and join in the search on foot. But I'm afraid my old hips and knees just will not let me go afield like they once did," he said regretfully. Then he gestured to several leather seats and a couch surrounding a coffee table about 15 feet in front of his desk, and said, "Please, won't you come in and sit down."

As I took a seat, I noticed on a nearby credenza an old picture of the judge and a group of other men, maybe 30 years ago judging by hairstyles and the judge's then-dark hair color, all standing in a field in hunting clothes, the beautiful walnut stocks of their shotguns gleaming in their hands.

He saw me looking and said, "That is one of the fields at Somerset, my family's ancestral home on the James. Every September for years, some of my cousins and other male family members would join together for a dove hunt. There used to be quail and even some pheasant hunts too, later in the fall, but that was many years ago. I'm afraid I don't get down that way as often as I would like any longer."

I nodded, knowing dimly that Judge Carter was a first-families-of-Virginia type, a descendant of the old English families that had arrived in the 1600s and established country seats in southeastern Virginia on the banks of the James River, not all that far from where tourists now stampeded through Williamsburg.

"Enough of that," Judge Carter said. "Much more importantly, how is the search coming along?"

"I guess it's going all right," I said. "Luke is up with several groups of searchers in the National Forest. They're searching campsites."

"That is hard work, climbing over those ridges on foot. Do you know where they are, or where they're planning to go next?"

"They're mostly in Augusta County today," I said. "We have other groups knocking on doors all over here in Jameston County, hoping that someone saw something. Plus the sheriff has sent deputies to every vacant house they know of to see if Legrand was using one of them as a hideout."

Judge Carter nodded approvingly. "I released as many of my bailiffs from courtroom duty this week as possible, so they could join in the search. The bailiffs are all deputy sheriffs, you know, assigned to me for courtroom work. Unfortunately, I just had to recall three of them to provide security for Mr. Legrand's arraignment this afternoon. Three is more than necessary – we usually just have one for an arraignment – but given his recent escape from jail, it is wiser to have too much security than too little. As soon as the arraignment is over and he is locked up again, I will release them back to the search. We will have your children back to you safe and sound very soon, Mrs. Andrews."

Almost on cue there was a knock at the door, and in came the bailiff who had escorted me back to the judge's chambers. A beefy, barrel-chested man, his brown deputy sheriff's uniform and star-shaped badge looked a little cheap compared to the polished, rich wood of Judge Carter's chambers.

"Are we almost ready, Billy?" the judge asked him.

"Yes sir. Do you still want to do this here in chambers?"

"Yes, I think so," the judge answered, then looked at me. "We hold sensitive hearings in chambers on occasion, and this will only take a minute or two. Back here in chambers, only the defendant and courtroom personnel – and you, if you wish – may attend. But out in the courtroom, everything is public by Virginia law, and we cannot control who walks in and who walks out, even on a weekend. We know Mr. Legrand had some kind of assistant involved in the kidnapping of your son, and that man has not yet been apprehended. I see no reason to take even the slightest chance that he shows up in the open courtroom, so we will do this back here."

The old judge paused for a moment before he continued.

"Now, Mrs. Andrews, are you sure you would still like to attend? It is your right as a victim to attend, but I certainly understand if you would prefer not to see him. And, in fact, I perhaps would gently recommend that you wait outside, if you will permit me to say so."

"No. I want to see the man who did this to us," I said firmly.

He looked at me steadily with an understanding nod of his head and said, "Then you shall."

He turned back to his bailiff and said, "Billy, I want all three deputies in here at all times. And I want Legrand handcuffed at all times."

The deputy asked, "Should I handcuff him in the front, so that when he signs his plea form, we do not need to take off his handcuffs at any time? Handcuffing in front is not quite as secure as handcuffing him behind his back, but if he makes one wrong move, I'll tackle him."

"No," the judge said. "I have no doubt about your physical abilities, but handcuff him behind his back, and never take them off. I do not want him to have any freedom whatsoever. I will waive signature of his plea form."

"Yes, sir," the bailiff answered. "And I doubt he will be a problem, anyway. He is on some pretty heavy-duty painkillers. He had his jaw wired this morning after they pulled those broken teeth out of his gums, and he has been on oxycodone ever since he came out of anesthesia."

I was surprised. "What happened? Did he fight the deputies when they were arresting him last night?"

It was the bailiff's turn to be surprised. "Oh, I thought you knew," Billy said. "Last night, when Dr. Andrews came to the interrogation room, Legrand lunged at him. And your husband, in self-defense, hit him back. Really hard. Legrand's upper jaw was broken. You don't see that very often. Usually it's the lower jaw. Four of his teeth were broken, too. We had to get an oral surgeon to come up this morning from Richmond to patch him up. Your husband packs one heck of a wallop," he said, delivering this last line with a satisfied grin, his look telling me that he knew I must be proud of my husband.

"Oh," I said.

Billy looked at the judge and said, "Sir, if you're ready for the prisoner, I'll go get him from holding now."

"Go ahead," the judge said.

When the judge and I were alone again, he pushed a Queen Anne chair to the far side of his cavernous office, near built-in bookshelves filled with a library's worth of old legal tomes and casebooks.

"Ma'am, if you would sit over here, you will be able to see what is happening, but you will be well away," he said. "We will put him over there," and he nodded at a leather couch that was in front of his desk, flanked by matching leather chairs. "His attorney, Mr. Wajda, will sit on one side of him. I will have Billy sit on the other side. The prosecutor, Mr. Reynolds, can sit in one of the chairs."

"Ok," I said as I sat in the chair where he directed me. He walked over to his coat rack, plucked up his black judicial robe and shrugged it over his dark-gray suit. Then he settled down into the deep reddish-brown leather chair behind his desk and waited.

Within a few minutes, the whole ensemble was there. First the two lawyers came in. Mr. Reynolds shook my hand and said a few nice words before finding his chair. The defense lawyer, Eric Wajda, sheepishly introduced himself at some distance before settling down in the couch where the judge directed him. The court reporter, an older woman, came in with her laptop and recording device in tow and headed over to a small chair just to the side of the judge's desk to be in good position to make a transcription of the hearing. Then the heavy wood door of the chambers swung open again, and in came the three bailiffs with Hiram Legrand in tow.

Legrand didn't even give me a sidelong glance as he shuffled in. He was a tall man, sizable, but not as big as Luke. The side and upper part of his mouth were discolored and very swollen from where Luke apparently had hit him. I realized as he turned his head that he still had a wad of gauze stuffed under his lip and one cheek from his surgery this morning. He was handcuffed behind his back just as the judge directed, so Billy had to grab one of Legrand's arms plus a fistful of Legrand's shirt to lower him to a seated position on the couch with his hands crunched behind him. Then Billy directed one of the other two bailiffs, a youngish man with a crew cut, to stand at the door leading into the chambers. He had the third bailiff, an older, heavyset man with a thick, steel-gray walrus moustache, stand to the side of the judge and his court reporter.

Billy himself settled his bulk down next to Legrand, and Mr. Wajda sat on Legrand's other side. Wajda looked surprised when he saw Legrand's facial injuries but said nothing.

"All right, gentlemen, let us get this procedure done effi-ciently," the judge said, and the court reporter sprung to life, rap-idly taking down every word he said on her machine. "Mr. Legrand, you are here to be arraigned for unlawful escape from the custody of the Commonwealth and for the kidnapping of Henry Andrews, a minor child. You are here on charges filed by Mr. Reynolds, the Commonwealth's Attorney for Jameston County."

As the judge went through a preplanned script he obviously read at every arraignment, I stared intently at Legrand's face. He hung his head and gazed at the wine-colored rug on the floor be-tween the couch and the judge's desk. His head was down so much that small ripples of double chin formed under his jaw, and a tattoo on the side of his neck showed above the collar of his shirt. His hair was long on top but cut severely short on the sides. I could see the pale-white scalp contrasting with his almost-black hair.

The judge's voice broke into my conscious thought again.

"Now, Mr. Wajda, do you have any objection to Mr. Legrand's being held in custody at the sheriff's office until such time as Capt. Hudson, the warden of Cent-West, can determine the method of Mr. Legrand's alleged escape?"

Wajda looked a little uncomfortable being put on the spot, knowing that he alone stood for Legrand in this proceeding. He cut a quick, apologetic glance at me before he spoke.

"Yes, your Honor, I'm afraid I must object," Wajda said. "Being held in the sheriff's office is highly irregular, as you know. He would not be given access to the amenities of the jail, I mean the medical care, the law library, and so on. He would not even have a bed in the sheriff's office. More importantly, the jail has pay phones so that he can call me when he needs to, but the sheriff's office does not. It is very difficult for me to meet with him at the sheriff's office for confidential attorney-client conversations, because they do not have a secure room there that is also completely private, at least as far as I know. The jail has such rooms reserved for attorney-client use only."

Mr. Reynolds's body language became animated as Wajda spoke. When Wajda was done, he hardly needed the prompting the judge gave when he turned and said, "Mr. Reynolds."

"Your Honor, the Commonwealth does not believe the Court should care even one little bit about Hiram Legrand losing the benefit of 'the amenities of the jail,' as Mr. Wajda puts it," Reynolds said, stabbing his index finger on the back of a nearby chair.

182

"He does not need a recreation yard. He does not need a law library. He does not need a pay phone. He forfeited those benefits when he chose to escape from Cent-West."

"Allegedly escaped," Wajda put in.

"There's nothing 'alleged' about it, Eric," Reynolds retorted.

"Gentlemen, even in chambers, this is a formal proceeding," the judge interrupted, looking sternly at the two lawyers. "You are both much too experienced to behave in this way. Mr. Wajda, you will not interrupt Mr. Reynolds again. Mr. Reynolds, you will direct all of your comments to the Court, not to Mr. Wajda. Is that understood? Is it? Very good. Now, continue."

"Yes, sir," Reynolds said. "As far as the specifics of Mr. Wajda's objections, I am sure we can find in the sheriff's office an adequate place for private attorney-client conversations. For security reasons, we may need to have a deputy in the room at all times, and even then, Mr. Legrand will need to be handcuffed. Now, if Mr. Wajda still objects to that, what we can do is arrange to have Mr. Legrand transported to the Richmond City Jail and held there pending trial. That way we no longer have to worry about a potential security breach at Cent West. They have plenty of cots available down in Richmond. But I am guessing that Mr. Wajda may object to that as well."

Mr. Wajda waited until the judge's eyes were back on him, giving him permission to speak, before saying, "I'm sorry, judge, I must object to that as well. Having a client nearly 100 miles away, especially when he is charged with felonies that come with the possibility of life in prison, is just unheard of. The Public Defender's Office doesn't even have money in the budget to pay for the gas back and forth. Maybe there is a way to work out something with Mr. Reynolds about housing Mr. Legrand in the sheriff's office temporarily. That said, I can't agree to a deputy in there listening to us all of the time."

"All right, well, I anticipated you two would have to thrash this out," the judge said. "And I would prefer that you reach an agreement without my having to make a ruling here. So I'm going to ask you two to step outside of chambers, out in the hallway, and work this out among yourselves. I will give you ten minutes to do so. After that, I will send one of the bailiffs to go get you. If you have not reached an agreement, then I will tell both of you what is going to happen, and that ruling may not be what either of you wants. So I strongly urge you to reach an agreement on your own. Is that understood?"

"Yes, sir," the two men said simultaneously.

"Very well," the judge said, then nodding his head at the young bailiff at the door, "Please let these gentlemen into the jury room so they can have some privacy."

After the door closed behind the young bailiff as he led the two lawyers down the hall, the judge gave me a reassuring smile and a nod of the head, then turned back to the couch, where Billy was still next to Legrand. The older bailiff with the walrus moustache was still hovering behind the judge.

"Billy, do you want to take Mr. Legrand back to holding while we wait for Mr. Reynolds and Mr. Wajda to work this out?" the judge asked his big bailiff.

"No, judge," Billy said. "You only gave them ten minutes. By the time we get him down to holding, we'll just have to bring him back."

"Very well," the judge said. "I probably will not –"

From my angle, I could see perfectly well what happened next. Hiram Legrand's right hand was supposed to be handcuffed to his left hand behind his back. But it impossibly swung free, seeming to have sprung to life out of the couch cushions behind him. In that hand was something short and black, and I did not register what it was in the split second that Legrand whipped it around to Billy's side. Then I heard the deafening blast of a powerful handgun going off indoors as Legrand squeezed the trigger and fired a bullet into Billy's barrel chest. Billy immediately made a whooshing sound and fell forward off the couch, landing face down on the floor.

Hiram Legrand stood up, the handcuffs dangling from his left wrist. He raised his gun and pointed it at the shocked older deputy standing next to the judge. The older deputy was still fumbling with his holster strap when Legrand shot him twice, and he went over backwards and landed with a nightmarish thud.

The court reporter was screaming when I jumped behind the Queen Anne chair. I lost sight of Legrand briefly as I hid behind the chair. Out of the corner of my eye, I saw the door to chambers burst open as the young deputy ran back into the room with his gun drawn and Mr. Reynolds right on his heels, but he abruptly slid to a stop so suddenly that Mr. Reynolds literally ran into the back of him.

From my crouch behind the Queen Anne chair, I peeked over at where the judge was to see what had made the young deputy freeze.

Legrand had his left arm clamped around Judge Carter's neck and had hauled him out of his chair. The silver-colored handcuffs still attached to that wrist dangled in front of the judge's chest.

With his other hand, Legrand was pushing the muzzle of his handgun against the judge's temple.

"Don't move, or I'll blow his damn head off right here!" Legrand yelled, his eyes convincing the young deputy that he was telling the truth. Then, looking at Mr. Reynolds, Legrand commanded, "You, close the door and lock it!"

Mr. Reynolds did as Legrand ordered and swung shut the heavy door to the judge's chambers, closing us all in the judge's chambers. As the door was closing, I caught a glimpse of the defense lawyer, Mr. Wajda, running away down the hallway.

After the door was closed, the young deputy and Mr. Reynolds stood shoulder to shoulder next to the door, both staring wide-eyed at where Legrand had his gun shoved up against Judge Carter's temple. The judge's slender fingers reached up and gripped the arm Legrand had clamped around his neck, but Legrand was 40 years younger, and the judge had no chance of freeing himself. Behind them the court reporter was cowering in the far corner of the judge's chambers, her knees up to her chin as she tried to curl up into the smallest ball she could, her hands covering her mouth as if to stop any involuntary noise that might catch Legrand's attention.

"Holster your gun," Legrand said to the young deputy. The deputy hesitated, but then the judge's reddening face convinced him to obey. He carefully put his firearm back into the holster on his hip. Legrand then took the muzzle of his handgun off the judge's head and pointed it directly at the deputy.

"Move slowly when I tell you what to do," Legrand said to the deputy. "Slowly. If you make any fast move, even a little one,

I'll blow your heart clean out your chest. Then I'll off this old bastard. You understand? Now, unlatch your belt and let the whole thing drop to the floor. Do it now."

The deputy complied, working the buckle of his thick black belt very slowly and then dropping it on the floor. It was weighed down by his sidearm, handheld radio, flashlight, and handcuffs, so it made a heavy thud when it landed.

"Kick it away from you," Legrand said. "Keep kicking it until it's under the couch. Good. Now go back to the door. No, better yet, turn around and face the wall. Press yourself up against it. Hands on the wall, over your head." Then, looking at Mr. Reynolds, he said, "You too, pal."

I saw that both Mr. Reynolds and the deputy were facing the wall with their hands pressed against it over their heads. Legrand started to drag the judge by the neck backwards toward a small hall at the back of his chambers. I hadn't paid any attention to it before, but as I looked down it, I could see a bathroom down that hall through an open door, then a slight red glow near the ceiling, though I couldn't make out what it was.

Then Legrand's eyes were searching for and found me behind the chair. I ducked down behind it.

"Hey," he called. "Hey, Sarah."

I recoiled as he used my name.

"Sarah," he said again. "C'mon, I want you to watch."

I hid behind that chair and could see my hands quivering.

"Suit yourself," he said, and a beat later his handgun blasted again. Mr. Reynolds shouted out, and then I heard a thud and running feet. Ambient sunlight flashed down the small hallway near the bathroom before darkening again. Then the young deputy was cursing and darting over to the couch, fumbling to retrieve his gun.

I peered from behind the chair and saw the judge on the ground, lying on his side and trying to catch his breath. The deputy skidded to his knees as he came to the judge's assistance, but the judge smacked away his hands and croaked at the deputy to go after Legrand. The deputy scrambled on his feet and ran down the small hallway with his gun drawn, past the bathroom. At the end of the hallway he pushed open a door I hadn't seen. The soft red glow I had seen was an exit sign.

After a few seconds, the deputy backpedaled back through that door and then ran back into the main part of the judge's chambers. The court reporter was weeping quietly as the deputy first checked on both his fellow bailiffs. His body language told me he could not find a pulse in either of them. Then he dashed over to the main door of the judge's chambers, where Legrand had made him face the wall. Mr. Reynolds was on the ground, with a red splotch in the middle of his back. He was awkwardly trying to reach his hand around behind him.

"Oh, Christ," the deputy said, then he reached under the couch to retrieve his handheld radio. He knelt next to Mr. Reynolds, clamped his hand down in the middle of the growing red splotch on Mr. Reynolds's back, and used the other hand to talk into his radio.

"Code zero, code zero," he bawled into his radio. "I have two deputies down, repeat, two deputies down. We need immediate assistance. Judge Carter is hurt. Jimmy Wayne Reynolds is shot. I have two ladies crying here in the judge's chambers, and I don't know if they're hurt. Send every damn ambulance we've got."

188

Gibberish came back at him on the radio, but evidently he understood it.

"Yes, damn it, yes, I said code zero!" he yelled into the radio. "Billy and Cal are both down, and I think they're dead."

More gibberish, and then the young deputy answered, lower and more in control this time.

"No, he has escaped custody. Repeat, Hiram Legrand has escaped custody. He ran out the judge's fire exit out the back. I saw a gray sedan driving fast down High Street, and I think he was in it."

The young deputy paused for a moment. He used the back of the hand holding the radio to wipe the sweat on his forehead and brow, and with his other hand he visibly increased the pressure he was putting on Mr. Reynold's gunshot wound. As he put the radio back to his mouth and hit the transmit button again, he was looking directly at me, watching me shiver uncontrollably as if it were freezing here in the judge's chambers.

"Dispatch, tell all officers. Legrand is armed," he said. "I have no idea how, but he is. Tell them he's armed, and dangerous in the extreme."

Chapter 45

For me, the long pandemonium following Hiram Legrand's escape from the courthouse ended when Luke came barreling into the courtroom, which was being used as a staging area following the ordeal back in chambers.

Luke's eyes darted all around the huge crowd of law enforcement, rescue workers, and hangers-on in the courtroom until he spotted me. Then he ran to me, his boots thudding heavily on the floor. When he got to me he bent down, wrapped his arms around me and effortlessly stood up to his full height, carrying me bodily for a few steps before he stopped and just held me, thanking God over and over in a whisper that I was ok.

I always felt petite in his arms. An overwhelming sense of relief gushed over me, of finally feeling safe. I hugged his neck tightly and kissed him on the side of his head, and then I pressed the side of my face against his and told him I loved him. We stood there like that for a while, my feet off the ground, my chest pressed high atop his chest, my cheek against the side of his face.

Most of the people in the crowd stopped what they were doing and looked at us as I stroked Luke's hair and kissed him again on the side of his head. My hands dropped to his back, and I felt burrs and prickles sticking to the back of his fleece pullover. His boots were covered in dried mud, and he had streaks of dirt all over him from his day searching through the mountainous woods up in the National Forest. I grabbed a fistful of hair on the back of his head, gently pulled his head back so we could look each other in the face, and said, "You're a mess."

We both smiled through our tears, and he put me down, but I didn't let go. I held him by his cheeks and looked him in the face, his stubble rough on my palms. I took in his mouth, his jaw, his cheekbones, his eyes. Finally, after long moments of just looking at him, I said, "I'm so sorry for what I did and said last night, Luke. And for what I said today. I didn't mean any of it."

"I know, baby," he said. "Are you really ok?"

"I'm ok," I said.

"I would have died if he had hurt you," he said.

I nodded, my throat too choked up to say anything back, instead just hugging him even more tightly around his neck. After a long minute, he started talking again.

"I heard a ton of stuff about what happened in the judge's chambers on the way over," he said. "I couldn't make any sense of it."

I could only shake my head and say, "It didn't make sense to see it in person, either."

"What the heck happened?"

"I don't know where to start," I said truthfully.

Agent Byram, who had been watching us amid the crowd of law enforcement, strode over and answered the question.

"Someone planted a gun in the judge's couch," Byram said.

"What?" Luke asked incredulously.

"Someone planted a gun in the judge's couch," Byram repeated. "Had to happen that way. There's no way Legrand had the gun with him coming into the judge's chambers. He was in custody in the sheriff's office from the time he was arrested to the time he sat down on that couch during the arraignment. He'd been frisked by half a dozen law enforcement officers, including me. All three of the bailiffs in chambers, including the two dead ones, still had their firearms with them after Legrand's escape. So it's not like he swiped one of theirs. No, I think the gun was planted there."

"By who?" Luke asked.

Byram cut a look at the various uniforms milling around near us. In addition to local deputies, Virginia state troopers were busily working, their light gray, long-sleeved uniforms in some contrast to the brown, short-sleeved uniforms of our locals. Byram ushered us over to the back corner of the courtroom for some privacy.

"I think Legrand may be getting help from a member of local law enforcement," Byram said.

My heart gave a jump at that. "Really?" I asked.

"Yes," he said. "It explains a lot. A deputy could help spring him out of Cent-West. A deputy also could plant a gun in the judge's chambers. And what agency handles both the local jail and courtroom security? The regional sheriff's office. Somehow Legrand got out of those handcuffs. A deputy could have planted a handcuff key in there as well."

Luke nodded thoughtfully, then said, "Legrand also managed somehow to evade the sheriff's roadblocks after he kidnapped Henry."

"Exactly," Byram said. "And where did you get knocked out when someone snatched Emma?"

"The sheriff's own parking lot," Luke said.

"Right," Byram said. "Agent Healey and I were already working on a law enforcement connection as a theory, but as soon as we heard what happened during the arraignment, we put a call in to the lieutenant colonel of the Virginia State Police BCI. That's Bureau of Criminal Investigation. Any state trooper who could be spared is here. Officially, they're here because of the murder of two local law enforcement officers and because of violent crimes on a member of the judiciary and a prosecutor. And they are investigating those, that's for sure. But they're also here as a backstop. If one of the locals is helping Legrand, maybe taking a bribe to do it, it'll be a lot harder for him with the troopers around. A lot more of them will be here later tonight and tomorrow."

"How about getting more of your people, federal agents?" I asked.

Agent Byram nodded. "Agent Healey and I already reached out early this morning, after Emma was snatched. This is a no-brainer, even for Washington. We have two related kidnappings, and another one unrelated, for a total of three, all perpetrated by the same man or someone working with him in less than a week. This is unheard of. Now this same man has escaped twice and murdered two law enforcement officers. My boss has called in the cavalry. I would anticipate having as many as a dozen agents here, some arriving tonight, others by tomorrow."

"What should we be doing in the meantime?" I asked.

"The same," Byram answered. "That friend of yours, the lawyer? He's doing a great job of getting all these volunteers to search in an organized way. I can hardly improve on his plans."

"That's Stumps," Luke said. "My old college roommate."

"I'm going to have him make sure the volunteers work as separately from local law enforcement as possible. Until we can look into this law enforcement angle, I'd rather the local deputies don't really know where those volunteers are at any given point in time."

As I nodded, Rev. Rigsby came through the crowd toward us. He had walked over from the church when he heard what had happened. Agent Byram took his leave, telling us he'd be in touch with any updates.

"I'm so sorry, for everything," Rev. Rigsby said to us. "Luke, I tried to find you earlier today after the terrible thing that happened last night with Emma, but they told me you were up in the mountains searching all day. Then the next thing I knew, bam, this happened. Can I get either of you anything? Or do anything for you?"

"Thanks, but no," Luke said. "Just keep asking church members to help with the search for Henry and Emma."

"Oh, absolutely, that's a given," he said. "I saw you were talking with that man from the FBI. Do they have any idea where the kids are?"

"No," Luke answered. "I wish I could say yes, but I can't. They still just don't know."

"I'm so sorry," Rev. Rigsby said. "You'd think they'd have some kind of lead by now. Maybe the state police will be able to help."

"Well, they think Legrand might have help from a cop," Luke said.

"Really?"

"Yeah, it's just all this amazing luck Legrand has had. An escape from jail. Getting out of handcuffs. Having a gun right when he needs it."

"Makes some sense," Rev. Rigsby said. "But enough of that. Y'all have been through so much. Do you think now might be a good time for a prayer? It's times like these that we need to understand --"

"I'm exhausted," I interrupted. "Luke and I hardly had any sleep at all last night."

"Oh, of course," he said. "You should go home and get some rest."

"I don't know that I want to do that just yet," Luke said. "We still have a little daylight left. I should circle back with Stumps and see what we can do, maybe here in town."

"I want to stay with you," I said, squeezing Luke's hand. He smiled and nodded at me.

"I understand completely," Rev. Rigsby said. "I'll swing by your house later tonight. Don't worry about dinner. I'll bring you a big Tupperware bowl of pasta and meatballs. In about an hour, we'll be feeding the law enforcement officers from outside of town over at the church kitchen, so they don't have to stop working to find someplace to eat. It'll be no problem to bring y'all some once you get home."

Chapter 46

In the rapidly fading light, Henry and Emma were sitting with their legs crossed, facing each other, with a tic-tac-toe game drawn in the dust between them. During the boredom of the afternoon, Henry had shown her how to play. On the other side of the room, a complete alphabet with both upper-case and lower-case letters written in the dust in a child's handwriting was left unattended. The thin streams of setting sun slipping through the cracks in the wall had already retreated from that side of the room and left it dark.

The two men were arguing outside, just out of earshot of the children. Hiram Legrand kept touching the swollen part of his face.

"Why are you still wearing that mask in front of them?" Legrand asked.

"I've already told you," Ski Mask said. "I don't want them to know who I am yet."

"It ain't smart to keep them around," Legrand said. "We need to get rid of them, throw the bodies in the woods somewhere, and then move. We can't hide here forever."

"Not yet," Ski Mask said. "First we need to break Luke."

"Ain't we already done that?"

"No, we've got to finish taking everything from him. It'll happen tonight, if we get a little lucky. Hand me the phone. We'll need to get moving soon."

Chapter 47

8:30 p.m.
Saturday night

<u>Luke Andrews</u>

After Sarah and I quickly ate the spaghetti dinner Rev. Rigsby brought by, she excused herself to make some phone calls to the volunteer searchers, and I walked him to his car. Out in the darkening night, he got me to talking.

One morning a few weeks ago, I told him, I had taken a break from work to watch a recital by Emma's little music class for three-year olds. I parked myself in one of the stackable chairs they had set out for the parents. There were 16 little kids in her class. Eight of them were playing miniature instruments, and the other eight were singing and making hand motions. Miss Susan, their music teacher, was kneeling with her back to the audience, mouthing the words and doing the hand motions along with them.

There was no point to this story I was telling Rev. Rigsby, but I couldn't stop describing to him everything I remembered of Emma from that day, everything from the blue headband that kept her wavy hair out of her face, to her little fingers as they clutched the mallets of her miniature xylophone. Finally Rev. Rigsby had to put his hand on my shoulder to steady me.

"Luke, I feel terrible seeing you hurting so much," Rev. Rigsby said. "I wish I could help you. All I can tell you is to remember that there is a reason for everything, even if it's hard to understand now."

I exhaled loudly, closed my eyes, and said in a husky voice, "I don't understand it at all."

I was quiet then, looking out into the dark and listening to the nighttime noises. The peepers were peeping in the distance, probably on the marshy pond where the little frogs liked to overwinter and come alive each spring.

"Emma and Henry didn't do anything to deserve what's happening to them," I eventually murmured.

"I'm sure they didn't," he said. "But God only allows hurt to come to us when there is good reason for it. There is some wisdom in the Bible for this."

"Like what?"

"Deuteronomy tells us, 'Know then in your heart that as a man disciplines his son, so the Lord your God disciplines you.'"

"You think God is punishing me?"

"Maybe."

I paused only a moment or two before tiredly shaking my head. "Even if I did something to deserve this, Emma and Henry are just little kids. They haven't done anything wrong."

Rev. Rigsby said, "The Old Testament has an answer to that, in Exodus. 'I, the Lord your God, am a jealous God, visiting the sin of the fathers upon the children unto the third and fourth generation.'"

"I can't accept that," I said.

"It's in the Bible."

"Rev. Crosley says that Jesus is the measure of the Bible."

Rev. Rigsby patted me on the hand again and said in a lighter tone, "Well, it is difficult to know about these things. Perhaps you should talk with Rev. Crosley about this tomorrow. I'm sure he'll be there for you."

"He's too sick now," I said. "I wouldn't want to bother him."

"You're right, he is a little bit sick," Rev. Rigsby said. "When I visited with him earlier, he had quite a cough. I'm sure he'll be fine soon enough, though. What I meant to say before about the Bible was --"

"Rev. Crosley was coughing a lot?" I asked. "Tonight?"

"Yes," he said. "But it's no big deal. Probably just post-nasal drip. Once that tickle gets in your throat, it's hard to stop coughing. I'm sure he'll be fine once his cold clears."

A bright ray of concern for Rev. Crosley streaked into my fogged mind. It sounded like the amoxicillin hadn't made a dent in Rev. Crosley's pneumonia, which he obviously had not told Rev. Rigsby about, characteristically keeping his troubles to himself.

"Did you happen to notice his lips?" I asked.

"Lips?"

"Yes, lips. Did you notice whether they were normal color or not?"

Rev. Rigsby was quiet for a few moments, then said, "Well, it's funny you ask that. He was so chilly sitting on his front porch that they were turning a little blue, even though it's not all that cool this evening. But he's an older man, plus he has that cold bug. So I made him go inside and get under a blanket on the couch. He needs his rest."

Oh man, I thought to myself. Those blue lips weren't related to temperature. With pneumonia, blue lips probably meant low oxygen levels in the blood. My mind flashed across the symptoms for ARDS, Acute Respiratory Distress Syndrome, a pneumonia complication that was dangerous for a man of Rev. Crosley's age, especially as weak as he was already from the cancer. On Thursday, just before we got the news from Jan that Henry had been snatched, Rev. Crosley had really been hacking on his porch. That was two days ago. I had been so wrapped up with my family that I had not thought to have anyone else look in on him. I glanced at my watch.

"I should go see him," I said.

"Oh, Luke, I'm sure he'll be fine. You and Sarah need your rest."

"No, you don't understand, it could be serious," I said and quickly pulled out my phone and started dialing.

Rev. Rigsby said, "He probably did manage to fall asleep by now. You shouldn't wake him."

"I know," I said. "I'm calling Stumps."

Just then, Stumps picked up his phone.

"Hey, Luke," he said. "Are you ok?"

"Yeah, we're ok," I said. "We're at home. Sarah is exhausted, so I'm making her stay home and get a good night's sleep."

"Good," he said. "I sent most of the volunteers home at dark. I want them to get a lot of sleep so they can get rolling again at dawn."

"I need a favor," I said.

"Anything."

"Can you swing by my house and keep an eye on Sarah?" I asked.

"Yes, of course," Stumps said. "I'm not even that far from you. I was putting up more of the new posters, the ones with Emma and Henry both on them, at a few more spots outside of town before turning in for the night. I'm maybe 15 minutes away."

"Thanks, man," I said. "I'll be back home within an hour or two. How soon can you be here?"

"I'm on the way now," he said. "Where are you going?"

"Out. I need to go see a patient."

"You can't be serious."

"I am."

"Luke, there's other doctors. You are in a horrible crisis. No one expects you to see patients now."

"I know," I said. "But this one is special. He was my childhood pastor. I just need to see him in person and decide whether I need to get him admitted to the hospital. I'll wait until you get here before I leave."

"Are you sure?"

"Yes."

"You're nuts, but ok. I'm on the way."

Rev. Rigsby was rocking briskly in his chair on my porch. I said to him, "I already was planning to ask Stumps to stay the night here with us, so he doesn't have to drive all the way home to Richmond to get a bed. Let me just go inside and tell Sarah, and then I'll be on my way back to town to look in on Rev. Crosley."

***

202

Stumps had rolled up my gravel driveway a few minutes after Rev. Rigsby left. Sarah at first had been alarmed that I was going to run out for a little while, and she wanted to come with me, but then she relaxed some when I told her Stumps was coming by to keep her company.

The solitary ride in my truck back to town was tough. I hadn't had a quiet moment to myself all day. I was aching to dwell on Emma and Henry, to visualize them and remember everything about them, but I shoved that fiercely out of my mind. I couldn't hold myself together if I gave in to that. So I rolled my truck windows down to let the nighttime air rush in. It was rich with the fragrances of spring, and I occupied my mind by trying to identify each sweet smell blowing over me.

Eventually I rolled up to the curb in front of Rev. Crosley's house. It was completely dark. He probably was asleep, but I knew under which planter on his porch he hid his spare key. Just as I was getting out of the truck to walk on up to his front door, my phone buzzed with a text. It was from Sarah.

> *With Stumps in car. He had flyers left over + he needs somet'g to eat, so we did a few more postings. Heading to Catesville store for sandwiches. Love u.*

I texted her back, telling her to be careful and that I loved her. Slipping the phone back in my pocket, I walked up Rev. Crosley's sidewalk, climbed up his porch steps, and knocked lightly at his front door to see if he was awake. As I expected, he didn't answer. So I found the spare key hidden under the planter where he had started a tomato plant and let myself in his house. I groped around in the dark until I found a light switch. Then I went to his bedroom, eager to see him with my own eyes and decide if he needed to get to a hospital. He wasn't there. I checked the spare bedroom, his little office nook, and then the couch in the living room. To my surprise, all were empty. He wasn't home.

Mildly alarmed, I glanced at the neighbors' houses on either side. I knew dimly who they were, but that was all. I scrolled through my contact list and called Jan, my head nurse, to see if perhaps she had arranged another doctor to look in on him.

"Luke," Jan answered her phone without preamble, her voice tight and rushed. "Did Dr. Bridges call you? I know this timing is awful, and I wasn't going to bother you given all the horrible things going on, but the ER doc really should hear from you."

Dr. Bridges was the Richmond oncologist to whom I'd referred Rev. Crosley.

"What are you talking about?" I asked her.

"You don't know?"

"No!"

"Oh, Luke, I'm so sorry, I thought you were calling because you just heard," she said. "I stopped by Rev. Crosley's house about two hours ago, to check on him. He was a big help today. He dug up some names of former church members who have moved away, younger pastors he has mentored, friends, you name it. He has a lot of them coming to Jameston tomorrow. I think he alone has brought in 50 or 60 volunteers to help with the search. Then he went with one of the in-town groups to put up the new flyers this afternoon. But he was working way too hard, so I wanted to check on him after he went home."

"Jan, I'm going to explode if you don't tell me what has happened."

"Sorry," she said quickly. "When I got to Rev. Crosley's house, he didn't answer the door. It was unlocked, and I let myself in. I found him on the floor, unconscious. We haven't been able to wake him since then."

Oh, no. No, no, no.

"Where are you?"

"WMC," she said, meaning Wilson Medical Center, the closest big hospital to Jameston.

"Vitals?" I asked.

"Better now," she said. "I rode in the ambulance with him myself. In the ambulance his heart rate was really high, around 125, and his blood pressure was way down, 75 over 55. I'm sitting in the ER with him right now. His pulse is at 110, and now his BP is 85 over 60. Better, but still not good at all. I gave the ER doc the medical history I could remember. Then I called Dr. Bridges at home and had him give the rest."

"This has pneumonia complication written all over it," I said. "Is that what they're thinking?"

"They're not sure," she said. "The EKG came back good, so that eliminates heart attack. A worsening of the pneumonia is what they're thinking, of course. But we still can't wake him up. CBC came back ok except for a high white blood cell count. Pulse oximetry is at 88. The ER doc says that's low, but not crazy low."

I tilted my phone away from my mouth and exhaled hard in the darkness of Rev. Crosley's porch. Typical ER confusion. She was telling me that Rev. Crosley was stable, but they couldn't figure out why he was unconscious. The EKG would have told the ER doc if he'd had a heart attack, so they had at least eliminated one of a hundred things that could be causing his unconsciousness. The CBC – complete blood count test – had been run, and they had learned that his white blood cell count was high, but that was hardly news. White blood cells spike when the body is fighting an infection, like bacterial pneumonia. And his blood wasn't as well saturated with oxygen as it should be, but the ER doc was right that 88 wasn't awful.

Bottom line, they didn't know jack.

"He's been admitted, right?" I asked.

"Yes, it's happening right now. We're also waiting on the results of the toxicology screen."

"That's going to come up negative," I said. Unless Rev. Crosley drank some antifreeze out of his car or gobbled down a bottle of Tylenol, the usual ER first-tier drug screen wasn't going to find anything. I started to list to Jan the tests I wanted her to get the hospital doctors to run on Rev. Crosley, telling her to make sure they were very aggressive with this. She let me go on for a while, but eventually she cut me off.

"Luke, it's all being taken care of. The doctors here are on top of things. I'll be here and make sure nothing is getting missed, and I'll call you if there's anything I don't know."

I exhaled again.

"Ok," I said reluctantly. "Just make sure they take good care of him, Jan. I'll get there as soon as I can get away. Maybe tomorrow."

"Of course," she said. "We'll take good care of him."

After I got off the phone, I sat on one of the rockers on Rev. Crosley's front porch and breathed in the nighttime air. I was so tired that I could hardly think straight. So I concentrated on my breathing, pulling the cool air deeply into my belly, then exhaling fully before taking another breath. When I felt calm and focused enough, I took stock.

I remembered back five years ago, when Sarah was pregnant with Henry, and her obstetrician had done the ultrasound and told us we were having a boy. We sat in her old car afterwards, both saying over and over in disbelief that we had a son. Something about learning the baby's gender made Sarah's belly so much more alive then, so much more real. It was the day we became parents.

The first night we had Emma home from the hospital after she was born, we'd swaddled her and rested her in the cradle right next to our bed. After Sarah had fallen into an exhausted sleep, Emma started to stir and cry. I lifted Emma out of her crib, and lying back in our bed, I gently placed her on my bare chest. Her tiny ear had been right over my heart, where she could hear it beat. Emma quieted down and eventually fell back asleep, her warm little body rising and falling with my own breathing. I had lain there with my newborn daughter nestled on my chest, enamored, knowing that it was one of the greatest moments in my life.

My phone buzzed, breaking into my thoughts. Seeing it was Sarah, I picked it up.

"Hey, sweetheart," I said. "What's up?"

"Hi, honey," she said. "Stumps and I just finished the last of the flyers. We're at the country store in Catesville. They're closing up but they're making a few sandwiches for us, one for Stumps tonight and then some to take for tomorrow. Do you want me to get anything for you?"

"No, thanks," I said. "I'm not hungry. I'm heading home now."

"Hang on, I can't hear you," she said. "Let me get outside so I can get a better signal. Ok, what did you say?"

"I said I'm heading home now."

"How's Rev. Crosley?" she asked.

"It's a long story. I think he'll be ok, though."

"Good," she said. "Hurry up and get home so we can get to sleep, and then get going early tomorrow."

"I was just going to say the same thing to you. You are way overdue for sleep. Is Stumps --?"

My question was cut short by a hard knocking sound coming from Sarah's end, as if she had dropped her phone on concrete. Then I heard her make a surprised noise, followed by an angry noise.

"Get off me!" Sarah shrieked at someone, electrifying my nervous system instantaneously.

I shouted her name at the top of my lungs, my voice exploding in the quiet of Rev. Crosley's neighborhood. Even so, I knew my voice would be only a tinny squeak coming out of her phone on the cold parking lot of the Catesville store. I could hear a struggle going on between Sarah and someone else. She was yelling in short bursts, as if she was hitting whoever was grabbing her.

Hit him, baby, my mind blared as I ran back into Rev. Crosley's house to call 911 on his landline and keep my phone line open. *Hit him hard, and then run as fast as you can out of there.*

Sarah was still fighting her attacker as I fumbled with the old wall-mounted phone in Rev. Crosley's kitchen. I was about to dial 911 when I heard an angry shout burst out on Sarah's side of the call. It was an angry male shout, yelling at Sarah.

Then an earsplitting gunshot cracked over the earpiece of my phone, and Sarah went silent.

That silence persisted for several seconds before the roar of a car tearing out of the parking lot came through my earpiece, ending with the sound of a crunch as it rolled over and crushed Sarah's phone.

As my trembling hands dialed 911, I replayed in my head that angry shout at my wife. I knew that shout. I knew the shout that had overpowered my wife's screams in the moment before the gunshot silenced her. The voice that made that shout belonged to someone I much loved.

It was the voice of Arthur T. Dixon, Esq., the esteemed member of the Virginia State Bar, equity partner in the vaunted Huntington & Powell law firm.

Stumps.

***

God no, God no, God no, the begging prayer spilled from my mouth as my truck flew at 90 miles per hour along Route 620 to the country store where Sarah had said she was. *Please God, please God, please God.*

I tried to think how maybe what I had heard didn't mean Sarah was dead. Maybe I was wrong, maybe it hadn't been a gunshot. I mean, it had sounded just like a gunshot. I'd been shooting guns all my life, growing up on our farm. I knew what a gunshot sounded like. Then again, maybe someone had an old car nearby and it had backfired at just that moment.

Sarah had fought her attacker. I could hear that. Maybe she had fought him off? And besides, Stumps was there with Sarah. He wouldn't let any harm come to her.

But Stumps had been the man who had angrily shouted Sarah's name. Of that I was sure. Yet it wasn't possible that Stumps had been the one to attack her. There was no way. We'd been best friends since college.

But *someone* who knew my kids had pointed out Henry to Hiram Legrand. And *someone* had gone in that jail, maybe like a lawyer visiting a client, and slipped Legrand a master key to let him escape the first time.

But there was no way. Stumps was doing everything he could to help us. He was leading the volunteer search effort.

Of course, the volunteers hadn't found anything yet.

The open fields let me see from over a mile away the flashing red and blue lights slicing through the darkness of night next to that country store. My stomach rolled, knowing what those lights meant. The blue lights meant that I had directed police on my 911 call accurately to where my wife had fought for her life less than 15 minutes ago, before a single cracking gunshot had ended that fight. And the red lights flashing up ahead meant an ambulance and a first aid squad, and a gunshot victim.

Sarah.

I already had the gas pedal pinned to the floorboards, but I pressed my foot even harder on it, until I was practically standing in the cab of the truck. Roaring down the road toward the flashing red and blue emergency lights, I strained to remember my emergency medicine rotation in my first year of residency, right after medical school. Three of us student doctors, two women and myself, were tagging along with the attending physician in that ER. He was a chunky, older guy and, though he was pretty sharp, he also was very full of himself.

Whenever he had a break in the action, he gave us short, impromptu lectures. He had given one such mini-lecture on gunshot wounds after he had satisfied himself that his patient in bed #5 was not having a heart attack, but instead had only consumed way too much bratwurst and beer at his company picnic earlier that day. He had said, "GI cocktail," briefly to a nurse to get her to make the patient a blend of an anti-nausea med, some lidocaine for pain, and a big dose of Maalox, a foul concoction that would nonetheless soothe any upper GI tract problem. After appreciatively watching the nurse's backside as she walked off to do what he said, he had turned to three of us student doctors and gave the information I would use in about 30 seconds to try to save my wife's life.

All right, here's the deal, he had said to start his little lecture. *Gunshot wounds simply are puncture wounds that result in catastrophic tissue damage. Three factors determine the severity of the wound and what an emergency practitioner must do to treat the patient. The first factor is the size of the bullet. The second is the speed of the bullet. And the third is the location of the injury.*

Of these, the third one is by far the most important. You don't believe me? You all are too young to know this, but President Reagan was nearly killed by a tiny .22 caliber round, which is the sort of cartridge 11-year-old farm boys use to pick off squirrels in the woods. That bullet was small and slow, but John Hinckley, Jr., managed to place that bullet under the president's left arm, where it broke through a rib and lodged in his lung, stopping less than an inch from his heart. An inch difference in location was all it would have taken for the country to have had another presidential assassination less than 20 years after Kennedy.

I shook the steering wheel as I strained to remember what that attending ER doc had said next.

Now, all of you are here just to do your obligatory rotation in the emergency department. None of you are going to be working in emergency medicine, so you may never deal with a gunshot victim in your careers. Good. I hope you don't. But just in case you do, let me imprint this on your frontal lobes – A, B, C, D, and E. Remember that. A, B, C, D, and E.

He had ticked off each of these five on the fingers of one hand as we three student doctors crowded around him. One of us had taken notes. I hadn't.

The letter A is for airway. If the victim can't talk or is unconscious, sweep her mouth for obstructions. A tongue might be swollen, or she may be bleeding in the mouth. Clear it, right away.

B is for breathing. Is the victim breathing? If not, start rescue breathing immediately.

C is for circulation. Put heavy pressure on any bleeding, then check to see if she has a pulse. If not, begin CPR immediately. And don't be a wimp about it. Compress that chest hard. If you don't squeeze that heart and get the blood circulating again right away, her brain will start to die in three minutes.

D is for disability. If the victim is awake, see if she can move her hands and feet. If not, she may have damage to the spinal cord, anywhere from the base of the skull to near the tailbone. Be very, very gentle. No heaving her on a gurney. She might be just a jostle away from permanent paralysis.

Then he had asked us if anyone knew what E stood for. The other two student doctors, both from the suburbs, had no idea. It was me, the country boy who had come of age hunting in the woods with his father, who had guessed correctly.

Very good, Dr. Andrews. E stands for exit wound. Find it. Very often your patient will have been shot in her belly or chest, and she presents supine. Presenting supine means she's laying on her back, in case you missed that day of medical school.

When she is supine, you probably will find a small, neat entrance wound to her front. Do not make the mistake of focusing solely on that while she bleeds out of a much larger and more insulting exit wound to the back. Check the victim as thoroughly as possible for that exit wound. Left untreated by a stupid practitioner, it is the exit wound that kills more often than any other trauma caused by that bullet.

Hoping that the paramedics on the scene treating Sarah had heard a similar lecture when they took their certification classes in the meeting room of a volunteer firehouse somewhere, I kept the truck at its very top speed until the last possible moment. Then, when I had brought my speeding truck recklessly close to

213

the emergency vehicles blocking the country store's parking lot where Sarah probably was presenting supine with a gunshot wound to her chest or belly, I crushed the brake pedal and fishtailed my truck to a stop. The sound of the screeching tires was barely out of the air when I threw open the door and darted out.

The first deputy evidently didn't recognize me and held up a hand as if to stop me, but I blew past him on a dead run and weaved around the emergency response vehicles and first responders in their various uniforms, trying to get to my wife so I could elbow the paramedics out of the way and save her myself. I finally burst around the ponderous ambulance parked right next to the scene of the shooting. Then I stopped short, frozen in place, stunned by what I saw.

Unconscious and lying supine, bleeding heavily from a gunshot wound with paramedics working feverishly on him, was my friend Stumps.

I looked wildly around the parking lot for Sarah, but all I saw was Stumps's car. It was empty and parked off to the side. Right next to it was Sarah's phone, resting on the pavement where it had been knocked out of her hands as I had been talking to her. Looking back over to where Stumps lay, it looked like he had made it to within about 35 feet of her when he'd been shot.

Sarah was nowhere to be found.

I cried out her name as I ran over to Stumps, completely innocent Stumps, to try to save his life.

Part Four

Chapter 48

<u>Sarah Andrews</u>

A half hour earlier, I had been on my phone with Luke in the parking lot while Stumps was inside the country store, waiting on our sandwiches. A man had come out of nowhere and grabbed me from behind, knocking the phone out of my hands. He had reached around my head, trying to clamp his hand over my face. I'd turned my head just fast enough to avoid it and somehow struggled free and turned to face him.

In front of me, with a hellishly predatory look on his face, had been Hiram Legrand. He held a rag in one hand, and the other was balled up in a fist. For a moment I had frozen in panic, and in that moment he'd drawn his fist way back to take a huge swing at my face in a bid to knock me unconscious. But as Legrand's swinging punch had been arcing widely towards my head, everything Luke had ever taught me for a moment like this had welled up in me.

Even as far back as college, Luke always had insisted that I learn to defend myself. Back at William & Mary, he'd made me go to self-defense classes at the campus women's center. He also had spent hours with me himself, first in our college gym, then years later in the gym in our old barn. He showed me how to break free from various holds an assailant might have on me, how to get out of the way of the wide, swinging punches that most men throw, and how and where to strike back. I thought he was a little nuts, but I gave in just to humor him.

> *Blocks are usually stupid,* Luke would say. *Even if you can get your arm up in time to block his punch, he could hurt your arm badly, and then you'll be left open to a second punch. It's better to take a quick half step back when he takes a big swing at you, so that he completely misses you.*

So a half hour ago in the parking lot, when Legrand's wide punch had been arcing towards my head more slowly than the athletic punches Luke threw at me when we practiced, I'd reflexively taken a quick half step back. Legrand's punch had flown past my face. Then I had kicked my foot as hard as I could at his crotch, with the earnest intention of crushing his testicles flat against his pelvic bone.

> *It isn't like the movies, Sarah, when the girl saves herself by a single kick to the bad guy's crotch,* Luke had said. *Most men will react quickly enough to avoid a direct hit to the family jewels. They'll either be able to squeeze their thighs together, or they'll move their hips away just fast enough. But what's also true is that almost every man, when defending himself against a hard kick to the groin, will drop his hands away from his head and down to his lower belly in a*

218

reflex to protect himself. That's when you can smash
him in the face with your fist. He'll be wide open for it.

My foot had connected hard against the inner part of Legrand's upper thigh as he jerked his hips away from me just quickly enough to avoid a crunching shot. In so doing, he dropped his hands to his lower gut and scooted his hips back, leaving himself slightly hunched over and his face wide open. Legrand had howled in pain as my fist slammed into his face and jolted his broken teeth and jaw.

After you pop him in the face, don't run yet, Luke
had instructed. *If you turn to run after that one pop,*
some men will be able to recover in a few seconds and
then chase you and catch you. So if you've popped him
one, take that opening before he recovers and really
hurt him with the hardest kick you have. Then you
run. And scream your head off.

In the instant that Legrand had been frozen by pain and held his hand over his broken jaw, I'd kicked him with all my strength in his belly. His breath had whooshed out in a sudden rush, and in that instant I heard Stumps shouting my name. Glancing in his direction, I saw Stumps tearing out the door of the country store and sprinting powerfully toward us.

I'd known then that I was not going to have to run away from Legrand. Stumps was a three-time All-American wrestler at William & Mary. So I had turned back to Legrand, fully intending to kick him again. Even if he recovered and grabbed me, Stumps would plow him over in just a couple of seconds. Then I would

219

tell Stumps to break Legrand's bones until he told us where my children were.

An instant later the deafening percussion of a gunshot had cracked open the cool night air. I'd ducked reflexively, and out of the corner of my eye I saw Stumps fall down to the pavement, clutching his side. He'd been shot.

In that moment of shock with my back to Legrand, he had reached around me again and clamped his rag hard on my face. As I tasted and smelled that chemical vapor roiling down my throat and into my lungs, I knew Legrand had beaten us again. The last thing I'd seen was Stumps struggle to get up off the pavement, one hand reaching out to me and his other hand on a huge splotch of red spreading across the lower left side of his shirt. Then he had collapsed back down on the pavement, and my world dimmed and then went black.

***

As I slowly regained consciousness in the backseat of a car, Hiram Legrand smiled at me. The smile was abbreviated because of the swelling on the side of his face where Luke had hit him, but his mirth was there. It was dark outside, but I could see he had slid all the way to the other side of the backseat to create enough distance to keep the shotgun in his hands pointed at me. His smile grew wider as he saw me realize that my hands were bound tightly at the wrists with coils of thin, strong cord.

The last of my grogginess quickly dissipated as he poked the muzzle of his shotgun in my side.

"The worm done turned, ain't it, Sarah?" he asked me, sounding pleased with himself, albeit with his voice a little muted because of his jaw being wired shut. "Six hours ago, we was sitting in court, and I was the prisoner. Now you is."

A man wearing a black hoodie sweatshirt with the hood pulled up over his head was sitting alone in the front, silently driving. I could only see the back of his head.

I looked back at Legrand and said, "You are disgusting. You are evil. And when my husband finds you, he's going to kill you."

Legrand smiled and nodded like he had been expecting me to say something like that. Then he abruptly leaned forward and smacked my face hard before quickly leaning back and pointing the shotgun at me again. The cords binding my hands together sunk painfully into my wrists when I strained against them. Legrand laughed as I made a frustrated noise in my throat.

Then the driver issued a single word without turning around. "Stop," he said, speaking more to Legrand than to me.

My head swiveled back in the direction of the driver. I knew that voice. It took me several seconds to place it, and then when I did, I slumped in shock.

"Oh, you indescribable bastard," I said.

Legrand tittered at that for a while, and then he said to his driver, "Oh, c'mon, man, she knows who you are. You gotta be hot in that sweatshirt by now, and it ain't even yours."

The driver was quiet for a moment, and then he sighed heavily. After a pause, with one hand on the wheel, he used his other hand to pull the hood from his sweatshirt off his head and immediately smooth his distinguished gray hair back into place. When he dropped his hand, the dashboard lights illuminated his dignified profile.

Sitting behind the wheel, driving me wherever Hiram Legrand wanted me to go, was a genuine, blue-blooded member of the eastern Virginia aristocracy, that scion of the Somerset Plantation, the Honorable Judge S. Dalton Carter.

Chapter 49

When the car Judge Carter was driving rolled to a stop on a dirt path in the middle of the dark woods, Legrand pushed me out and got out with me. Keeping the shotgun pointed at me, he quickly stuck his head back in the car and said something under his voice to Judge Carter.

Judge Carter then pulled away, and I saw that I had been in a gray sedan. I knew it was the same car that had been used to steal Henry away from the soft little cocoon of his preschool at the neighborhood park.

Outside the car, I could hardly see where we were. The night sky was cloudy, completely blocking the moon and the stars. Legrand made me crunch through the woods. With my hands tied in front of me, I got caught in a briar patch in the darkness of the night. The wiry branches of thorns stuck into me through the denim of my jeans, making little pricks into the skin of my legs underneath. As I tried to disentangle myself with my tied-together hands, Legrand impatiently jabbed the shotgun into my back and told me to keep moving. So I had to push through it, making the thorns press painfully deeper into my skin until the tough branches of the thorn bush broke off.

Finally we came into a clearing in the woods. In the darkness of night I was able to make out the outline of an old log cabin. It took me a few seconds to register what I was seeing.

I knew exactly where we were.

"Here?" I said more than asked.

"Yes, ma'am. Here is where you'll be staying," Legrand said mockingly, as if he were a well-trained bellhop at a five-star hotel. Then he chuckled, having amused himself with his fake agreeability.

When we both stepped up on the old, sagging boards of the cabin's porch, he reached around me, undid the lock on the door, and quickly pushed the door open. Then he roughly shoved me through the doorway and slammed the door shut behind me, locking it. I heard him walk back off the old porch and crunch away into the night.

The interior of the cabin was even darker than the night outside. Before my eyes could adjust, I heard a hesitant movement across the room. Great, I thought to myself as I lifted both bound wrists to scratch my forehead. Of course there'd be a field mouse or maybe even a raccoon sharing this place with me.

Then I heard two soft voices ask me a one-word question simultaneously.

"Mama?"

Lightning exploded in every molecule of my body.

"Emma! Henry!"

Henry and Emma were scrambling to their feet as I darted across the room and slid on my knees to meet them, finally seeing them in the darkness as I drew near. Then I felt their blessed little hands and arms hugging me. They put their heads on my shoulders as they both wrapped their arms around my neck and

224

squeezed me tightly. Straining vainly to break out of my cords to hug them back, I couldn't break free, so I settled for grasping one leg of each of them with my hands.

"Are you ok?" I asked, knowing already from their happy wiggles that they were unhurt and completely healthy.

"Yes, mama!" they answered in unison.

"Thank God," I said. "Thank you, thank you, thank you. Oh kids, I missed you so much. I'm so, so, so glad to see you."

Then my two children pushed me over onto my back and climbed on me like we were playing on the rug in daylight in our living room at home. Their knees dug wonderfully into the front of me, and I loved every single ounce of their living, breathing, safe bodies. Emma's hair was in my face, and Henry's breath warmed my cheek when he kissed me. Their presence over-whelmed me, and I could not help but start weeping from the most intense joy I had ever felt in my life.

"Mama, why are you crying?" Henry asked.

"Oh, sweetie, I'm just so happy to see you both. Mommy isn't sad at all. I'm just so happy I can't hold it in, and it's coming out as tears," I said. "Now tell me – are you sure you're not hurt in any way?"

"No, mama," both kids said, and my heart soared. Then I lifted my arms and, with my wrists bound, I winged my elbows out to form an O with my arms. Then both kids wriggled right up into that O until they were wedged tight and I had them both in a bear hug. Lying there on my back with their heads warm and snuggled up near my neck, tears of joy and relief streamed out of my eyes and tickled my ears before they dampened my hair spread on the dusty floor.

"Are we going home now, Mama?" Emma asked me.

"Not yet, baby."

"Why not? Are we waiting until Daddy gets here?"

"Yes," I said, without thinking. Then, after a moment, I repeated, "Yes, baby. We're waiting for Daddy to come up here."

"Then will we go home?" Emma asked.

"Yes," I said, making certainty come into my voice for them to hear. "When Daddy comes up here, we'll get to go home. You two weren't scared up here, were you?"

"No," both children said together.

"That's good," I said. "There's no reason to be scared at all. This is kind of like a game, isn't it?"

"When we go home, can we go to Applebee's?" Henry asked randomly.

"Applebee's? Oh, um, sweetie, I'd say that just as soon as we come down off the mountain and get home, Daddy will probably take us out to Applebee's. Tell me what you'd like to get to eat when we go there."

"Grilled cheese with applesauce," Henry said.

"Mac and cheese," Emma said.

"Well, you definitely can have them. And dessert too, if you're good."

"I want a chocolate sundae for dessert," Emma said.

"I want a caramel one," Henry said.

"Like I said, if you're good, you can have them," I said. "That means being very good while we're up here. And listening to what I tell you. Can you do that?"

"Yes, mama."

"Ok, then."

"Are those men coming back?" Henry asked. "The one that smells bad and the man in the funny mask?"

226

"I don't know, sweetie," I said. "They might, but they might not. Did the man in the funny mask ever show you what his face looks like or tell you who he is?"

"No," Henry said.

"Uh-uh," Emma said, shaking her head in the tight confines of our bear hug together.

"Ok, then, it's a secret for now. It's part of the game. I came up here to finish the game with you."

"I don't wanna play anymore, Mama," Emma said.

"Emma, just finish the game," Henry said. "Daddy hasn't had a turn to come up here yet."

"That's right," I said. "Daddy hasn't had a turn yet."

"When's it gonna be Daddy's turn?" Emma asked.

"I bet he'll find us up here by tomorrow."

"Like hide and seek?" Emma asked.

"No, Emma, it's not like hide and seek," Henry said.

"Well, it's a little bit like hide and seek," I said. "Daddy just has to come here and find us. And when he does, we're all going to go home, take some baths, and then go out to eat."

Emma seemed to puzzle through something in her head. Then she said to me, "Mama, Daddy fell down."

"Do you mean in the parking lot last night?" I asked her.

"Yes," she said. "Is he hurt?"

"No, baby," I said. "Daddy's not hurt at all. I just saw him before I came up here to be with you. He's completely fine and looking so forward to seeing you kids again. Now kids, remember, who's the strongest man in the world?"

"Daddy is," both Emma and Henry said together.

"That's right, baby," I said. "Daddy is the strongest man in the world. Nothing can hurt him. He'll be up here in no time."

"Ok, mama," the children said.

"Now, look," I said, "if we want to be sure we're really well rested for when Daddy finds us, we need to get plenty of sleep tonight. Have you said your prayers tonight yet?"

Both kids shook their heads in my arms.

"Well, let's do it now. Let's say one together. Who wants to pick one?"

"How about *Now I Lay Me Down to Sleep?*" Henry asked.

"Mmm, that's a good one. But maybe we can save that one for when we get back home."

"Can we do that Christmas one?" Emma asked.

"Sure, sweetie. Let's do that one."

And that was how, in the darkness of an old cabin, two children who did not know they were kidnapped sang with their mother a simple little Christmas carol:

Away in a manger, no crib for a bed,
The little Lord Jesus laid down His sweet head.
The stars in the sky looked down where He lay,
The little Lord Jesus, asleep on the hay.

When the last note softly faded from the air, I let the quiet of the night soothe us for a good long while before I said, "Let's go to sleep now. Ok?"

"Ok, mama," the children said together.

In just a few minutes, both kids were fast asleep, and I could relax. Emotion as warm and soft as bathwater flowed over any conscious thought. For a long time I simply lay there in it, letting it softly stream over me, reveling in the glorious feelings of my children sleeping in my arms.

At some point, when the current receded enough to expose thought again, I considered what I was going to do. I had to have a plan for when . . . when . . . but there were too many 'whens' to think of. When the kids started asking harder questions in the morning. When Luke didn't show up as I had said he would. When Hiram Legrand came back.

So I prayed to God. I prayed real prayers, serious prayers, scared grownup prayers. I prayed for my children, for my husband, for myself. Then, done without being finished, I lay quietly and looked up at the rough boards that served as a ceiling in this place.

Eventually I started humming *Away in a Manger* again in the softest of tones, so as not to wake the children. The warm flow of emotion gradually rose again until it covered the rocks below, and the gentle current flowed smoothly over the top of them without showing even a ripple.

Chapter 50

Luke Andrews

I woke up in our bed at home, and for the briefest of moments, I thought everything was normal, that Sarah and the kids were just down the hall, and we'd have a long breakfast and then a lazy day relaxing around the house.

A blink, then reality. I reached for my phone on the nightstand, checking for any texts with good news or any news at all, but there was nothing.

Settling back down in the bed in the pre-dawn silence of the house, I thought about last night. I somehow had held myself together for a while after Hiram Legrand's driver shot Stumps and together they had abducted Sarah. Then, around midnight, I'd asked Agent Byram the question that was pounding in my brain. I asked if he thought Legrand planned to murder my entire family.

Put on the spot, Byram had offered up some kind of reassuring answer, but the look on his face told me what I already knew.

I tried to drive home after that, but I hadn't made it. As I was driving through the dark of night, I felt like I was covered in a maddening swarm of bees. That swarm had grown thicker and heavier until they were suffocating me. Finally at one straightaway on the road home, with a thick hardwood forest on either side, I hit the brakes hard enough to make my tires slide on loose gravel and dirt on the side of the road. Then I burst out of my truck and ran into the woods, gulping air like it was water, sprinting faster than I ever had on my best day on a football field. I might never have stopped if I hadn't suddenly lunged for the solidness of the nearest tree and bear-hugged its big trunk. My momentum nearly took my running feet out from under me, but I had fiercely held onto the tree. My arms couldn't quite get all the way around the trunk, but I hugged it tightly, pressing my forehead against it. Then my knees had unhinged, the rough bark scraping my forehead as I sagged to the ground.

And then I had bawled. Not cried. Bawled. There on the ground next to the big tree with my hands and knees crunching into the dried leaves of last fall, I had shrieked Sarah's name into the darkness of the woods. Then I had shrieked Henry's name, then Emma's name, then all three names together, over and over, until my lungs had ached and I couldn't seem to get enough air. I had come apart right there in the woods last night, nearly becoming animal-like, pounding on the soft ground with my fists and cursing at God for what He was letting happen to my family.

I could not recall how I had managed eventually to peel myself from the ground. I could not recall walking back through the woods to my truck. I could barely even remember coming home and crawling under these covers, on this bed, where Sarah and I had loved each other and created Henry and Emma, and where I had just awakened this morning to the reality that they were gone.

Looking up at the ceiling, I listened to the empty silence of my family home, and let it speak to me.

My father had come back to this house as soon as he got out of the Army. He had brought my mother here, and together they had raised Eli, Trish, and me. This quiet house had been filled with music back then. Dad would put on country music and perch Trish or Eli on his broad shoulders, singing along with exaggerated arm motions like he was an Italian opera singer rather than a karaoke Johnny Cash. A great barrel-chested man with a salt-and-pepper stubble and huge, calloused hands, Dad had been a splendid father.

Mom had liked country music too – one could not be a Virginia mountain girl of her generation and not like country music – but her tastes had been broader. She would sing the popular music of every year in her beautiful voice. If the finest, most delicate china you ever saw could sing, it would sing like my mother. One of my childhood memories was hearing her sing a few lines to my father as she handed him a cold drink. I was about six years old at the time, and my father and I were painting our four-board fence outside. A wood fence was a luxury, but my mother had liked a pretty homestead, so my father had built it for her along our driveway and up in the front of the farm by the road. He had been painting the top three boards while I was crawling around his ankles to paint the bottom board, and she'd come out of the house to us with sweet tea for him and juice for me, singing her little song. When she finished, he had whispered in her ear over my head. She burst out laughing then, a good, hard laugh that lasted. She was still giggling as she walked back into our house.

I lay there in bed for a little longer, comforted in the remembering.

When the lifting darkness outside the bedroom window on Sarah's side of the bed told me the day was almost ready to break, I forced myself out of bed and walked barefoot down the old heart-pine floors. At our side door, I stepped into my boots and went outside. The early-morning air immediately cooled my bed-warm skin, and I breathed it in deeply, filling my lungs to their bottom before exhaling again.

In those last moments before dawn, a reddish-orange glow grew out of the tops of the hills to the east, softly lighting the high cirrus clouds above them. My eyes focus on those clouds, miles up in the sky, their textured ruffles filling the vast sky. Of all the fertile fields in this area, my great-grandfather had picked this place for his farm because of the high land and distance. Except for the mountain behind the house, the surrounding forests were all lower than our open pasture, and it made the sky huge. Its reddish-orange expanse eased my mind.

After Sarah and I graduated college and got married a few weeks later, I had wanted to see real big-sky country out west. So that summer we took a long road trip to see Yellowstone, Salt Lake, the Tetons, and anywhere else that our gas-money budget could take us. We were young and broke, so we pitched tent night after night, making love on blankets in that wide open country as elk bugled, wolves howled, and owls screeched, feeling as raw and alive in that western air as any two young people had ever felt in any century.

I remembered one spectacular night lying on my back on our blanket with Sarah atop me, her delicate hands pinning my own hands down above my head. Our fingers had been interlocked, the new wedding rings on them still feeling unfamiliar and new and exciting. A million stars filled the night sky behind her head. I told her how much I was in love with her, feeling my own words with an intensity and vulnerability that only a young man making love with a beautiful young woman can feel. She had silently smiled at me, squeezing my hands tightly until our interlocked fingers seemed to become one before bringing her head down to kiss me. Later, we hadn't gone back inside to our tent, choosing instead to cuddle outside on our blanket and sleep under the huge star-filled sky above us. After she fell asleep in my arms that night, I'd felt so in love with her that I had looked up at the honest western sky and simply thanked God for that moment in time.

Calmed, I walked along our side pasture under the early-morning Virginia sky. The dew on the grass quickly wet my boots as I headed down to the woods, down to Corby Creek, where I had spent many quiet hours when I was growing up. I had almost reached the tree line when I heard the rumble of a car on our long gravel driveway.

I looked back and saw Rev. Rigsby's car rolling toward the house. I wasn't alarmed, because I could see through the windows of his white Volkswagen that he was by himself, so I knew he didn't carry any bad news. He would have come with one of the FBI agents if that was his mission. He spotted me and stopped his car before getting to the house, sliding out from behind the wheel. I trotted over and met him at the side of the driveway. We talked over the four-board fence my father and I had painted for my mother years ago.

"How you holding up?" Rev. Rigsby said as I got up to his car. I appreciated his understated manner. I didn't need profound expressions of sympathy. He had woken up in the parsonage before dawn and driven out here to be with me when I got up in the morning, and that was enough.

"Hanging in there," I said.

"Any news, any leads?"

"Not really," I said. "I'm heading to town in a little while. I'm supposed to meet the FBI agents at the sheriff's office at eight this morning. They know Legrand took Sarah. They're virtually certain he had a driver helping him again. They're still thinking law enforcement, maybe, but who knows."

He nodded and said, "I checked with the hospital before I came out here this morning. Rev. Crosley is recovering. They're still not sure why he passed out, but he's getting better. And your friend, the lawyer from Richmond, is a very lucky man. Turns out he was hit with buckshot from a shotgun, not a bullet. Took two pellets above his left hip, on the side, and they tore him up but didn't hit any important organs. He'll be in the hospital for a week or so, but he should be ok, too."

I had learned all of that late last night, but I nodded anyway. I was glad there were good doctors over at the Wilson Medical Center taking care of them. Still, I made a mental note to call Jan and ask her to drive over there and check on Stumps and Rev. Crosley at the hospital for me.

"Tell me, Luke, how are you doing?" Rev. Rigsby asked meaningfully.

It wasn't meant as the usual pleasantry, and I considered the question.

"I don't know," I said after a few moments. "I always thought losing my parents and my sister in the accident was the worst thing that would ever happen to me. But at least then I still had a future. Emma, Henry, Sarah – they *are* my future. And Legrand has stolen them from me. All I can do is hope that I get them back."

Rev. Rigsby looked thoughtful and said quietly, "I'd hazard a guess that you're pretty mad at the world."

I exhaled audibly and gave an abbreviated nod, then looked away.

"That's ok," he said. "When God appears to be silent in the face of our suffering, it's natural to be angry."

I didn't say anything. After a pause, Rev. Rigsby asked softly, "You want to hear from God now, do you not?"

"Yes," I said quickly, the word slipping out of me. Rev. Rigsby had nailed it on the head. I wanted to know *why* this was happening to my family. And I wanted to know what to do.

"It can be hard when God is silent," he said. "It's natural to expect God to tell us what His plan is. I can't tell you what His plan is. No pastor can. We're all fallible. You've seen the contradictory messages from the televangelists who run those so-called megachurches. And even traditional pastors, educated in the best seminaries, can come up with different meanings from the same Scripture. No, there are times when we need to hear from God Himself, directly."

"I'm not hearing much of anything right now," I said.

He was about to say something more, but my phone buzzed with a text in my pocket just then. The text was from Byram, and it stopped our conversation in its tracks.

> L – We have in custody a suspect for Legrands co-conspirator. He's law enforcement. Come now if u can. Lets bump 0800 meeting up to 0730.

The time on my phone said 6:55 a.m., and I immediately texted back that I was on the way.

"What's up?" Rev. Rigsby asked.

"They have Legrand's driver," I said excitedly. "He's a cop of some kind. I've gotta run. This is how we get my family back. If we find Legrand's driver, we find Legrand, and if we find Legrand, we can find my family."

"That's great, Luke," Rev. Rigsby said. "Go get them."

***

"Amos Hudson, the warden of Cent-West Jail," Agent Byram said to me in the sheriff's office, which by then was overflowing with federal agents wearing suits and Virginia State Troopers in their light-gray uniforms. "We think he is the one who has been helping Legrand. Helping Legrand with driving; helping him with his escapes. And we owe the breakthrough to Agent Healey. She figured out three different things overnight to bring it all together."

Ms. Healey shrugged and kept a professional frown on her face as Byram continued.

"Obviously, when Legrand escaped from Cent-West using Capt. Hudson's own master key, that got our attention," he said. "But we didn't think Hudson would leave such a clear trail to himself. When we questioned him after the first escape, he agreed to take a polygraph. A lie detector test. And he passed with flying colors. So we initially eliminated him as a person of interest."

"Ok," I said uncertainly.

"Last night," Agent Byram said, "everyone assumed that when Legrand escaped, he kept the handgun he used yesterday in Judge Carter's chambers. But when a lot of extra law enforcement personnel showed up last night, Agent Healey came up with a list of long-shot work items they could do overnight. She figured we had the manpower, so why not? Anyway, one of the items on her list was to do a shoulder-to-shoulder search around the courthouse, just in case we found something interesting. She thought perhaps Legrand might have dropped something during his escape that might help us. So overnight she sent out some of the state troopers to do it.

"Sure enough, this morning at about 2:00 a.m., one of the troopers found in the bushes, near the back door Legrand ran out of, a .40 caliber Glock. Model 22, to be specific. That is a semi-automatic, black polymer handgun popular among law enforcement agencies. It also happens to be the very sidearm issued by the Jameston County Sheriff's Department to all sworn law enforcement officers employed by the sheriff, including the ranking corrections officer at Cent-West.

"That Glock is chambered for rounds of the size and type Hiram Legrand used on Thursday in Judge Carter's chambers to murder two bailiffs and to wound the prosecutor. So we checked the serial number of the Glock against the sheriff's records. The firearm found in the bushes next to the courthouse was issued two years ago to Amos Lee Hudson, age 50, captain in the Jameston County Sheriff's Department and the administrator of the Central Western Regional Jail. Hiram Legrand escaped and shot two deputies guarding him with Capt. Hudson's firearm. After he escaped earlier this week with Capt. Hudson's own key."

I was reeling. I knew Amos.

"When we woke Hudson up at 2:30 a.m. this morning at his home and brought him in, he acted like he was shocked that his firearm was not in its usual place in the top drawer of his dresser," Agent Byram continued. "But of course we had plenty to bring him in to the station for questioning. Besides, his boss, the sheriff, ordered him to come in and explain himself.

"After he came with us, our people did an initial search of his home for any evidence. Judge Carter had already gotten up in the middle of the night and signed the search warrant for us in his bathrobe. We haven't found much yet, but we have technicians going over it with a fine-tooth comb."

"Where is Amos now?" I asked.

"Right here. He's still down in the interrogation room down the hall," Ms. Healey said.

"He is?" I asked sharply, starting to get up out of my chair, but Byram put a firm hand on my shoulder.

"No, no, not again," he said. "Your giving a smack to Legrand is a closed matter, but don't you go re-open it by barging back in the same room and going after Amos Hudson."

"A couple of our colleagues in the Bureau, from Washington, are already interrogating Hudson," Ms. Healey added. "They're the best. If he's going to talk, they'll be able to get him to do it."

Reluctantly sitting back in my chair, I asked, "Is he saying anything now?"

"Nope," Byram said. "He's claiming he doesn't know a thing. Says he didn't know his firearm was missing, just like he didn't notice his master key missing two days earlier. He says he worked his standard 5 a.m. to 3 p.m. shift at the jail, came home, put his firearm in its usual place in his top dresser drawer, went for a jog, and then took a shower. Then he claims he was working in his woodshop in his basement at the time Legrand escaped yesterday at about 5:30 p.m."

I thought back to my confrontation with Legrand in Cent-West the afternoon before he escaped. It'd been the second time that day I'd seen Legrand, and he'd been angry about how I'd torpedoed his future insanity plea in court earlier that day. Right there in the jail's medical exam room he had threatened to go after my kids. I had jerked him across the table and had been ready to wring his neck when Capt. Hudson and a whole platoon of his corrections officers intervened. Hudson had given me a half-baked story about how someone had noticed Legrand was all fired up beforehand and that this is why they were so close by to intervene.

"We might not have been able to hold Hudson, if what he said checked out," Agent Byram said. "But there's more."

"What?"

"We found an email address for Legrand," Byram said, "and we have some emails between him and Capt. Hudson. Agent Healey here struck gold."

"It was luck," Ms. Healey said. "Yesterday morning, we were getting thin on leads, so I decided to just do some blind fishing, and that means computers. We had no reason to believe that Legrand uses a computer. But like I said, we were getting pretty thin on leads, so I decided to take a few stabs at free email services, you know, like hotmail.com, gmail.com, riso.net, things like that. I have a contact at RisoNet, which runs riso.net. I asked her to look for any riso.net address that had the word 'Legrand' in it anywhere."

She handed me a manila folder with "Legrandmaster666" written on the tab before continuing.

"Besides just the email address itself, from the context of the emails, this clearly is Hiram Legrand's email. I printed out a hard copy of one chain and put it in this folder."

I flipped open the folder and looked at the email chain:

To: Legrandmaster666@riso.net
From: capnhudson@horizons.net
7:05 p.m.
Don't call again. I will not help you.

To: capnhudson@horizon.net
From: Legrandmaster666@riso.net
7:55 p.m.
I got yor key

To: Legrandmaster666@riso.net
From: capnhudson@horizons.net
8:10 p.m.
I don't care. They already know that. I have explained it to them, and they're fine with me.

To: capnhudson@horizons.net
From: Legrandmaster666@riso.net
8:55 p.m.
I can sqweel on how u helped and thell know u did it

"Son of a *bitch*," I said.

"We've confirmed that capnhudson@horizons.net is Capt. Hudson's personal email address," Agent Healey said. "We pulled his computer out of his house, and we'll send it out for forensic analysis, to see what might be stored on his hard drive. In the meantime, we got the CEO of Horizons out of bed this morning at around 4 a.m., and he got his chief technical guy to give us the scoop. These emails were sent to and from a computer with an IP address matching the IP address on Capt. Hudson's computer. It was him."

Looking at the date and time stamps on the email exchange between Amos Hudson and Hiram Legrand, I said, "Thursday night was two nights ago. Henry already had been taken, and Legrand was still on the loose. What was Legrand trying to get Amos to do?"

"We don't know. He obviously was extorting Capt. Hudson for some kind of help. Capt. Hudson appears in his first email to reference a telephone call he received from Legrand, and we're in the process of pulling Hudson's mobile, home, and office phone records to see what incoming calls he received."

I asked, "So what now?"

"This is a big break, Luke," Agent Byram said. "We have a forensic team at Capt. Hudson's house right now going over every inch of his house and car. He was sloppy enough to use his own email address and let Legrand use his own master key. He even was risk-taking enough, or blackmailed strongly enough, to plant his own gun, and probably a handcuff key, in the couch in Judge Carter's chambers. If he was that sloppy, the chances are good that we'll find something else we can use. More to the point, if we can make Hudson believe that there is light at the end of the

242

tunnel for him, that he might not spend the rest of his life in prison if he talks, he might break and spill his guts about everything. Where Legrand is. Where he's stashing your family. And how to get them back."

Chapter 51

10 a.m.
Sunday morning

<u>Sarah Andrews</u>

On the outside, I was happy Mom, relaxed and smiling and playing little games with the kids. After Henry tried unsuccessfully to untie the cords binding my wrists, I even made that seem like part of the fun.

Inside, my mind was racing over my options about how to get us out of this cabin and away from Hiram Legrand

The cabin was a little small for our game of Spin-and-Find, but with just three of us playing, it worked. Henry had on a blindfold I had made from a strip of cloth I had clumsily torn off the front of the T-shirt I was wearing underneath my sweatshirt. He was spinning around in place the requisite ten times in the middle of the cabin. Emma was smiling quietly in one corner of the room, and I was on the other side, where I kept glancing at the locked door whenever the kids weren't looking at me.

Dizzy, Henry staggered away from both of us

"Colder," Emma giggled, and Henry changed direction.

"A little warmer," I whispered.

"But colder for me!" Emma laughed, too loud, and Henry headed straight to her. She cheated and moved a few steps to the left, and Henry kept going until his fingertips touched a wall.

The rough-hewn beams of the cabin were huge and as solid as they'd been the day the cabin was built. But the chinking, the filler between those logs, was cracking and falling apart. I didn't know what kind of mortar people used way back when, but it obviously didn't last forever. It had deteriorated enough that I could see to the outside in some places.

A new piece of board had been nailed into the wall. Together with the pair of ruined, child-sized sandals in the corner, it wasn't hard to figure out that this was where Legrand had held Mary Beth Marshall, and that she had tried to kick her way through the crumbling chinking.

Peering at the chinking, I thought I could kick away at what remained if I worked at it, but there was no way a grown woman could squeeze through that space. On the other hand, a little girl like Mary Beth Marshall just might be able to squeeze through that space.

If she could, so could my kids.

Still, I wouldn't get the chance to find out so long as Legrand was hanging around. I knew I would make a lot of noise if I started trying to kick the chinking out, and he had a shotgun. I couldn't see him now through any of the cracks in the wall, but I had spotted him earlier in the morning in the nearby woods. I figured that he probably was nearby.

"Mama, do you think Daddy will find us this morning?" Henry asked me. He had tagged Emma and pulled his blindfold down to a loose kind of handkerchief around his neck, while Emma was pulling up her own blindfold to go around her eyes

245

for her turn to spin in the middle. It was easier to make two blind-folds, one for each kid, than to keep tying and untying one. Underneath my sweatshirt, my T-shirt was missing its lower front.

"Maybe, sweetie. But I think it'll probably be tonight. So we should plan on spending the day up here. That way, if we get found earlier, it'll be fun to win the game earlier."

"We win when Daddy finds us?" Emma asked.

"Yup," I said. "That's how we win."

"Who's that man that brought you here?" she asked.

"Oh, he's just a man who Daddy knows. He has to pretend to be the bad guy for our game, and Daddy gets to play the good guy."

Both kids seemed to accept that. In just another couple of years, probably just one for Henry, they wouldn't be little enough to fool like this anymore.

I was debating what other kinds of pleasant fibs would work for the rest of the day with the kids when, through a gap in the chinking, I caught a glimpse of Legrand walking back from the woods and in the direction of the cabin. My heart fluttered in my chest.

"Part of the game is doing exactly what I say," I said to the kids. "So, if I tell you to pretend to be asleep, will you do that?"

Both kids nodded.

"And if I tell you to run into the woods as far as you can, will you do that?"

Both said they would.

"Ok, then." I said as Legrand was getting closer. "Now, go face the wall, lie on your sides, and close your eyes. Pretend to be asleep. Even if the man who's pretending to be the bad guy comes in here, I want you to pretend to be asleep until I tell you that you

246

can stop. Even if it takes a long time. It's really, really important that you pretend to be asleep. Ok?"

"Ok, Mama," both kids said.

"Good. Go, do it now. And be very, very quiet."

The two kids scooted over to where I had told them to go and closed their eyes. But their eyelids were a little twitchy, and anyone looking closely would know they were faking it. Plus I wanted to make sure they couldn't see anything.

"Put on your blindfolds, both of you, right now, and then pretend to be asleep," I whispered to both of them. "It's part of the game."

Hiram Legrand's footsteps clomped on the porch of the cabin. I stood in front of my children, facing the door, my hands still bound with cord in front of my lower belly.

"Remember, don't move. Keep your eyes closed, even behind your blindfolds. No cheating!" I whispered to them as Legrand worked the heavy black padlock on the door outside. Then the door swung open, and there he was, standing in the doorway with a pump-action shotgun in his hands.

Legrand's eyes flicked down briefly at the kids lying on the floor, facing away from him, and I stopped breathing. Then he brought his eyes back up at me again.

"Come on," he said.

I didn't want to leave the children, but he had that shotgun in his hands, and I wanted to get him away from the kids. He followed me as I walked out the door. He kept his shotgun pointed at me, and keeping me in front of him, he made me head to the nearby woods.

247

Once we got far enough from the cabin that I was positive the kids couldn't hear, I fought down my fear enough to ask him, "So how'd you get Judge Carter in on this?"

"That's my father you're talking about," Legrand said, then snickered as I gasped.

My mind raced through what I knew about Judge Carter. His wife had died a few years ago. He was Virginia aristocracy all the way. But money and land didn't make a man any more likely to be faithful to his wife. Decades ago, could he have taken some fancy hunting or fishing trip to Arkansas where Legrand was from, found some local girl, and had a secret child out of wedlock? It was possible.

My thoughts were cut off when Legrand ordered me to stop and turn around to face him. When I did, I saw that he had the shotgun shouldered and pointed at my chest. He backpedaled a few steps until he was perhaps 20 feet away from me. Then he took a knife out of a leather sheath on his hip, and he tossed it at my feet.

"Pick it up," he said.

My breath was ragged, and I didn't move.

Legrand cursed at me, then said, "I got this here shotgun loaded with three-inch buckshot shells. Pick up that knife right now, or I'll blow your heart and lungs right out your back. Make 'em hit the trees over yonder."

I bent over and picked up the knife, using both hands at once because my wrists were still tied together.

"Put the point of the blade against your neck," Legrand said. "Right up against it. No, not the front. The side. I wanna see your face."

The cords around my wrists dug into me as I awkwardly twisted my arms to point the knife at the side of my neck. Legrand stepped back a few more feet, lowered his shotgun to his hip and held it there with just his left hand. Then he pulled a phone out of his pocket and peered at its screen to line me up for a photo, but then stopped and looked back up at me.

"You don't think you can rush me before I can drop the phone and pull the trigger on this here shotgun, do you?" he asked.

I looked at the distance between us.

"No," I said, and I wasn't lying.

"Me neither," he said. "I figure if you try it, I'll be emptying this in your gut at maybe ten feet. A load of triple-aught buckshot at that distance will cut you in half. And if I go to that effort, I might as well drag the top half of you back to the cabin with your kids. So don't try it."

Wondering whether he was planning to kill me on camera, I forced myself to show him a face that was fearless and angry.

"Make the point touch your skin," he said. "Push it in some. I want to see a little dimple in the side of your neck."

I did as he said, but not before waiting a few seconds as if I was deciding whether I would do what he asked. The sharp point of his knife poked maddeningly into the sensitive skin on the side of my neck, but I refused to let my face change expression.

"Close your eyes. And I want you to push the knife against your neck deeper," he said.

I closed my eyes but said irritably, "If I push it any more I'll cut myself."

"I don't give a damn. It'd make a better picture anyway. Now stop giving me that badass look on your face and push it deeper into your neck, or I'll stop playing games and just kill you and then go back to the cabin and kill your kids."

I immediately pushed the knife hard into the side of my neck until I felt a trickle of a single drop of fluid. I knew without looking that I had pierced my own skin, and a drop of my blood was rolling down my neck and come to a rest on my collar bone. Then I heard the fake electronic sound of a camera shutter come from his phone, and I opened my eyes and let my hands fall away from my neck without asking permission. Legrand was taking a look at his screen to see the picture he'd just taken.

"Drop the knife at your feet," he said. "Then go walk to that pine tree over there."

I did as I was told, and once I was far enough away, Legrand retrieved his knife and quickly texted something on his phone. Then, pocketing his phone, he pointed the shotgun at me again, and ordered me to go back to the cabin.

As I got back to the porch of the cabin, I said a prayer that Henry and Emma weren't up and moving around inside. Legrand had me open the lock and the door, and I blocked the view from the open door with my body as best I could in case the kids were up and moving. But they were still pretending to be asleep in the exact position I had left them.

When the door was locked behind me again, and Legrand had stomped back off the porch and wandered off into the nearby woods again, I whispered to the kids that they had to stay still for just one more minute. I licked my finger and rubbed the thin stream of drying blood off my neck. When I could no longer hear the crunching of dry leaves under Legrand's feet, I told the kids that they could take off their blindfolds and get up. I made much of how good they'd been to listen to me so carefully.

"Where were you, mama?" Henry asked, his eyes blinking even at the dim light in the room after having been wearing his blindfold for ten minutes.

"Oh, I was just outside."

"What were you doing outside?"

"I was looking to see if Daddy was coming up the mountain yet."

"Did you see him?"

"No, not yet," I said. "But it's still morning. Maybe I'll get out there and check again this afternoon."

I sat down, and using my pointer finger on the cabin's dusty floor, I drew a large pound sign.

"So," I said. "Who wants to play another round of tic-tac-toe?"

Chapter 52

Luke Andrews

An unexpected truth is that no matter how desperate a man is when looking for his whole family, he soon runs out of things to do.

After talking with Byram and Healey earlier in the morning, I had checked in with Sarah's friends, who were working to update the social media. They also had produced and printed out updated paper flyers with Sarah's picture along with the kids' pictures on them. A number of volunteers were quickly posting them. By now they were pros, having hit for a third time every store, gas station, restaurant, bulletin board, and telephone pole that possibly could hold a flyer.

Even so, I had learned that finding missing people was more about computers and forensics and phone calls than on-foot searching. Wandering around the woods or knocking door to door was a tiny net compared to the far larger one based on technology. Still, a sizable group of volunteers was searching in the vastness of the mountainous federal land within driving distance of Jameston, on the theory that Legrand might have a camp of some kind in the woods somewhere nearby. I couldn't sit still; I had to keep moving forward and do *something*. So, after I ran around all morning, I was getting ready to rejoin the volunteers out in the National Forest when I got a call from Rev. Rigsby asking me if I'd like to come over to the parsonage for a quick break.

The parsonage, an old house that served as the home of the pastor of our church, was comfortable and familiar to me. Situated just across the street from the church, it had been Rev. Crosley's home throughout my childhood. Rev. Rigsby put out a plate of Entenmann's pastries and poured cups of store-brand coffee for each of us as we settled into old upholstered chairs in the living room.

I got him up to speed on what had happened that morning. The euphoria from having identified Amos Hudson as Legrand's accomplice had already faded. He was clinging stubbornly to his claim that he was innocent. The forensic team had spent all morning combing through his house and cars, but much to Agent Healey's disappointment, they still hadn't yet come up with anything. Tips were still pouring in to the toll-free hotline the FBI had set up, but nothing sounded promising. Bottom line, we were no closer to finding my family.

Rev. Rigsby nodded and said a prayer aloud right then. At least he made it short. He talked about how much I loved my family, and that he hoped that it was God's plan to bring them back home to me. I kept my hands folded and my head bowed, but I didn't really join in.

When he was done, I said, "I guess I should be getting back up to the National Forest. Though to be honest, there's not really any hard proof to believe they're up there. Now that we've hit all the public campsites and are just starting to look into the real backcountry, it's like looking for a needle in a haystack. But it gives all the volunteers something to do."

He nodded and asked, "What does the FBI think is the best way to find your family?"

"Travel," I said. "That's what Agent Byram told me this morning. Travel means driving a car. They have publicized a general description of the car Legrand has used, and transporting Sarah, Henry, and Emma means that their faces are out in public. Pictures of those faces have been seen all across Virginia by now."

And they had. Sarah's friends' work on social media had helped, but it really was the Amber Alerts and its massive audience that got us millions of pairs of eyes. Every television station in Virginia had run stories on the kidnappings, as had many stations in North Carolina, Tennessee, and other neighboring states. National cable news networks had caught wind of the story and ran segments on their morning news updates, all of which was rapidly being tweeted, blogged, and linked all over the place. If only Legrand would run, drive, get out on an interstate or state highway and expose my family's beautiful faces to observant eyes, we could find them. This was the FBI's theory behind putting as much pressure as they could throughout Jameston County. If he was still in the area, applying hard pressure could cause him to run.

When Agent Byram had explained the strategy to me this morning and saw that I was not encouraged, he asked me whether we had problems in Jameston County with coyotes going after livestock. We did. The coyotes, having learned that young sheep and calves enclosed in a pasture were easy prey, killed a good number of the younger and smaller members of flocks and herds in the county. Plus coyotes were elusive. You couldn't just use the old farmer's standby of keeping a rifle around while you were working and hoping to spot one by chance. You had to hunt them specifically. Byram had nodded and said his uncle had similar problems with coyotes on his farm in Ohio, and that he planned to hunt for Legrand the same way his uncle hunted for coyotes. When I had looked quizzically at him, he explained that every farmer with a coyote problem becomes a hunter, and every hunter knows that it's easier to spot a running coyote than one that is completely still.

The analogy had grabbed hold. Hiram Legrand was a coyote. Run, Hiram, run.

After I shared this with Rev. Rigsby and was getting ready to make my exit, a text buzzed at my hip. I pulled my phone out, hoping to see Byram's or Healey's number, but it was an "unknown" number.

"Who's this?" I murmured as Rev. Rigsby stirred a little more sugar into his coffee. A lone word, "hello," appeared, and my phone took a second to download an attached picture. When it popped on my screen, I retched and barely held in my coffee.

It was Sarah, with a knife against her neck. The photo captured a close-up of her from the shoulders up. Her face filled my screen. I could only see the blade of the knife. The handle and the hand of the bastard holding it was off screen. Her eyes were pinched shut. When I pulled my phone to within inches of my eyes, I could see the tip of the blade pushing into the side of her neck and a stream of blood running out of it.

My screaming of Sarah's name filled the parsonage as Rev. Rigsby scrambled out of his chair to get to his old landline phone in the kitchen and call the FBI.

The FBI got their techs working on the text right away, just as they had when Legrand had called me on Thursday. Again, it was untraceable. Again that almost certainly meant a prepaid cell phone. They tried right away to match the unnamed cell phone to a cell tower, but again the signal was dead, probably because someone had yanked the battery out of the cell after using it.

I left that conversation feeling beaten. Legrand had my wife and my children and was actively mocking me over it. The combined might of hundreds of law enforcement officers and volunteers wasn't making a dent in Legrand's plan, whatever it was. He'd been caught twice, only to slip away seemingly effortlessly. I'd had calls all morning from friends, well-wishers, law enforcement, and others, and none were bringing me any closer to getting my family back.

Only God could do that, and right about now, it sure didn't seem like He had a whole lot of interest in stopping Hiram Legrand.

I decided to go to the Wilson Medical Center to see both Rev. Crosley and Stumps. The drive seemed to take no time at all, and when I got there I walked straight up to the intensive care unit on the fourth floor. I found Stumps sleeping, with his mother quietly sitting at his side.

"How's he doing?" I whispered to Mrs. Dixon after she got up to hug me, but I already knew he was going to be ok. He still had to recover from hemorrhagic shock – massive blood loss – but upon his arrival in the hospital they had quickly given him the units of O-negative that he needed. With his superb health he would recover from his blood loss within a matter of days, not months. But he would be very sore for a lot longer than that. Most of the buckshot blasted at him had missed, and the two pellets that did hit him had not punctured any of his internal organs. Still, they had done a number on the lower left portion of his abdominal wall, especially the oblique muscle near his hip. He was torn up enough that they had him on morphine, which was the reason for the sleep in midday.

"He's doing just fine, Luke," Mrs. Dixon whispered back at me. "My Arthur is strong. Always has been, even when he was a little boy. It's going to take a lot more than a bad man who can't shoot a shotgun straight to keep Arthur down."

I smiled at her use of Stumps's given name, and also that she had worn her Sunday best to be with her son in the hospital. So many families waiting in hospital vigils showed up in old sweats, ball caps, and other such comfortable clothes meant to double as pajamas. But Mrs. Dixon, a class act through and through, would never be seen in public looking like that. She was wearing a half-sleeved floral dress, ankle-length on her short stature, spotless white shoes, and a pearl necklace.

"Have your nieces and nephews come by to visit?" I asked her.

Back in college, I once had gone home with Stumps to have Thanksgiving dinner with his family, and dozens of cousins throughout Richmond and Southside Virginia had congregated under his parents' roof for the holiday. Their extended family was very close.

"They're all out with the searchers, looking for your family," she said in her gentle way. "Arthur wouldn't have it any other way. He sent them out to keep searching. The only person he couldn't get to leave was me."

Overwhelmed by the simple goodness of my best friend and his mother, and the kindness and generosity of her family, I swallowed hard several times and blinked back the mistiness in my eyes.

"I'm sorry," I said, wiping my eyes with my wrists. "You have so much on your own mind, you don't need the burden of my troubles. I should leave you be. I need to go down to the second floor anyway."

"You hush," she chided me kindly. "I already told you my Arthur will be just fine. You're fighting for your family. It's right that your mind should be on them and only them. You're very nice to come by and see Arthur at all."

"He's my best friend," I said. "And he's done so much for me. He got hurt trying to save my wife yesterday. He might have even taken a shot meant for her."

Mrs. Dixon's eyes shined with pride for her son as I made my exit. On the way out, I stole a yellow sticky pad from an unoccupied nurse's desk at the end of the hall, and I left a note asking Stumps's attending physicians to call me if anything happened. It wasn't entirely proper to do so, but under the circumstances, I doubted anyone would complain about my request for the doctor-to-doctor professional courtesy.

Walking past the elevators and throwing open the metal door of the stairwell, I found that the stairs were empty, utilitarian, and still smelled of dried concrete and metal. The smell brought me back to a different hospital on one day that happened years ago, when I was just a teenager.

258

That day, my whole family -- Eli, my sister Trish, Mom, Dad and me -- piled into Dad's pickup truck for a rare trip to a restaurant, to celebrate Trish's 13th birthday. The front tire on the passenger side blew out on the interstate and sent the pickup rolling. By the time it came to a rest, Dad, Mom, and Trish were gone. I was 17. Eli was just 9. While our parents and sister were being transported to the morgue, the on-call pediatrician at the hospital had checked out Eli and me and found us to be completely unharmed. We had stood numbly in the hospital's hallways until Rev. Crosley had hustled over to the hospital and taken us home.

The memory flickered like an old movie in my mind as I hit the push-bar of the metal-door entry to the second floor and headed to Rev. Crosley's room.

Introducing myself as "Dr. Andrews" at the nurse's station and a flash of my identification was all I needed to have the nurse turn the computer monitor around to let me see Rev. Crosley's information. The hospital doctors still didn't know what had caused him to pass out. He was stable now. They still suspected a transient ischemic attack – a mini-stroke – but they weren't sure, so they were keeping him for some testing and observation.

Rev. Crosley had been dozing under a thin blue hospital blanket but awakened when I slipped into his room. He welcomed me warmly, shushing my apology for waking him up. Then, once he installed me in the chair next to his bed and asked me to tell him everything that was going on, I gave him something of an update, but the poor man was sick and weak, and I didn't see a reason to burden him with the hard reality. So I emphasized, well past the point of fibbing, every possible sliver of a reason for optimism about finding my wife and children.

I guess I ran my mouth for longer than I intended, and when I realized he probably was going to see right through me if I kept it up, I clumsily cut it short by saying, "And I'm just trying to accept God's will in all of this," sounding phony even to myself. I was just trying to say something I thought Rev. Crosley would want me to say. But he pulled up when I said it.

"Oh, Luke, I'm not sure this is God's will at all," he said. "That would mean that Hiram Legrand is an instrument of God's will. I can't believe that."

I didn't say anything in response. I didn't even nod my head. Instead, I just looked away, staring at an empty corner of the room.

The seconds ticked past in the pregnant silence. For no reason I could have explained at the time, sweat started to pop on my forehead, its cool moisture spreading thinly atop the reddening heat of my face. Then my breathing quickened and grew heavier in the quiet of the room. When the pulse of my own heartbeat throbbed in my inner ears, I couldn't hold back any more, and I turned back to him and burst out bitterly.

"You don't think this is God's will? Well, that's just great. If God isn't doing this, He sure as hell isn't lifting a finger to stop it."

Those words had rushed out me before I had even thought of them, but Rev. Crosley didn't seem taken aback. Not in the least. If anything, he seemed to have expected it.

"Luke, what has happened to your family is evil," he said calmly. "Evil doesn't come from God. But evil *can* cause you to get angry with God. It can even make you question whether God exists at all."

I tried then to keep my thoughts buried inside. But I just couldn't, and it wasn't even close.

"You're damn right I think this might all be a lie," I said furiously, pounding my fist on the wooden armrest hard enough to crack it. "Everything. All of it. I've looked up at the skies over and over, begging God to save my family. But God's been silent. He hasn't lifted a finger. God has *abandoned* my family. And He's abandoning me, too."

Embarrassed, my eyes filmed over, and I looked away from Rev. Crosley again, waiting for him to reproach me. But he didn't. When he remained quiet, I turned back to him and saw that his face was composed, almost peaceful, and he was looking vaguely upward at where the wall met the ceiling of the room. Then he breathed in deeply, and let it out slowly. His chest and belly rose and fell with his breath.

In the moment before it actually happened, I knew he was going to sing.

His gentle tenor softly stroked a familiar hymn's lyrics in the warm air of the room. The words were sweet and simple, and somehow it wasn't weird for him to sing. Even there amidst the institutional furnishings of a hospital room, his singing seemed to be the most natural thing in the word. I just sat there and listened to him. As the stanzas progressed, I felt the tension in me gradually release. Soon the hymn's piano accompaniment in G-major key was playing in my mind from memory.

After Rev. Crosley finished the hymn, he was quiet for a few moments. Then he looked at me, his kindly face brimming with compassion.

"Luke, frustration with God is not a barrier to faith. It's a sign of it. When we are frustrated and even angry with God, it's because we *believe* in God. Remember the story about how the disciples saw Jesus after His resurrection and asked Jesus when He would come back? They asked that because they *believed* Jesus was the Messiah, and had the power to set matters right. What's more is, they were impatient for it. The same is true now. You believe God has the power to help you, and you want that help just as soon as you can get it."

He looked down at his hand on mine, gathering his thoughts, and then he continued, "Being a person of faith is not about knowing when and how God will rescue us. Rather, it's about what to do in the meantime."

He paused, then looked up at me.

"And now you're asking yourself, 'So what am I supposed to do now?'"

I nodded, unable to speak.

"Luke, there is only one answer. You should do all the good you can. In all the ways you can. In all the places you can. For as long as you can. And then, be at peace."

Chapter 53

<u>Sarah Andrews</u>

Pebbles on the cabin's floor dug into my knees as I knelt to peer outside through the largest crack in the chinking. The day was sunny and nearly perfectly still. No wind was there to rustle the leaves in the trees outside. The birds' morning songs had quieted down, and the squirrels were taking a midday siesta.

I had seen Legrand outside a few times as he walked about, but Judge Carter was gone. Probably he had headed back to his other life in the courthouse, where he could continue his charade, lording it up before sycophant lawyers, fawning staff, and needy litigants. I kept looking for Legrand for a while before I turned back into the room.

"You kids have another guess yet?"

"Florida," Emma said.

"Texas," Henry said.

"Nope, but they're both good guesses. Try again."

I already had done the "I'm thinking of a number between 1 and 100" game several times, letting them keep guessing at the right number until someone picked it correctly. Now we were playing Guess the State. The answer was California, but if they guessed that early I was going to fib and change it to Minnesota to keep the game going longer.

I was burning time. The Guess the Sport game had flopped quickly after Emma ran out of sports she knew about once we got past the old standbys of football, soccer, and baseball. But they were pretty good at the Guess the State game, because we had put together a United States map puzzle over Christmas. Luke had sprayed the puzzle with an adhesive he bought at a hobby store and then framed it. The framed puzzle was still hanging in the kid's playroom at home, presiding over the Thomas the Tank Engine throw rug, two beanbag chairs and overflowing toy boxes.

My breath stopped when my ears caught Legrand's voice droning, almost inaudibly, at some distance away from the cabin. I held up my hand to quiet the kids.

I couldn't spot Legrand, but his voice just barely floated over to me. It sounded like he was on the phone. I strained hard to hear him, but the kids were still fidgeting and whispering between themselves.

"Kids," I said. "Do you remember the most important part of the game today, where you have to do exactly what I tell you until Daddy gets here? Ok. What I need you both to do is go all the way across the room for me, and be perfectly still and quiet. Can you do that for me?"

Emma and Henry obediently scrambled to the far corner of the room, and I turned back toward the crack again. As I did so, a small movement in the woods caught my eye, and I spotted Legrand. He was some distance into the woods with a phone to his ear, looking absently at the ground as he talked. Cupping my hand to my ear, I was just barely able to make out his side of the conversation.

"I think it's time to move," Legrand said.

A pause.

"Yeah, I know," Legrand said. "But it ain't gonna be long now. Once you get him there, we can show him a body."

Another pause.

"Which one, the girl or the boy?"

Another pause.

"All right. How long?"

One last pause.

"Make sure you bring more duct tape. Works good on kids, easier than cord. Their arms and legs are too small and they can slip out of cord."

As Legrand hung up and the woods went nearly silent again, I wiped at the beads of sweat popping on my forehead. Carefully keeping my back to the kids, I strained at the coils of cord binding my wrists for the hundredth time that day. My skin whitened above and below the knots as I strained, then flushed red again when I relaxed. Not even close.

Turning back to the kids, I walked over to them and plopped myself down brightly.

"Ok, Emma, it's your turn to guess," I said in a cheery voice.

Chapter 54

<u>Luke Andrews</u>

"What are you doing here?" I asked Stumps and his mother incredulously, stunned to see them standing outside the front door at my house.

"Agent Byram told me you were here," Stumps answered. His hospital johnnie was gone, and he was dressed in his own loose cotton sweats, running shoes, and a tee-shirt through which I could see the lumpiness of the heavy bandages taped to his left side.

"That's not what I mean," I said. "What I mean is that you should be in the hospital. Stumps, you're at a huge risk for infection, and even with the blood they gave you, you must be weak. There's no way they discharged you already."

"They didn't," his mother said. "He woke up maybe a half hour after you left this morning. I tried to stop him, but he said he had to get out and come help you. The doctors argued with him and told him that they could make him stay. Then he told them what-for. Illegal this, patients' rights that, and before I knew it,

266

Arthur was signing paperwork discharging himself against medical advice. Though I did insist that I drive us here. He's on pain killers now."

"What can I do to help?" Stumps asked me.

"No, sir," I said. "You need to get back in the car and have your mother drive you back to the hospital."

"What can I do to help?" Stumps repeated.

"Come on. You're crazy."

"Luke. I'm here. I'm not leaving. And I'm not some sucker who sleeps in a hospital and lets rip-off artists like you charge me 250 bucks for an aspirin," he said with a smile. "Now, what can I do to help?"

I sighed and shook my head.

"You can start by coming in and lying on the couch."

Chapter 55

<u>Sarah Andrews</u>

"15 minutes?" Hiram Legrand asked a few moments after he answered the call on his phone. He was much closer to the cabin now, not more than 100 feet away. I could hear his side of the conversation when I got next to one of the bigger cracks in the chinking.

"Did you remember the duct tape?" Legrand asked.

A pause.

"Oh, come on, you couldn't have bought some?"

Another pause.

"Oh, screw that, no one woulda' thought nothin' about you buying duct tape," Legrand said.

After another pause listening to the caller, Legrand's scowl deepened, but he said, "All right, whatever. I'll get them ready so we can load 'em up as soon as you get here. Yeah. Bye."

I hurried over to the kids.

"Henry, Emma, do you remember how you pretended to be asleep this morning?" I asked. "Well, I need you to do it again, but this time even better. I want you to lie down facing that wall over there. Close your eyes and get those blindfolds back on. Then do your very, very, extra-very best to keep your eyes closed and not move a muscle. Not until I tell you otherwise. No matter what you hear. Can you do that for me?"

Both kids obediently did exactly as I told them, for which I thanked God. Then I sat down next to them, with my back against the wall and my legs straight in front of me. Soon I heard Legrand walking to us, his steps crunching the dried leaves in the old yard around the cabin. My heart was pounding, but I forced a tired and beaten look on my face. Then Legrand was working the lock to the door of the cabin, and with a last glance at Henry and Emma to be sure they were still, I faced the door.

In one hand, Legrand had a large spool of the same kind of cord that was digging into my wrists. In his other hand, he had the knife I had pushed into the side of my own neck that morning. He looked at my sleeping kids.

"Why they wearing blindfolds?"

"They're tired but it's too sunny outside to sleep," I whispered. "This makes it dark enough for them to sleep."

He shrugged his shoulders and walked closer to us. "Just as well," he said. "Easier this way. I'll do you first. Now, squeeze your ankles together."

"What?"

"Squeeze your ankles together. Now."

When I did as he ordered, he cut off a few arm lengths of cord off his spool. Then, instead of bending in front of my feet where I might have kicked him, he carefully crouched to the side of my legs and put his shin directly on both of my shins, letting his full weight painfully crush down, pinning my legs to the ground. I grimaced at the grinding bone-on-bone pain and the awful stench of him.

Situated as we were, I might have been able to hit him once using my arms, but seated and with my hands tied together and all his weight on my legs, it wouldn't be much of a hit. I just couldn't generate that much force. And he had the knife. If I hit him, he'd stab me, leaving the kids alone with him. So I sat there quietly as he efficiently wrapped the cord tightly around my ankles several times, finishing his knot with a flourish like a cowboy. Then he got up off my shins, stood up to his full height, and smiled at me, his nasty teeth looking greasy.

"Now for them," he said, nodding at my kids and starting to cut several more lengths of cord.

*****

Luke Andrews

Stumps had finally agreed to stretch out on the couch, his mother sitting on one end with his head on her lap. Watching her tenderly stroke his head while he and I talked earnestly about how to make Amos Hudson tell us what he knew by force was comforting.

We were debating whether Judge Carter would order the police to let us question Hudson privately, when we heard the rumble of a car in my driveway. I swung open the front door right after the first knock. In front of me stood a shame-faced woman and a little girl whose picture Ms. Healey had shown me in my office on Wednesday.

"I'm Mary Beth Marshall," said the little girl.

"And I'm Allison Marshall," said her mother. "Mary Beth wants to help."

***

Sarah Andrews

After Hiram Legrand finished cutting several lengths of cord meant to hogtie my kids, he dropped all but one of the lengths of cord to the floor and looked over at me. Then he gave me a little mocking salute with his knife, and he crouched at Henry's legs.

"Think it's time for him to wake up?" he asked.

***

Luke Andrews

"Honey, I think you're describing a cabin," I said to Mary Beth. "That's an old-fashioned kind of house. People hundreds of years ago used to build them out of trees they chopped down."

"Oh," she said. "I didn't know."

"That's ok. You're being a huge help. Can you please tell me everything you remember about that cabin?"

Allison looked uncomfortable but said nothing. Stumps was sitting up on the couch and listening carefully. His mother was bustling in the kitchen, making coffee for everyone.

"I don't remember much," Mary Beth said. "It was dark in there."

"Could you see outside?"

"Yes," she said. "I could see outside through some cracks in the wall. I even tried to get outside. But he came back before I could get out."

"What could you see outside?"

"Mostly just woods. And some squirrels and birds."

"The woods, were they grown right up next to the house?"

"Not really. There was kind of a field, I guess. Not much grass. It was all full of weeds and bushes and little trees."

"Do you mean like saplings?" I asked. "Saplings are young trees, maybe about as tall as your mom here. They grow wild in what used to be a yard or field, if no one is taking care of it. Is that what you saw?"

"I guess so."

I looked outside the window, deep in thought. The clear pasture on that side of our house went for a few hundred yards before it stopped at the tree line, where the woods were thick with oak, hickory, and beech. The window was open, and the familiar scent of honeysuckle growing outside reached me. I thought about where we were on the calendar. It was mid-spring, when everything bloomed, and the fertile Virginia fields around us were renewed for the year.

"Honey, were there any big trees in that old yard?" I asked her without quite knowing why. "Something that stands alone, like it was planted there by someone a long time ago?"

"Yes."

"How many?"

"Just one. I could barely see it, but if I strained my eyes hard to the front, I could just about see it. It was almost around the corner."

My breath started to come short.

"Mary Beth, did that tree have flowers on it?"

"Yes."

Goosebumps roared across my arms and chest, and every muscle in my body clenched at once.

"Were the flowers a whitish pink? Were they? *Were the flowers a whitish pink?*"

"Yes. They were. How did you know that?"

I said nothing for a moment, my mind reeling with the truth. Then I screamed for Stumps to call the FBI as I bolted toward the back door.

***

Sarah Andrews

As Hiram Legrand turned his attention to cutting lengths of cord meant for my children, who were lying quietly and obediently with their little Spin-and-Find blindfolds on, I had slowly been curling my legs underneath me. My legs were bound together at the ankles, so my feet moved in perfect tandem. In the moment that Legrand crouched down to Henry with his knife in one hand and a length of cord in the other, I was coiled as tightly as a snake.

Then, when he announced in his high-pitched twang that it was time for my son to wake up, I suddenly struck.

Pushing off with my feet, I leapt at Legrand, stretching out to my full length and seizing his knife hand. He gave a cry of surprise and yanked away hard to try to free himself, but I held tight, and his yank helped me drag my knees back under me.

When he couldn't immediately break his knife hand free from my grip, he dropped the length of cord he held in his other hand and drew back a fist to smash me in the face. With my two hands on his knife hand, my face was completely exposed to the blow he was about to deliver. He had already broken the nose of Henry's preschool teacher, Claire Michaels, and I could see in that flash of a second that he planned to crush mine. But it was the wrong move for him to make. In that moment as he drew back his fist, I pushed off on my knees again and shoved as hard as I could on his knife hand.

It was all I could do to mute a triumphant scream when I buried his knife, to the hilt, in the middle of his throat.

***

Luke Andrews

Once every July when Trish, Eli, and I were young, my father would take us up to the abandoned cabin my grandfather's family had left when my grandfather was a little boy. Grandpa's cabin, as we called it, was about two miles up the mountain behind our farmhouse, on a steep and winding trail that deer used just enough to keep it visible. A person in good shape could make the walk up the trail from our farmhouse to the old cabin in about an hour. If he was in great shape, and ran hard, he might make it up those two miles in 20 minutes.

That meant running up the trail to Grandpa's cabin from our farmhouse was faster than driving to it, for it was within the borders of the National Forest. Except for the Blue Ridge Parkway, no roads were allowed to be built in that protected wilderness. From our house, a driver would have to go a number of miles up a winding country road, then over on a state highway to one of the entrances to the Parkway, and then back down the Parkway until he found an old dirt path so overgrown that a car could barely squeeze down it. Even then, he'd have to know what he was looking for, because the dirt path died before it got to the cabin. By car it was at least a half hour, and farther yet if you were starting from town.

When Grandpa's cabin was part of a working mountain farm, they had planted a few standard pear trees in his yard. Far bigger than the dwarf varieties that they sold in nurseries today, over the years the trees grew to some 40 feet high. Eventually they died off, but one had dropped a fruit that took hold and the deer had somehow overlooked, and the seeds germinated, so that by the time I was a child another full-grown pear tree was blooming again every spring next to the old cabin. Each July it would be filled with fruit, so my father would lead us up the mountain to the old cabin, and we'd stuff our backpacks full of the ripe pears. Then, for over a week afterwards, the whole family would eat pears at breakfast and lunch, and then for dessert after dinner, pear pie or pear cobbler with vanilla ice cream. Even after all of that chowing down on the pears, my mother still would have to can the majority of the pears and stack them in mason jars, to be pulled out of our pantry months later during the winter while the land rested.

Apart from our summer trips for pear picking and my father's use of the cabin as a little hunting shelter, we didn't get up to the cabin often when I was young. Years later, though, when Sarah and I were dating in college, I was inspired to walk with her all the way up there with a picnic basket in hand. At the summit, the gentle Blue Ridge mountain breeze fluttered the tops of the trees. The big pear tree was covered with the pinkish-white blossoms that year, and the springtime weather was glorious. We spent a romantic springtime afternoon on a blanket under its shade, with a little petal of one of the blossoms occasionally fluttering down from the tree and onto us.

Mary Beth Marshall had just described that tree to me. When she did, what had been burbling below the surface of my consciousness exploded into full view. As I bolted out the back door, I yelled at Stumps to call the FBI agents, and to find one of the old people in town who could show them the way to my grandfather's cabin.

***

276

Sarah Andrews

Fighting the shock of having just stabbed Hiram Legrand, I got my breathing under control, then said, "Kids, you're being really good. Just keep your eyes closed just a little longer. Ok?"

Both kids nodded at me, their Spin-and-Find blindfolds still in place, giving no sign that they had any understanding of what they had just heard. And there hadn't been much to hear. Hiram Legrand had made very little noise after I had stabbed him with his own knife in his throat just below the Adam's apple. His body lay not more than eight feet away from my children.

I looked up at the door, which Legrand had left ajar behind him, and knew immediately what I had to do.

"Just another few minutes, kids," I said as I sawed Hiram Legrand's knife back and forth on the coils of cord binding my ankles. My ankles were freed easily after just a few swipes, but cutting the coils of cord on my wrists was more difficult, because I had to twist the knife awkwardly to get the point in the right spot. When I finally cut through one coil, the others loosened, and soon my hands were free and I was rubbing my chafed, sore wrists.

"Kids, are you all right?" I asked.

"Yes," both of them said back.

"Ok, you sit tight for just one more minute."

I dragged Legrand's body across the dusty floor and peered cautiously out the door, looking around outside for any sign of Judge Carter. Nothing.

I finished pulling Legrand's body out the front of the cabin and around the corner, where it couldn't be seen from the porch. Then I walked back into the cabin and looked at the blood on the floor underneath where I had stabbed him.

"Kids, you can stand up now, but keep on your Spin-and-Find blindfolds for just another few seconds. No peeking."

I led my children out of the cabin and onto the porch, and looking again to make sure no one was around, I shut the cabin door behind us. Then I let the kids take off the blindfolds and open their eyes, and they squinted and blinked against the sudden brightness of the springtime sun outside.

"What are we doing now, Mama?" Emma asked.

"We're going home, baby," I said, picking her up and grasping Henry by the hand. The start of the trail that led down the mountain to our home was not even a hundred yards away. I wanted to get in the woods; I didn't like to be exposed in the open.

I was just about to hurry them across the open yard when the sound of a car coming reached my ears.

***

Luke Andrews

About three-quarters of the way up the mountain, my thighs and lungs were burning in equal measure. At the bottom of the trail, Stumps had wordlessly joined me. I yelled that he'd never make it, and he yelled back that his mother was calling the cops and that he was coming with me. I had taken no time to argue. I simply ran, and he ran with me, clutching his own side as we charged up the mountain to Grandpa's cabin, where Hiram Legrand and

278

Amos Hudson had stashed away the little Marshall girl and where he probably had my wife and kids hidden right now.

A quarter of a mile up, Stumps fell back, and I looked behind me quickly. His normally warm-brown color had become a sickly gray, and despite his outstanding level of fitness, his body had suffered far too heavy an insult yesterday to make this run. He stumbled and fell to one knee.

"I'm so sorry," he said, gasping. "I just can't keep up. I'm lightheaded and dizzy. You go. Keep going."

"You're lightheaded and dizzy because your blood pressure is way off," I said back to him, my own chest heaving. "Sit against this tree, and put your head between your knees before you pass out."

"Go," he said, pushing me away from him. "Keep running. I'll be behind you. Just let me catch my breath."

Without another word, I had taken off running up the trail again. After 100 yards or so, I had glanced back in time to see him stagger to his feet and start following me. Now that I was most of the way up, I figured he probably wasn't even halfway. And Byram and Healey and the cops were still at least 30 minutes away.

I was going to have to do this myself.

***

Sarah Andrews

I froze in place on the cabin's front porch when I heard the car. The tree line and the start of the trail that led home was straight in front of the kids and me, across an overgrown field dotted with pine seedlings, thorny briar patches, and other wild bushes. To our sharp left, the car slowed where Hiram Legrand and Judge Carter normally parked, maybe 75 yards away, where what remained of an old trail was choked off by the thick growth of saplings and brush. The car came to a stop, but I didn't hear the telltale change in engine noise of a driver putting a car into park. The driver seemed to be hesitating.

Just as I was thinking about how we could slip off unobserved to the right side of the cabin and get under the cover of the woods in that direction, the engine of the car revved hard. Then the car bucked as it popped over a big fallen branch and started to tear through the brush toward us, smashing the small saplings and wild thorn bushes that had grown there.

We'd been spotted.

"Race me, Henry!" I yelled. "Race me right now!"

Without another word, I sprinted away from the cabin and toward the trail, with Emma bouncing in my arms and Henry running alongside me as fast as he could. Even so, we were making achingly slow progress. The car was easily going to beat us to the trail, but finally the heavy growth of pine saplings and brush in the overgrown field forced the driver to stop the car not 40 feet away from us.

"Keep running!" I yelled to Henry.

Emma clung tightly to me and Henry moved his little legs as fast as they could go. I looked back and saw Judge Carter hurrying out of the car with the walnut stock of a double-barreled shotgun in his hands.

I kept running, but Judge Carter was quickly cracking the shotgun open and pulling shells out of his breast pocket, looking up at the three of us like we were upland birds he hunted on his plantation. We were never going to get out of his range before he loaded it. I dropped Emma to the ground.

"Kids, run that way as fast as you can!" I pointed at the trail. "Run down that hill as far as you can go, and you'll get home where Daddy is waiting for you. Go! Go now!"

I pushed both my children, and they ran off toward the trail. Then I wheeled around and ran in the opposite direction, intentionally racing right in front of Judge Carter to give him an easy shot at me. When he snapped his shotgun shut and shouldered it, I cut hard to my left, running away from him again, and zig-zagging as fast as I could as he curled his finger around the trigger.

The percussive boom of his shotgun was terrifying. He came so close to hitting me that I felt a pellet of shot tear through the loose cloth of my sweatshirt, not an inch from my side. And he didn't drop his shotgun from the shoulder. Following me steadily with his muzzle, he pulled the trigger again just as I dove behind a wild bush. The second load of shot shredded the bush above me.

Scrambling to my feet, I watched Judge Carter crack open the shotgun to reload it. In the distance, Henry and Emma were almost to the tree line, but Judge Carter was groping for shotgun shells in his breast pocket, and they still weren't out of his range.

Without any hesitation, I charged straight at him.

Luke Andrews

The muscles in my legs and lower back were on fire as I raced past the huge white pine tree that told me I was just a couple hundred yards away from the end of the trail to Grandpa's cabin. I was getting to the last cutback when the thunder of two shotgun blasts rolled down the mountain at me, less than three seconds between them.

The screaming plea that was about to burst from my chest was abruptly silenced by the astonishing and sudden appearance of Henry and Emma, running down the trail at me no more than 50 yards away. Huge smiles spread across the kids' faces as soon as they spotted me.

"Daddy!" both kids shouted, laughing and stumbling down the trail.

The most powerful feelings I'd ever known collided within me. The overwhelming joy of seeing my children crashed into horror that Hiram Legrand was unseen in the woods nearby and shooting at them. I swept both kids up in my arms and skidded behind a big poplar tree.

"Daddy, did we win the game?" Henry asked as Emma scrambled up my chest and kissed my cheek.

***

Sarah Andrews

I got to Judge Carter just as he slipped two more shells in the barrels of his shotgun, but before he could snap it shut. I slammed myself bodily into his chest and knocked him over backwards. His shotgun spun away, the shells falling back out of the two barrels and onto the grass a few feet away from the shotgun.

Judge Carter tried to scramble away from me, but I slammed my fist down on the man who had loaded a gun with shells he meant to shoot at my children. He howled in pain when I connected, and I began to pound on him with both fists. He was using his arms to try to fend me off, but I was taking any opening to hit him as hard as I could. But just as he started to panic underneath me, someone with enormous strength suddenly grabbed me from behind under both shoulders, bodily pulled me off the judge, and threw me to the ground.

Towering above me was a large man wearing a ski mask.

Stunned, I stole a glance back at the cabin. I saw Hiram Legrand's body right where I had dragged it, around the corner from the front. And Judge Carter was on the ground, trying to scoot away from us.

Looking back at the man in the ski mask in front of me, I scrambled back to my feet and away from him. He looked big and athletic. I didn't think I could outrun him, at least not without slowing him up first, and I couldn't run in the direction of my kids anyway. So I held my ground when he moved toward me. Then, just as he got in range, I kicked my foot hard at his crotch, just like I had done to Hiram Legrand in the parking lot of the country store.

But this man seemed to expect it. Before my foot got near to hitting him, he threw his knee up and across him, blocking my kick. My foot slammed into the heavy bone of his upper shin. In that moment as I reacted to the sharp hurt in my foot, he buried a punch into my belly with hellishly athletic precision, knocking all of the wind out of me. I doubled over, and the last thing I saw was a glimpse of his other hand arcing in a blur toward my neck.

***

Luke Andrews

"You remember Mr. Dixon? Turner's daddy?" I breathlessly asked Henry, who had just told me about the game Sarah invented for the kids. Henry knew Stumps's son Turner; they had caught some crawfish together last summer down at Corby Creek when Stumps came up to visit.

"Yes, Daddy, I remember," he said.

"Ok then," I said. "The last part of the game that Mommy was playing with you is this. You and Emma have to keep running down this trail as fast as you can. It won't be long until you see Mr. Dixon. You tell him what you're doing, and you do exactly what he says. Now I'm going to run back up to the cabin and get Mommy, and then we're going to chase you back down to the trail. If you get to Mr. Dixon before we do, you and Emma win. If Mommy and I catch up to you before you get to Mr. Dixon, then we win. So you have to run fast. Got it?"

"Yes, Daddy," Henry said. "Me and Emma have to get to Mr. Dixon first, and he's down the trail."

"Thatta boy," I said. "Now you and Emma just stay on this trail and run as fast as you can. No matter what, you keep running down the trail. You're not allowed to go back up to the cabin, no matter what. Ok? Now, ready, set, go!"

I pushed them off me and watched them scurrying downhill until they swung around a switchback and went out of view. Then I tore up the mountain. In those last steps up the trail, I begged God to watch over my children for me.

Then, without a plan of any kind about what I would do, I burst into the open.

Grandpa's cabin was in front of me, maybe a 10 second sprint away. The big pear tree in its whitish-pink glory stood in front, surrounded by pine seedlings and oak saplings and thorn bushes. Then, jarringly, just off the side of the cabin, I saw a dark gray sedan. Crossing behind a large autumn olive bush on his way to the car was a big man who looked like he was dragging something.

He hadn't spotted me yet, and in that second that I was watching, he came from behind the autumn olive bush. His back was to me, and he pulled what looked to be a ski mask off his head and tossed it in the car. Then he reached down and dragged an unconscious woman into the back seat. Though I couldn't see her face, I recognized the long hair and the green William & Mary sweatshirt right away. Sarah.

I screamed my wife's name and sprinted at the car. The man turned and looked in my direction upon hearing my scream.

In that moment before he hopped in the driver's seat and pulled away, long before I could reach him, I had a good look at his face. That face belonged to someone I'd known from the day he was born. It belonged to someone my parents named Elijah Emory Andrews, but who we all called Eli.

Eli Andrews, my younger brother, was supposed to be in a prison cell 150 miles away, in the Wytheville State Prison, serving time for being a small-time drug dealer. Instead, he had just thrown my wife into the backseat of a car and drove off from the overgrown yard where our grandfather's family had made their homestead in the 19th century, and where our father had brought us up to pick pears every summer.

The Final Part

Chapter 56

4:20 p.m.
Sunday afternoon

Luke Andrews

One of the old deputies who used to hunt with my father knew the way to Grandpa's cabin, and he was in the lead car with Byram and Healey with a caravan of cars behind them as they raced up the old dirt road off the Blue Ridge Parkway. Within a minute, the overgrown field around the cabin was flooded with police in various uniforms and FBI agents in their business suits and blue blazers.

An hour later, the surreal, dream-like feel up on the mountain was still ongoing. In that hour since I'd seen my brother drag off my wife, I'd borrowed Ms. Healey's phone and learned that my kids had run into Stumps about halfway down the mountain, and he had led them home. At that very moment, Mrs. Dixon was baking cookies with them in our kitchen, and half a dozen law enforcement officers were sitting in chairs around my house, keeping guard. Keith Watson, the kids' pediatrician, was in his car on the way to my house to do a checkup on them, but I'd already seen them with my own eyes and knew they were fine.

We found the blood in the cabin and the telltale evidence of Hiram Legrand's body having been dragged from there to the side of the cabin. He had a deep knife wound in his neck, and we found a bloody knife back in the cabin. One of the agents carefully bagged it for fingerprinting later.

Ms. Healey told me she thought my wife had killed Legrand herself. I wasn't so sure, but our conversation was cut off by Agent Byram's side of an angry exchange with the director of the Virginia Department of Corrections over the abrupt appearance of Eli Andrews. Ms. Healey whispered to me that Byram had done a routine check of the DoC's inmate information system right after Henry had been snatched on Wednesday. He had no cause to be suspicious of Eli, but instead he was routinely checking up on all of Henry's family members, as was standard operating procedure in any kidnapping. And he had confirmed online that Eli was still incarcerated in the Wytheville State Prison, over a two-hour drive away, thereby checking him off the list as being a person of interest in the crime. Which we now knew was wrong.

While I was standing nearby, Byram gave his opinion of the DoC's inmate information system to the director. The director's response was loud enough that I could hear him over Byram's earpiece explaining how only a dumbass fed could overlook calling the facility's warden personally to confirm an inmate's location. After barking at each other for a minute or two, Byram and the director cooled off enough to curtly discuss plans for the director's return call in 15 minutes as he looked into the status of inmate Elijah Emory Andrews.

At the same time, the deputies on site had done a search of the overgrown field around the cabin. They had found two empty red-plastic shotgun shells, 000-buckshot, recently fired, not more than 10 or 15 steps from where I had seen my brother throw my wife in the back of the car. But they didn't find a body or telltale blood anywhere in the field. I knew enough from hunting with my father what buckshot would do to a deer or, by extension, a person. The deputies concluded, and so did I, that both shots had been a miss.

More federal agents were showing up in black sedans. They would be doing an inch-by-inch forensic investigation of the area.

"We're not so sure anymore Amos Hudson is involved in any of this," Byram said to me as agents and deputies swarmed around the cabin.

Surprised, I asked what he meant. I'd already figured that Hudson somehow knew someone else in the corrections system and managed to spring my brother, for what reason I couldn't imagine.

"Well, for one, our computer techs found a very specific kind of malware on Hudson's computer. It would enable someone from afar to control his computer. Including sending email."

"What about the fact that Hiram Legrand used his key and his gun?" I asked.

"Yeah, you're right, there's that," Byram said. "But our techies are saying that this malware is sophisticated. Not something you might pick up by looking at a sketchy website or something like that. They say that someone installed it on Hudson's computer and used it from afar, remotely. Interestingly, they think Hudson's computer might have been controlled by a phone, not a desktop or laptop computer. In any event, those emails we saw on Hudson's computer may be fakes. Increasingly, we have to consider the possibility that this is a set-up job."

I shook my head, more out of confusion than disagreement. When I saw Byram had nothing more to say, I started to walk over to the pear tree. Soon they would ask me why I thought Eli would do this, and I wanted to think about my answer. But before I got there, I heard Byram's phone ringer go off, so I stopped and came back. Again I heard his end of the conversation.

"Tuesday, you mean Tuesday of this week, four days ago?" he asked his caller.

After a pause, he asked, "Are you 100% sure that's who signed the release order?"

After another pause, he said, "Ok. Send it up to us right now. We're going to have to reach out to him and ask him about that order. Wait, hey, I've got another call coming in. You send that up now and I'll get back to you. Thanks again for the help."

Then, looking at his phone to find the right button, I watched him take the incoming call.

"This is Byram. Whaddya got?"

A long break this time. Byram's eyes widened, and he motioned for Healey to break away from her conversation with some of the other agents and come over to him.

"You've positively traced the number to him?" he asked his caller as Healey came up with a questioning look on her face. When he heard the caller's answer, his jaw muscles clenched, and in his face I saw him make his decision.

"All right. Go to his chambers, to his house, anywhere you can find him, and take him into custody. Do it right now, on my authority. I'll call Washington to inform the public corruption unit."

He hung up the phone and looked at me, then to Ms. Healey, then back to me again.

"Luke, your brother was released by court order on Tuesday of this week," he said. "It's called a writ of habeas corpus ad testificandum. It's the way a judge can spring an inmate temporarily to testify at a trial, which is a common enough occurrence. So it's a pretty routine order, and in this case that order releasing your brother was issued by the Circuit Court of Jameston County, endorsed by Judge S. Dalton Carter, presiding."

"*What?*"

"Yeah, I know," Agent Byram replied, before turning to Healey.

"Jeanne, forensics traced the host device controlling Capt. Hudson's computer," Byram said to her. "It was a phone, service provided by Verizon, phone number 434-555-1664. The subscriber was one Smith Dalton Carter. That is the given name of Judge Carter."

Agent Healey paused for a long moment, then said, "That son of a bitch. We kept him up to date on the investigation, step by step, because he was being so helpful with search warrants."

"Yeah," Agent Byram said. "We were played."

I felt slow and stupid, blinking and trying to understand what I was hearing. Byram saw me struggling and waited for my questions.

"Are you telling me that *Judge Carter* framed Amos Hudson for Legrand's escapes?" I asked.

"Yes," Byram said.

"And the judge himself got my brother out of prison with some kind of court order."

"Yes."

"Then my brother helped Hiram Legrand abduct my children and my wife."

293

"Very likely."

I blinked several times before I continued.

"So this whole thing, starting with the kidnapping of Mary Beth Marshall to now, has been some kind of plan by Hiram Legrand along with both my brother and the judge."

"Probably."

"This makes absolutely no sense," I said. "None."

We three stopped talking then, contemplating what we had learned.

After some time, both agents edged away to get to work, but I just stood there, looking without seeing. Absorbed in my own thoughts, the near-silence continued without notice.

Eventually I was brought back to the present by the song of an eastern bluebird floating over from the nearby woods. I imagined him finding a mate and then building a small nest with her. I imagined that nest high up in one of the towering poplars here on the mountain. They would be so far up in their nest that no one would know they were there, protected from the ground below, and they would have a beautiful view of the valley below without ever having to leave their home.

***

Coming down from the mountain on foot rather than by car somehow seemed right. It was faster than hitching a ride home with one of the deputies. Agent Healey looked dubious when I told her

I was going to take the trail back down to our farm, but I ignored her comment that I should have a police escort. Every available law enforcement officer needed to be looking for Sarah. I left the whole scene behind me without waiting for her reply, walking across the overgrown field to the trailhead.

When I started down the path, the dry pine needles on the trail crunched underfoot, and after a minute I began to trot. Within just a few steps I startled a group of deer that had been bedded down nearby. Their white tails flapped behind them as they bounded off through the woods. Then my downhill run gradually got faster and faster, until it finally became a breakneck sprint in which I just barely kept catching myself from falling forward on the steep trail downhill. I kept expecting my house to come into view, but the trail seemed to go on forever no matter how fast I ran. At some point a red fox sprinted across my path and out of view, and I forced myself to run even faster. The trees blurred past me, but the run seemed impossibly long, and I was sweating through my shirt as I turned at every switchback on legs that were turning to jelly from exertion. Still I forced myself to run on, minute after minute, until I could finally see the raised-seam metal roof of our farmhouse through the trees.

The house smelled of baking cookies when I burst into the kitchen from the backdoor. Both kids had chocolate-chip smears around their mouths and cups of milk in hand, and Stumps's mother was humming as she worked on her second and third batches. I swept the kids up in my arms and held them tight, then fell over on my back and let them crawl over me.

Over the next half hour, I heard all about tic-tac-toe, and Spin-and-Find, and word games and number games and all the rest that Sarah had them do. Mostly Henry did the talking while

Emma giggled her way through feeding me chocolate-chip cookies. I occasionally pretended to bite at her fingers like a shark, sending her into peals of laughter.

There is something different about loving a woman as the mother of your children. By then you have seen her as the attractive new girl you just met. You have fallen in love with her as a girlfriend; you have even loved her deeply as your wife. But it is a different thing to love her as your kids' mother. It was a natural completion to things, a sealing of a relationship. Never had I loved Sarah more than when I heard of the pretty lies she told our children.

Keith Watson, the pediatrician, was packing up to leave when I got there, but before he left, I listened to their hearts on his stethoscope. I had no real medical reason to do it, but I loved placing the stethoscope on just the right spots off to either side of their sternums, hearing the beautiful lub-dub sounds with each beat as healthy blood flowed through the clean vessels in their strong, young hearts. When I finally heard my fill, I picked both of them up, one in each arm, squeezed them to my chest and shook them back and forth in pure joy at their aliveness until they squealed and giggled in protest.

Later, when Agent Byram and Agent Healey pulled up to the house, I gratefully accepted Mrs. Dixon's offer to give the kids their baths upstairs. Stumps himself was asleep on the couch. He was lucky not to have a fever, and his wound had looked pretty clean when I changed his bandages with first aid materials I had in the house. Still, he was in real pain, so I made him take some of his Percocet to take the edge off. Between the exhaustion and the Percocet, in five minutes he was snoring under an old Scottish plaid blanket on the couch. Once everyone was settled in, I went outside to the porch to talk with the two FBI agents, who had come down off the mountain to talk with me.

"We picked up Judge Carter at his home just a little while ago," Byram said after we settled into the rockers on the front porch. "He drove up in his own car, a black Lexus. We had agents there waiting for him. The agents said he has one heck of a shiner on one eye and a fat lip. He apparently stammered his way through some kind of explanation about a fall. They're just getting started questioning him now.

"His Lexus shows no sign of being driven off road through brush. That makes sense; the car in which you saw your brother drive off with Sarah wasn't a black Lexus. Rather, it matched the description of the old gray sedan that had been used in the earlier kidnappings. That said, in the backseat of the judge's car, the agents found a very nice double-barreled shotgun."

Byram glanced down at some notes he had jotted down, then looked back at me.

"To be specific, the agents found in his Honor's backseat a Winchester Model 21 shotgun, side-by-side double-barrel, 12-gauge. One of our agents smelled the breech of the shotgun before he bagged it for forensics. It smelled to him like it'd been fired very recently. And in Judge Carter's breast pocket, we found one 3-inch shotgun shell, 000-buckshot, of the same make as the two empty shells and two live ones we found up there on the ground near the cabin. That's five shells total. Shotgun shells are sold in boxes of five."

Agent Healey broke it down for me.

"Our working theory now is that Judge Carter was the shooter you heard," she said. "We're thinking that he was up there on the mountain and was in the car already when you spotted your brother dragging Sarah into the backseat. We're not sure exactly how it happened, but we think that one way or the other, Judge Carter took two shots at your wife, missed, and your brother got control of your wife."

"'Got control of my wife?'"

"Given what Mary Beth Marshall told us about her abduction, we're guessing he used some kind of fast-acting anesthetic," she explained. "Mary Beth remembers a man rushing behind her and clamping a rag over her face. Our best guess is that this is how your brother did it to Sarah. With two shells fired and no blood on the ground at all, and with your brother taking Sarah with him instead of leaving a body there, we think Sarah likely is still alive."

Agent Byram's phone buzzed with a text. He read it and nodded his head.

"Looks like two different people left fingerprints on the knife found next to Hiram Legrand's body," he said. "Want to guess who those two people are?"

"Hiram Legrand and Sarah Andrews," Agent Healey said.

"Correct," he said.

"That makes it very likely that Sarah in fact managed to get the knife away from Legrand and kill him with it," she said.

"Correct again."

Eli wasn't likely to give Sarah that chance, I thought to myself. Hiram Legrand must have made a mistake to let Sarah get at him. Eli would not.

We fell quiet on the porch. Through an open window, I heard Emma inside giggling at something Mrs. Dixon said to her.

Byram's phone buzzed with a voice call. He picked it up, and though the conversation went on for quite some time, he said very little on his end. When he was done, he hit the off button and looked at both of us.

"Well, that explains that," he said.

"What?" I asked.

"Long story. The short version is, a few years ago, the governor of Virginia was facing a budget shortfall. And his budget people noticed that the previous governor had way overbuilt prisons. That left Virginia with a lot of unused prison space, just as other states were facing overcrowding. The budget people wanted to monetize that.

"So, Virginia began leasing its open cells to those other states. For a hefty profit, of course. Several states are doing that now. Pennsylvania has leased cell space to New York for years. And Arkansas was one of the states that took Virginia up on it. Looks like Arkansas sent several hundred inmates to Virginia to serve time."

"That's the connection," Agent Healey said knowingly.

"That's right," he said. "For almost a year, Hiram Legrand was incarcerated in a Virginia state prison in Wytheville, down in Wythe County, Virginia. And I bet you can figure out now who his cellmate was for that year."

"My brother."

"Correct."

Chapter 57

After we found the jailhouse connection between Eli and Hiram Legrand, Agent Byram headed back to town, while Agent Healey went inside my house to work on her laptop on the kitchen table. It was dark outside by then, but the moonlight was bright. So I stayed outside on the front porch with my phone on my ear, talking to news directors all over Virginia and national news organizations, trying to make sure Sarah's picture stayed on as many television and computer screens as possible.

Before I was done with the interviews, Agent Healey hit pay dirt. She sent her findings up to her FBI colleagues, and then she came out to the porch to show me. We sat at a small table Sarah had bought for the porch so our family could eat dinner outside during good weather.

"My brother had a LinkedIn account?" I asked incredulously.

"He sure did," Agent Healey said, clicking on a folder on her computer to show me. "He even used his own name. Probably to give a quick story that he was legitimately using LinkedIn if he was ever caught by a corrections officer, which he wasn't."

LinkedIn was a networking site used by business professionals to build contacts with other professionals. Executives, managers, lawyers, business owners, and such were on it. While Facebook, Twitter, and all the other social networking sites undoubtedly had been banned by the Department of Corrections, the buttoned-down LinkedIn was about the last place a corrections officer would think to look for any evidence of escape plans, porn, contraband smuggling, or anything else that jail guards cared about.

Looking at Agent Healey's screen, I saw she had a screenshot of my brother's LinkedIn profile. On LinkedIn, Elijah Andrews was a real estate broker.

"Your brother had 25 connections with legitimate people," Agent Healey said. "People are forever getting invitations to 'link' to someone else, and a lot of people accept those requests without thinking. We'll check it out to be sure, but it looks like your brother sent requests simply at random to people. That's not the main focus for now, though. Take a look at the top right of the page."

My eyes wandered over to the top right of Eli's LinkedIn profile. Sitting there was an innocuous little button that said, "Messages."

"Your brother had some Internet and email privileges at Wytheville State Prison as of last year," Agent Healey said. "You knew that already. But a lot of internet websites are censored by the prisons, for obvious reasons. Plus any emails he sent on the prison system all are subject to review, just like regular inmate mail. At any time, a member of prison staff can read the email, and they do so frequently for security reasons. So every inmate knows not to put anything in an email that they wouldn't want a corrections officer to know."

Agent Healey opened a folder on her computer.

"LinkedIn was the perfect workaround. Hiram Legrand opened a profile, too. Then he used the LinkedIn messaging service to contact your brother. So, your brother would login on the prison computer to LinkedIn, which is a safe, legitimate website that didn't arouse any suspicion. He'd look at his messages from Legrand, and respond with his own. There'd be no prison email for corrections staff to look at. After Hiram got out of the Arkansas state prison system, that's how they kept in touch."

"Does that folder contain messages between them?" I asked her.

"Yes," she said. "Actually, more than just the two of them. Your brother had correspondences with others as well. We just got these; we'll read all of them overnight. But for now, we're just triaging as fast as we can. Take a look at this strand."

LinkedIn Message
To: Hiram Legrand
From: Elijah E. Andrews

Is the judge ready to play ball?

LinkedIn Message

To: Elijah E. Andrews
From: Hiram Legrand

Hes ready

LinkedIn Message

To: Hiram Legrand
From: Elijah E. Andrews

When's he going to sign a release order?

LinkedIn Message

To: Elijah E. Andrews
From: Hiram Legrand

When you say

LinkedIn Message

To: Hiram Legrand
From: Elijah E. Andrews

Good. I need to be out. You make sure that judge gets me out of here. I need to see Luke face to face.

Agent Healey said, "These messages were sent over a month ago now. Who knows how long your brother and Legrand were working on this before then. Probably a long time. And that's a major problem when it comes to finding Sarah."

"What do you mean?"

She sighed, but she gave it to me straight.

"Luke, I think your brother is probably a very desperate man right now. We've been operating under the assumption that Legrand was staying local and had a good hiding spot from which to do it. And he did, with your brother's help. But now that hiding spot, the cabin, is gone. Now your brother is holding Sarah captive, and he knows you saw him. He also knows Legrand is dead. The game is up. Eli probably is figuring that his best bet is to leave the area, and get away as far as he can."

"Where?" I asked.

"Could be anywhere," she said. "He has lived in Richmond, so we've alerted the Richmond police department. Legrand was from Arkansas, and it may be that they had a backup plan to flee there, so we've notified our field offices in Arkansas. But it really could be anywhere. The target area is much broader now. That's what I'm talking about. With enough advance planning, your brother is able to take Sarah to anywhere in the country. Maybe even beyond. That makes it much, much harder to find her."

I nodded, taking that in. Then, after a long pause, I said, "There's something I need to know from you."

"What's that?"

"And I need to hear the truth."

"Of course."

"In your experience, when abductors are desperate, are they more likely to be violent?"

She flinched, and I could see the struggle in her eyes. Agent Healey was definitely a rules-following, black and white person. But it was her misfortune to also be profoundly compassionate as well. It was a rare combination. It ultimately made her the kind of person who would tell you the painful truth and then agonize about having done so.

"Yes," she said.

"Yes, what?"

"Yes, in my experience, a desperate man is more likely to be violent to the person he has abducted. That's especially so if his victim is female."

Nodding, I wordlessly rose out of my chair and stepped off the front porch to the cool grass of our front yard. My eyes focused far into the distance, and I looked deeply into the night, over our front pasture, across the road, and to our neighbors' fields. The moonlight was bright enough that the trees cast a shadow darker than the night.

I let my mind wander then, let it take a good long walk away from where I was.

Eventually I came across a memory from our wedding day in Sarah's hometown, on the campus of Washington & Lee, where her father had been a professor. We were in Lee Chapel that spring day, just a few weeks after we'd graduated college. Stumps was my best man.

Sporting our rented tuxedos, Stumps and I had made our way down a brick walk to the Victorian-design chapel. The chapel was well over 100 years old, but it rose out of the green grass as if the dark-red earth below had just birthed it that very morning. I'd taken a deep breath and then stepped through the arched white double-doors that led inside and then into the sanctuary, where 200 guests filled the pews to watch Sarah and me get married.

A few minutes later, as Stumps and I were waiting in the front of the chapel for Sarah to make her entrance, I had studied the chapel, committing to memory its warm white walls, light brown carpeting, arches, and wall sconces. Then the pianist switched to the wedding march, and everyone craned their necks to watch Sarah in her elegant white dress walk in on the arm of her father.

When she reached me, we had stood together facing the altar, holding hands, Stumps off to my side and Sarah's maid of honor to hers. I had felt every set of eyes in the chapel on us, and I could tell she did, too. The preacher began the first reading from the Bible, and I settled into the reality that I wasn't going to have another private moment with Sarah until the wedding was over.

Then she had squeezed my hand.

Her hand had felt feminine and small, the softness of each one of her delicate fingers squeezing into mine. Seeing her dimple up out of the corner of my eye as we both stood facing the preacher, I'd gently squeezed her hand back. It had been the only way we could communicate privately with each other in front of all of those guests. And we had stood there, just squeezing each other's hands in the middle of our wedding, that moment ours and ours alone among all those people. No one knew of that moment but us.

Standing beside the house where I had been raised, where Sarah and I had started our own family, where an FBI agent sat on the front porch with her laptop, I looked down at my palm, remembering the soft feel of my wife's hand.

Chapter 58

Sarah Andrews

Duct tape tightly bound me from my shoulders to my ankles when I awoke in the dark cellar. My elbows were pinched hard against my ribs. Even my hands were taped down flat against my hips. I looked and felt like a gray-colored mummy.

I was bewildered to see my brother-in-law sitting nearby. Light from a little oil lamp was holding back some of the darkness.

"Eli! What's going on?" I asked him.

"Shut up."

"What?"

"Shut up."

"Eli, what are you talking about? Help me. Get this tape off me."

"Sarah, either shut your mouth, or I'm going to shut it for you."

And then I knew. In a flash, I knew. Eli was the man in the mask who pulled me off of Judge Carter up on the mountain and then knocked me unconscious. Somehow, some way, he'd been part of this whole thing. The abduction of me. The kidnapping of Henry and Emma. Even the kidnapping of Mary Beth.

I tried to move, but the tape was incredibly strong. It had no give to it. Though I could breathe, I had to fight down rising panic that I was being suffocated.

"Eli, let me go. This tape hurts."

"No."

"Why are you doing this?"

"You want to know, ask Luke. In fact, you're going to have a chance to ask him. In person. Real soon."

With that, Eli stood up and poured some kind of liquid from a flask onto a rag and walked over to me. Unable to move anything else, I wrenched my head side to side, trying to avoid him, but he reached behind my head, grabbed a fistful of my hair, and yanked hard. Then he clamped the rag over my face.

I held my breath as long as I could, but eventually that chemical smell started to seep in, and things started to get hazy. Then finally my body's need for oxygen overcame my will, and with a mind of their own, my lungs drew in a deep breath, and the world gradually faded to black.

Chapter 59

9:30 p.m.
Sunday night

Luke Andrews

I'd left Agent Healey working on the kitchen table downstairs and spent a long time tucking the kids in their beds, waiting first with Emma and then with Henry until each fell asleep.

When I came back downstairs, I avoided the kitchen, instead going outside to thank the four deputies who had agreed to stay overnight at my house, just to keep an eye on things. I'd be willing to die before I let anyone get at my kids, but I'd been disabused of the notion this week that this would always be enough to keep them safe. I was very grateful to these men for helping me, and I told them so.

When I was done with that, I walked into the kitchen to find Agent Healey texting. She stopped when she saw me.

"How are you doing?" she asked.

"Fine."

"There's something else I need to show you," she said. "Come here and look."

She was sitting in what normally was my chair at our kitchen table, so to sit next to her and look at her laptop screen, I had to move Henry's booster seat off his chair and sit in that one.

"About an hour ago, this was found down at the Wytheville State Prison among Eli's legal papers," she said, gesturing to her screen. "We have an agent down there right now going through everything to see if there's anything that can help us. He found this and realized right away what he was seeing. So he scanned it in and sent it up to Rick Byram and me."

She turned her screen so I could see it.

"Eli was never supposed to see this," she continued. "But last year, your brother launched a new round of appeals, so he requested his whole legal file from his former defense lawyer. Sometimes the paperwork gets sloppy in the rush of things. This piece of paper somehow made it into his lawyer's file, and that file eventually got down to your brother last year. Eli would have seen this within the last year."

I read what was on her screen once, quickly, and I could feel the heat of blood flushing into my face and neck. Then I scrolled back to the top and read it again, this time more slowly. When I was done, I let all the breath out of my lungs slowly and closed my eyes.

When I finally opened my eyes again, Agent Healey was waiting patiently.

"Ok," I said. "I'll tell you about it."

***

Four years ago, before Eli had been in trouble with the law, he had been working side jobs and living in a dingy little apartment down in Richmond. I hadn't thought it was much of an existence, and I had largely ignored him and let him live his own life as I focused on building mine. But in the middle of one night, I had driven to Eli's apartment in Richmond after his urgent phone call. When I got there, he told me the story. He'd gone ballistic on some guy in a bar earlier that night. The guy had taken a drunken swing at him, and something in Eli had broken wide open. Eli was big, just as big as I am, and he said he had thrown a flurry of punches and kicks at the man until he hit him hard enough to knock him out. Then Eli had run out of the bar before the cops came.

I had shaken my head as Eli told me his story. Growing up, he'd always had a temper. When I was in college and medical school, I had received more than one phone call from an old great aunt or a cousin staying with Eli at the house, telling me that he'd been suspended from school for fighting. Distantly I had chalked it all up to not having our mother and father around. I would usually give him a quick pep talk on the phone, extract a promise that he wouldn't do it again, and then let it go.

But this wasn't kid stuff. This was a fight between two grown men in which the other man had been knocked unconscious. Still, as I had iced and then bandaged Eli's bruised knuckles, I had tried to talk him into turning himself in. He would get in some trouble, but a good lawyer probably could get him a deal for some kind of misdemeanor, something that admittedly would get a few weekends in jail and a record, but wouldn't ruin his life. I told him that if he turned himself in, I'd help him pay for the lawyer.

"I can't turn myself in," he had said. "I won't pass a drug test. It's cocaine."

I'd taken a long look at him then and known it to be true. His pupils were dilated, and he'd been talking very quickly, almost to the point of being frenetic. And during our whole conversation, he'd been sniffing back a runny nose that he'd seemed to have had for months.

If prosecutors found out that Eli had beaten a man senseless while on a cocaine high, they would put in him prison. He knew it, and I knew it. The cocaine wouldn't have been safely out of his urine and undetectable for at least five days, and he'd begged me to hide him until it all blew over.

And I had. In our grandfather's cabin.

At first, those days four years ago when he'd been up in Grandpa's cabin had been good days. I had stopped by several times, bringing him food and water, and talking with him for hours. He admitted to me that he was hooked on the expensive white powder, and that he'd financed his habit by selling marijuana to local potheads on the side. He had taken my lecture about that in stride. He'd even dutifully read the drug rehabilitation pamphlets I brought up with me on the third day he was hidden up on the mountain.

For five days after I stashed Eli away in Grandpa's cabin, I'd looked at the website for the Richmond Times-Dispatch, just to make sure there wasn't some squib in there about the police looking for the winner of a bar fight. I didn't see any, and I figured the Richmond Police Department had bigger fish to fry.

Then on the fifth day, I saw an article that made my blood run cold. Somehow, I had known right away. Even so, I was breathless at the casual way Eli had admitted to it when I confronted him.

"Yeah, that was it," he had said to me when I confronted him with it. "The man lived in my building. He also owed me money.

312

It got a little rough. He hit me, so I hit him back. A lot. One thing led to another. Then I called you. "

The newspaper article had described how a man had been found beaten to death in Eli's own apartment building in Richmond. The police said they thought it had been a drug deal gone awry and that the man had been dead for several days. The mayor of Richmond had even commented on the case, bemoaning the rising tide of drug violence in his city.

It hadn't been a bar fight at all. Eli had beaten a man to death in a fight over drug money, and then called me that very night to plan his evasion of law enforcement. And I had, while the man my brother had killed was lying dead just a few floors below us.

Eli had cut off my shocked blustering about needing to call the cops, his seeming warmth through the week abruptly freezing into solid coldness.

"We're not calling cops," he had said. "Not me. And not you either. You're in on this, too, Luke. You hid me up here. That's a crime, too."

Stunned as I was by the sudden change in him, I'd at least had the guts to throw him out of the cabin then. But I hadn't called the police. There was some truth to what he said. I'd hidden a murderer. No one would believe that I hadn't known that when I hid him.

And so I'd waited. Life had gone back to normal with frightening ease. Eli had gone back to Richmond when he deemed it safe. The homicide investigation went nowhere. I'd gone back to practicing medicine, acting like nothing had happened.

Then, finally, three guilty months later, I'd spent a long night looking at old family photo albums. There were pictures of all of us as kids jumping through a sprinkler in our yard. There were pictures of Trish and my mother doing their hair together, of Eli holding my father's tools as he worked on his truck, of Christmases and birthdays and first days of school.

At the end of one of the albums, one of the older ones from when I was really little, there was a photo of me sitting on my father's lap on his old tractor. I was about 6 years old. He was letting me steer the tractor, holding me around the waist with his big arm. He was pointing to a spot in our front pasture.

Even four years later, looking at the internal memorandum from the Richmond Police Department on Agent Healey's laptop screen, I could still hear the muffled sound the family photo album made as I closed it and reached for the telephone.

Richmond Police Dept. Memorandum
Subject: Elijah Andrews prosecution

Previously unknown subject's drug dealing was brought to the attention of the Drug Task Force by anonymous tip. The tipster advised that the subject was involved in a small marijuana distribution operation out of Spencer-Coleman Tavern.

Call was traced, and tipster was determined to be the subject's brother, Luke Andrews, a doctor in Jameston County, Virginia.

Subject was subsequently surveilled by the Task Force. Confidential Informant ("CI") 8 and CI 27 made multiple controlled buys from subject. The controlled buys were of substantial amounts of methamphetamine, along with small amounts of marijuana. Subject was arrested and charged with distribution of controlled substances. A Glock 9 mm handgun was found in his apartment.

Prosecution was successful. Subject went to jury trial and was found guilty. Due to the strength of the evidence against the subject, anonymous tipster Luke Andrews was not needed to testify and therefore was not notified that his identity was known to law enforcement. Richmond Circuit Court ordered 15 year term of imprisonment for drug distribution plus five years for the firearm violation, for a total of 20 years imprisonment.

File to be closed and archived. Recommend sealing of file for purposes of protecting identification of anonymous tipster.

End Memo.

When I was done explaining to Agent Healey how I'd ratted out my brother for selling a little weed to assuage my guilt for letting him get away with murder, only to learn he'd actually been a heavy dealer of meth and see him get 20 years for it, we sat there together in silence for a while before she spoke again.

"Luke, I wasn't going to show you this," she said, leaning over to click on her computer. "But based on what you just told me, I think you need to know." When she clicked on her mouse pad, there appeared on her screen a series of notes from the Virginia Department of Corrections during the first few months of Eli's incarceration, a few years ago.

"The agent we have going through Eli's papers down at the prison came across this," Agent Healey said. "Before you read it, just remember that no one ever followed up on this. So this therapist may not be right."

"What do you mean?"

"It's probably better if you just read it."

DOC Inmate Health Summary Notes

To: Samuel Axelrod, M.D., Medical Director
From: Carin L. Beth, LCSW
Re: Elijah Andrews, Inmate No. 041873

Having had multiple counseling sessions with Inmate Eli Andrews, I recommend transferring him to Shenandoah State Mental Hospital. I believe he has psychopathic tendencies.

Inmate Andrews is intelligent, but he has a marked lack of empathy. He is quick to anger, and he does not believably describe or display appropriate feeling when I use charged words such as "hurt" or "kill," or when I show him photographs of people looking scared or upset. His emotions seem shallow, especially fear and empathy, though I had the impression he is aware of this and was trying to hide it from me.

His history for violence is equivocal. His school records reflect many fights, but he does not have any violent crimes on his record. Still, I think he has psychopathic tendencies and the potential for violence. Diagnosing this is at the edge of my training as a licensed clinical social worker, but my thesis for my master's degree was on psychopathy, and he is showing signs of it. He is glib and egocentric. He lacks any guilt that I can see, and clearly is manipulative. I think he needs additional evaluation and treatment by a psychiatrist up in Shenandoah.

***

To: Carin Beth
From: Dr. Samuel Axelrod, M.D.
Re: Elijah Andrews

Carin, I appreciate your energy. That is why I hired you this past spring. But our medical budget is limited. I have two inmates who need back surgeries, several with HIV infections requiring extremely expensive medications, and any number of diabetics. A lot of the inmates here in Wytheville probably have some kind of psychological disorder, but the prison system does not have the funds to treat them all. Your request is noted, but denied.

***

To: Dr. Axelrod
From: Carin L. Beth, M.S., LCSW
Re: Elijah Andrews, Inmate No. 041873

For Inmate Andrews, I think the expenditure of funds would be worthwhile.

A psychopath functions differently from a non-psychopath. In my thesis, I noted that psychopathic serial killer John Wayne Gacy tortured and murdered

318

dozens of young men, but he saw himself as the victim because he had a poor childhood. I'm not saying Inmate Andrews has the potential to be a Gacy or a Ted Bundy. Still, many psychopaths view inflicting pain as an entirely acceptable tool to get whatever they want, whether it is money, revenge, or anything else. I see that potential in Inmate Andrews.

The research suggests that psychopathy is in part an adaptation, and that psychopaths can be made and developed rather than born. This is particularly true of males, who are more susceptible to environmental factors than females. His family history does include the death of both parents at a young age. I fear that if he were to associate with other psychopathic individuals in the inmate population, the tendencies I am seeing now will become full-blown and much worse. The incidence of psychopathy in inmate populations is much higher than in the general population. So this is a realistic concern.

***

To: Carin Beth
From: Dr. Samuel Axelrod, Medical Director
Re: Elijah Andrews, Inmate No. 041873

As the referring facility, any treatment of Inmate Andrews in Shenandoah will hit our budget. Your recommendation is declined.

In the future, please focus your efforts on cost-effective methods that are within your training, such as encouraging inmates to rebuild family relationships as they near their release dates. You are still in your probationary period, and I need to see better focus on the budgetary needs of our department before I can recommend you for a permanent position here.

The notes ended there. I looked at the goose bumps on my forearms tightening my skin until the hairs stood on end. Then I rubbed my forearms briskly as if to warm them up.

"I think I need to go to church now," I said.

***

The lights were dim in the empty sanctuary of my church. I stood in front of the altar and looked at the painting beyond. It was a copy of *The Transfiguration* by Raphael, some 20 feet high and 15 feet across. The copy had been painted there over 100 years ago, when this church was built to replace an older one that had burned. The top part of the painting depicted Jesus Christ floating in front of soft clouds, between the prophets Moses and Elijah. Below, the painting showed the Apostles trying to heal a sick child. They could not cure the child until the arrival of the recently-transfigured Christ.

Below, suffering and need; above, power and comfort.

When I silently knelt, prayer came not by words, but instead as a pouring forth that flowed smoothly, without resistance. But if someone had tried to force my prayer into the limited strictures of language, they might have heard me give thanks for the blessings of my children. They might have heard me asking forgiveness for not doing right by my brother and doing more to raise him after our parents died, and admitting that I had been selfish. They would have heard me asking God to help Sarah, to give her strength to endure, and to be with her now, wherever she was.

When I was done, I got back off my knees and walked back down the center aisle toward the heavy wooden doors that led to the slate steps outside. I needed to get back home. I had four armed deputies plus my best friend and his mother guarding my children, but all the same, I wanted to be there. I also wanted to make a list of things I was going to do to try to find Sarah. Tomorrow, as soon as the kids woke up, I was going to put them in my truck and work just as hard as I could, for as long as I could, everywhere that I could, to find their mother.

When I walked out of the sanctuary and headed to the side exit of the church, I saw that Rev. Rigsby's light was on in his office down the hall. He evidently heard me walking, and he poked his head out and saw me.

"Hey, Luke," Rev. Rigsby said, welcoming me into his small office. "You caught me working late. Come on in and have a seat."

"Thanks," I said.

"I heard about Judge Carter and Eli," he said, shaking his head sadly. "I don't know that any words of mine can comfort you now. I'm so sorry."

"Thanks," I said.

"How're the kids?"

"Healthy and happy."

"That's wonderful," he said. "Just wonderful. But what about Sarah? Any progress report on her?"

"No," I said. "Not a thing. Eli may have taken her to a backup safe-house or something like that as a contingency against being caught in my grandfather's cabin. But she could be anywhere by now. Maybe somewhere else in Virginia, maybe Arkansas. The kids are going to start asking questions tonight when Sarah doesn't come home."

"So what's the game plan on finding her?"

"Well, they've figured out how Hiram Legrand and my brother were communicating," I said. "They're reading through the messages now, but it's going to take a while to analyze. By then, who knows what Eli will do. He's desperate."

Rev. Rigsby nodded thoughtfully. When I was about to take my leave, he asked, "In all your interactions with Hiram Legrand, did he give you any hint at all about where he had been hiding that little Marshall girl? Or your own kids?"

"A little, but not much," I said. "He never said a word about my grandfather's cabin. When I first met him, he did suggest that storage facility, Midsouth Storage, the one with the big sign out front. But the cops checked that out right away and all the storage

322

facilities for miles around. The FBI has chalked that up to misinformation."

"Nothing else?"

"Well, the second time I met with Legrand, he was pretty fired up, and we got into it a little bit," I said. "He threatened to let my kids rot in a cellar somewhere. The FBI thinks that's misinformation, too. My grandfather's cabin doesn't even have a cellar. It just has a foundation of fieldstones resting on dirt."

"Oh," he said.

I nodded and we both stood up. He walked me down the hallway on the way out the door. As he held the door open for me, he said, "I'm really pulling for you, Luke. Maybe the FBI will be able to figure something out from those emails between Hiram and Eli. If they can cross-check between the two of them, they might be able to zero in on where Sarah might be. That's what you have to hope for, anyway."

"What do you mean, 'cross-check'?" I asked.

"Well, all along you've been looking at the hints from Hiram Legrand's perspective," he said. "So, when he hinted at a storage facility, you were looking at what storage facilities Hiram Legrand would think of. Now you need to think about what storage facilities your brother would be thinking about. It may be that Eli picked out the storage facility, and Hiram just spilled the beans a little."

That wasn't a bad idea. I considered it for a minute before I slowly shook my head.

"No, nothing comes to mind," I said. "Eli has been in prison the last few years. He doesn't know anything special about storage facilities, and there's only one in Jameston County, anyway."

"Oh, well, it was worth a try," he said. "Think on it, and maybe you'll come up with something. Maybe about that other thing he mentioned. The cellar."

"Yeah," I said. "But I can't think of any cellar Eli might be thinking about. The house we grew up in has a tiny crawlspace; that's it."

"What about those awful pictures Legrand sent you?" he asked. "I mean the ones of Henry, and then that one of Sarah. Anything about the locations of them?"

"No, not really," I said. "The one of Sarah from yesterday was a close-up, so you can't see much, but it probably was taken right outside in the woods near my grandfather's cabin. The first one of Henry, too. And the other one of Henry was taken outside this church. We figured it was just Legrand's in-your-face move about taking Henry out of his preschool here, which is just downstairs. Of course Eli grew up in this church as well, so he's familiar with it, too."

He nodded again and started to say something, but then he saw the look on my face and stopped.

"What?" he asked me.

I didn't say a thing. Instead I stared over his shoulder, looking without seeing.

"What?" he asked again. "What is it?"

Then my eyes focused on him again.

"Reverend, do you still keep the church unlocked all the time?" I asked.

"Well, yes," he said. "That was a tradition Rev. Crosley started, and I thought it was a very good one. The house of the Lord is always open to everyone. There's basically no crime in Jameston. Why do you ask?"

324

"Were you here a few hours ago? Was anyone here late this afternoon?"

"No, I wasn't here," he said. "The church is always empty late on Sunday afternoons. Everyone has gone to church already and is at home making Sunday dinner and getting ready for the week."

I kept staring at him, my breathing coming faster and faster until, for the second time that day, all the windows in my mind's eye aligned, and I could see straight through them all, deeply and clearly.

"He's in the cellar here, right here in the church, below us!" Running down the hall, I shouted back at Rev. Rigsby over my shoulder to call the FBI.

***

When our church had been rebuilt in the late 1800s, the builders had dug a very large cellar underneath it. It wasn't a proper base-ment – its floor was just dirt – and it initially had served in those pre-refrigeration days as a root cellar as well as a huge storage place. Over a century later, when I was 13 or 14 or so and getting ready for my confirmation, Rev. Crosley had taken our youth group down there. We each had only a candle to cut through the darkness. He tried to teach a serious lesson about the early Chris-tian catacombs, but we had all goofed around in the dark, so after about 10 minutes, Rev. Crosley had given up and sent us all back upstairs.

Eli knew about the cellar. Rev. Crosley did the same little lesson with each new youth group preparing for confirmation, Eli when it was his turn just the same as mine.

I ran down the hallway, and through some little nooks and crannies of the old church, until I got to the cellar door. I threw it open and ran headlong down the sloping ramp to the cellar before skidding to a stop at the bottom in the darkness.

Across from me, about sixty feet away and seated next to an oil lamp burning low, was Sarah. She was duct-taped around virtually her entire body, and she even had a strip of duct tape across her mouth. But her eyes were open, and she was breathing.

I looked wildly around the cellar in the darkness beyond the dim light of the oil lamp. Empty. Eli must be out doing some godforsaken thing, maybe posting a picture of my wife somewhere to torture me. Well, I was going to get the last laugh, I thought, as I ran across the room to her.

Chapter 60

10:30 p.m.
Sunday night

<u>Sarah Andrews</u>

When I regained consciousness, I was alone in the cellar, and a piece of duct tape was across my mouth. I tried to scream, but with my mouth held shut by the heavy tape, the sound in my throat was weak. Eli was gone. He had left the little oil lamp next to me.

I had been sitting there for an indeterminate time when the door to the cellar banged open and someone ran in. I couldn't see who it was. The light from the little oil lamp died out after 40 feet or so, and the cellar was much bigger than that. But there was just enough light from the door the person had left open for me to see that it was a man, and he was moving towards me.

Despite myself, I started breathing heavy out of fear, but when the man got within about 30 feet, there was just enough light to see he was Luke. And for one delicious second, I felt intense relief at being rescued by my husband.

Then, out of the darkest part of one corner, I saw a sudden blur of movement. Eli slammed into Luke at a full run, driving his shoulder into Luke and knocking Luke to the dirt floor below.

The two of them rolled on the floor. Luke shoved Eli's face with his hand to try to get Eli off of him, but Eli bit down on Luke's finger, and Luke yelled in pain. Then the two men ripped apart and scrambled to their feet, facing each other with their fists up.

"You bastard," Eli said to Luke, venom dripping from every syllable. "I'm going to kill her right here in front of you. You ruined my life. Now I'm going to ruin yours."

"Eli --," Luke started, but was cut off by Eli attacking him with a powerful, stomping kick aimed at Luke's knee that surely was intended to dislocate his kneecap. Luke saw it coming and pulled his leg back, but in so doing he was off balance, and Eli slammed a punch into Luke's jaw, sending Luke backpedaling until his back hit the wall of the cellar. Eli quickly followed up with a vicious kick aimed at Luke's gut. If he'd connected it might have ruptured something in Luke's insides, but Luke recovered just fast enough to sidestep it.

Then the two men were face to face just a few feet apart, fists up, feinting and moving in awful wordlessness for several seconds, the only sounds their breathing and the scuffing of their shoes on the dirt floor of the cellar. Luke spit red twice, and I knew blood was filling his mouth from where Eli had hit him.

Eli was moving a little faster than Luke, his anger driving him hard. I caught glimpses of Luke's face as the two men circled, and Luke still looked hurt from the punch. Then Eli quickly fired a kick aimed at Luke's ribs, and though Luke got his left arm down in time to block it, he yelped loudly as Eli's kick slammed into his arm. Luke's arm then hung limply, and he was grimacing in pain and unable to lift that arm.

Luke kept dodging Eli, trying to protect his limp left arm and his left side, but Eli kept cutting Luke off as Luke tried to circle away from him. Finally, when Luke stumbled just a touch, Eli seized the opportunity and threw another vicious kick straight at the same limp arm.

Almost quicker than I could see, Luke's limp arm suddenly sprang to life, and he caught Eli's kick in mid-air. For a split second, with Luke holding Eli's leg off the ground in the crook of his arm, Eli was standing on just one leg. Then Luke stepped in and stomped his foot hard into the shin of that leg on which Eli was standing, and it bent backwards at an impossible angle, breaking as audibly as a broomstick snapping in half. With a scream of agony, Eli fell to his back.

Luke stood over Eli, his fists still raised, listening to Eli's groans of pain. Eli was at Luke's mercy. Luke could reach down and kill him, literally with his bare hands. But he didn't. He waited, and when Eli scooted backwards to a sitting position ten feet away from Luke, his hands clutching his badly broken leg, Luke didn't follow. He just waited until Eli was quiet and looking him in the eyes.

"You fell for the oldest trick Dad showed us," Luke said. "Pretend you're hurt. Let the other guy get over-aggressive and do something stupid. Then take him out."

"Go to hell," Eli said through clenched teeth, breathing heavy and sweating from the pain in his broken leg. "I had nowhere near the time you had with Dad."

"I showed you, too."

"You didn't show me anything, you backstabbing bastard," Eli said bitterly. "You ran off when I was a kid. Completely ignored me. You know you did."

Luke was quiet for a few moments, then lowered his fists.

"I should have done more," Luke said. "I've always been sorry I didn't."

"Take your sorry and shove it up your ass. If you were sorry, you wouldn't have had me locked up like an animal for 20 years."

A shuffling of feet and a flashlight behind them caught Luke's attention, and he looked away long enough to see who was coming.

"Oh, thank goodness," Rev. Rigsby said, relaxing when he saw that Luke and I were safe. "I called the cops. They're going to be here in 10 minutes or less."

"Good," Luke said, then he turned back to look down at Eli.

"You see?" Luke asked Eli. "It was all for nothing. You're about to be arrested, at the very least for kidnapping your own niece and nephew. You were going to be released from prison when you were in your 40s, and you could still build a new life for yourself. Now you're going back, and you'll be there for the rest of your life."

"*You* put me in prison," Eli said, his face a mask of black rage. "And you robbed me of the best years of my life. All of this is your fault. I'm not going there the rest of my life. I'll kill myself before I spend another week there."

Luke shook his head.

"Mom and Dad would be ashamed of you right now," Luke said, and then he turned away from his brother, walked over to me, and knelt down. Ever so gingerly, he pulled at the duct tape across my mouth until it was free, and as soon as it was he kissed me on the lips.

"The kids are fine," he said. "Safe, healthy, and happy. They're at home with cops all around our house standing guard

330

over them. You saved them, Sarah. I have no idea how you did it, but you saved them."

I choked out, "Just get this stuff off my arms so I can hug you."

Luke found a tag end of the duct tape Eli had used and started carefully unraveling it around me. As he did, he kept glancing back over his shoulder at his brother to make sure he wasn't going anywhere, but with that broken leg Eli wasn't budging, and Rev. Rigsby was awkwardly standing guard nearby.

"I was watching you, Luke," Eli called over as Luke ripped the last of the duct tape off of me and threw it off to the side. "I came down from Grandpa's cabin and watched you. I could have killed you any night this week. It was all I could do not to kill you when I followed you to the sheriff's office and knocked you out cold in the parking lot. But I wanted you to live so that you could watch your own family disappear, then die."

Exasperated, Luke turned to his brother and said, "What in God's name happened to you, Eli? How did you turn out this way? We both lost Mom and Dad. Not just you. Both of us."

"God has nothing to do with it," Eli said. "There is no God. That's why I thought the church would be a great place to finish your family off. So you could spend the rest of your days sitting in this church, thinking about your hypocritical bullshit and trying to explain how this could have happened to you."

Scowling, Luke asked, "Where are you getting this crap? Some loser you met in prison?"

"It's the truth," Eli said defiantly. "There is no God. But you sure tried to play God, didn't you, big brother? You, the high and mighty Luke Andrews, decided what was going to happen to me. I came to you looking for your help, and you responded by putting me in that hellhole of a prison for years. But no, it wasn't someone in prison who helped me figure out that you're a hypocrite. It was Hiram's father."

"Hiram Legrand's father?" Luke asked. "Who's that?"

"Judge Carter," I answered.

Luke's head snapped back at me, his face stunned.

"Really?"

"Really," I said.

I heard an unpleasant chuckle behind Luke's back, over where Rev. Rigsby and Eli were.

"No, not really," Rev. Rigsby said, and he pulled a black revolver out of his pocket and shot Eli in the chest. Then he turned and walked a few steps to Luke and me, and pointed his gun right at us.

"No, not really at all," he said.

Chapter 61

10:55 p.m.
Sunday night

<u>Luke Andrews</u>

The blast from Rev. Rigsby's gun echoed loudly in the enclosed emptiness of the cellar. He had fired at Eli from not more than 10 feet away. The bullet tore a hole in Eli's sternum and ripped out his back, burying itself in the dirt below. It destroyed Eli's heart instantaneously, I knew. The life went out of my brother's eyes almost as fast.

"I am Hiram Legrand's father," Rev. Rigsby said, pointing the gun at me. "Or at least I was, until your bitch wife murdered him."

I couldn't breathe, the betrayal stunned me so badly.

"Wh-what, why?" I stammered.

"Where is God now?" Rigsby demanded of me. "You said your prayer. You knelt in front of your altar. You're in your church. So where is your god now?"

"What are you doing?" I sputtered, utterly bewildered, meaningful words escaping me. "I mean, you're supposed to be the pastor of this church."

"This church is a complete fraud," he said. "And every so-called Christian pastor is a big liar. I'm probably more honest than any of them."

I was speechless, unable to process what was happening. Rigsby saw that, and he flashed an unpleasant smile at my bewilderment.

"I just killed your brother, Luke," Rigsby said. "Eli said he'd protect Hiram if we would help him steal away your family. Eli failed. So I got rid of him just now. And now I'm about to kill you and your wife, too. What's more is, I'm going to get away with it. Everyone here is going to believe that Eli killed both of you. They'll treat me as a hero for being the one who finally stopped Eli."

Rigsby chuckled a little at that. He paused a moment to wipe sweat from his forehead with his gun hand. Then pointed the gun back at us.

"So say it, Luke," Rigsby said. "Say there is no God, and I might kill you first so you don't have to watch her die. I'll just put one in your head, instead of gut-shooting her first so you have to watch her writhe in pain until she dies. I might even give your kids a pass."

I looked back at Sarah, and I saw that her terror was complete. Rigsby was going to kill us. There was no doubt, and we both knew it.

"Come on, Luke," Rigsby said, cocking the hammer of his revolver. "At least say that God hates you, and that's why He's doing this to you. I'll take that."

I faced him for a few long moments, like I was thinking about it. Then, turning back to Sarah, I held her hand in mine and squeezed it gently.

"I love you, sweetheart," I whispered to her. "I love you so much. Tell the kids that I love them, too. Tell them that we'll all be together again someday." Taking one last look into her eyes, I squeezed her hand one more time, and said again, "I love you, Sarah."

With that, I wheeled back toward Rigsby and charged him, stretching to use every bit of my body to shield Sarah as I ran straight at the gun he was raising at me.

Epilogue

One week later

<u>Sarah Andrews</u>

I let Luke sleep late, as I had every day the past week. He was lying on his back next to me, wearing just his gray sweatpants. I was watching his chest and stomach peacefully rise and fall with each breath. The kids were downstairs, glued to a Thomas the Tank Engine video.

For the hundredth time, I thought back to a week ago when Luke ripped himself away from me to charge Rigsby in the cellar of the church. He was never going to make it. Rigsby had been at least 20 feet away from us. He easily had the time to fire off a shot at a range no one could miss, and Luke knew it. He had only hoped to live long enough after Rigsby buried a bullet in his chest to tackle Rigsby, and give me a chance to run, escape, and live.

But Rigsby himself hadn't lived long enough to take that shot. Agent Healey's bullet had seen to that. Her arrival in the church cellar had been nothing short of miraculous.

When it had all been over, Luke had come back to me and held both my hands. Then, even though I was not hurt, he had bodily carried me out of the cellar of the church. Somehow it was

339

just the right thing. Luke always knew how to make me feel safe, gloriously, wonderfully safe, without making me feel weak.

Propped up on one elbow in our bed, I watched him sleep for a while. His face was serene, and I was glad. The first few days this week, he'd awakened several times with a start and anxiously leaned over to check on me as I pretended to be asleep. Then he would kiss me softly before tiptoeing down the hall to check on the kids, lingering in each room before he eventually came back to bed. But he'd gained a little more peace every day this week, until last night for the first time he'd slept all the way through the night.

Using the tip of my finger, I curled one of the longer strands of Luke's hair. A soft breeze brought the warm morning air through the open windows of our bedroom, carrying in the clean scent of lilacs from the outside.

The sun was rising above the rolling hills and grassy fields outside our window. During the middle of the day, they were an intense green, as if God had inhaled deeply and, in that one great breath, pulled vibrant color from the moist earth below. Then later tonight, as brightness of spring gradually faded for the day, the evening shadows would soothe the land to sleep, releasing the smells and sounds and taste of springtime at dark.

Glancing at the door to our bedroom to make sure it was locked, I started kissing Luke's face gently to wake him, soft little butterfly kisses that just barely touched the skin of his cheeks, his chin, his forehead. When our eyes met, I walked my fingers across his chest and belly until he smiled and reached for me.

***

Luke Andrews

The FBI agents unraveled things the rest of the way within a few days after it was all over, though they respectfully waited until after my brother's funeral to tell me about it.

They confirmed that Eli and Hiram Legrand had been prison cellmates for nearly a year at the Wytheville State Prison. More than long enough for Eli to read correctly Hiram's near inhumanity, his joy for inflicting pain. And he had directed Hiram straight at me and my family. As awful as Hiram was, he had just been Eli's tool.

Even so, Hiram had been almost too much to handle. It was clear now that the kidnapping of Mary Beth Marshall was never in Eli's plans. Hiram was not nearly as smart as my brother, and he had jumped the gun and snatched Mary Beth away to feed his own rabid need.

I wondered if my brother had been calm or panicked when Legrand had proven unpredictable and got himself caught for kidnapping Mary Beth.

Judge Carter was trying to wheedle his way into some kind of plea bargain, but the federal prosecutors weren't biting. Judge Carter was no relation to Hiram Legrand; Legrand had just been jerking Sarah around. But it turned out that Judge Carter was quite broke. What remained of the family trust fund established over a century earlier had emptied due to bad investments. The fancy plantation was heavily mortgaged, and now, many generations after the first rich Carter ancestor had established it, it was co-owned by so many cousins, nieces, and nephews that his interest was diluted almost to the point of nothing. The job of state circuit judge came with lots of prestige but comparatively few dollars in the paychecks, and he'd simply been out of money.

Rigsby, with his fine nose for sin, had noticed months ago that Judge Carter was tough on most crime but strangely lenient on certain drug dealers. He learned that Judge Carter had been on the take for several years, taking hefty bribes to go easy on dealers and drug runners who happened to get caught on the 20 mile stretch of the interstate that ran through Jameston County. That money helped him continue to live the wealthy lifestyle to which he was accustomed.

Extorting Judge Carter with the threat of exposure had not been hard for Rigsby, because the judge was terrified at the prospect of going to prison himself. Even so, Rigsby knew better than to ask the judge for too much on the first approach. So he lied and told the judge that my brother just wanted to leave Virginia quietly, and move out west to start life over. The judge pretended to be reluctant, but in truth he was relieved that the request was not too big, and he signed the release order for my brother in exchange for Rigsby's silence.

But once the judge had done that, Rigsby owned him. Classic blackmail. It never ends. When Legrand snatched Mary Beth, Rigsby had the idea of making the judge get me involved in the case, and then making the judge keep him up to date on the FBI's search. Later, the judge had been much more resistant to helping Legrand escape from his own chambers. But Rigsby had described in colorful terms how some inmates would like to pay a visit to the unguarded prison cell of a disgraced ex-judge, and how Legrand had some particularly brutal friends still on the inside. Judge Carter's knees had turned to water, so he opened his chambers for Rigsby and went to get a cup of coffee. Rigsby planted the handcuff key in the couch, which the judge knew, and also the stolen gun, which the judge did not know.

After the escape and the shooting in chambers, the judge was utterly defenseless to blackmail. Rigsby had taunted him with the knowledge he had that could ruin the judge. He made sure to tell the judge all about the misery of prison for weaker inmates in the presence of stronger, violent inmates. Rigsby had threatened him with exposure so relentlessly and torqued him up so much that finally he was willing to shoot at my wife to cover up what he had done.

Legrand's first escape had been all Rigsby, though. Under the guise of stopping by to talk about the prison ministry at the jail, Rigsby had visited Amos Hudson at his home the evening Legrand first had been arrested. A visit to Amos's bathroom was all Rigsby needed to swipe Amos's master key from a keychain hanging on the peg rack in the hallway. Rigsby had followed up later that evening with an email to Amos. That email had an attachment that explained some of the new plans Rigsby wanted to suggest to expand the ministry. Amos guilelessly clicked on and read the attachment, which surreptitiously installed the malware program on his computer.

The frame-up for Legrand's second escape involved a much more low-tech approach. While Amos was out jogging after work just before Legrand's second escape, Rigsby apparently had slipped right into Amos's house and taken his service sidearm off his dresser, then stuffed it in the judge's couch a couple of hours later. Amos's shock later that night that his sidearm was missing had been genuine. If Rigsby had been just a little less aggressive about framing Amos Hudson, it may have stuck for a lot longer than it did.

Rev. Crosley had recovered completely from his recent hospital stay. The day after I brought Sarah home from the church cellar, I called over to Wilson Medical Center and asked the attending physician to run some tests on Rev. Crosley's blood. It had taken just a few guesses to get it right. Rohypnol has an active metabolite with a long half-life, and the tests had caught it. The night Rigsby had gone to see Rev. Crosley, he'd spiked Rev. Crosley's tea heavily with Rohypnol, or roofies, as the date-rape drug is commonly known. A massive dose would result in unconsciousness, coma, and if the victim was left untreated, even death. When Jan had stopped by and found Rev. Crosley face down, and raced him to the hospital, she had saved his life.

Rigsby himself was beyond understanding. Though no one had known it, Rigsby indeed was Hiram's father. He apparently had impregnated a 16-year-old girl, one Annie Lee Legrand, who had been a member of a backwoods congregation he led briefly some 30 years ago up in the Ozarks. Little was known of the relationship between Rigsby and Legrand as Legrand was growing up. Initial investigation revealed some recollections, by older members of churches in which Rigsby had preached long ago, of a young boy hanging around who Rigsby had described as a visiting nephew. Some thought that boy's name might have been Hiram. Others disagreed.

Due to some of the materials Agent Healey found on Rigsby's computer, she speculated that Rigsby himself had been abused when he was a child by a minister of some kind and was spending his adult life getting revenge. And indeed an investigation into his career as a preacher showed he'd been a one-man wrecking crew for a dozen small churches over the years. There had been a series of missing church funds, affairs with female church members, and sudden departures in the night from rural congregations throughout the South. Coming to our church to help Hiram and Eli get to me had been natural for him. Wherever he could hurt others, cause misery, or destroy faith, was home to him.

Agent Byram wasn't impressed with the speculation that Rigsby perhaps had been abused as a child. He wasn't convinced that this was why Rigsby worked hard to hurt the churches he snaked his way into, or how he knew how to strike such fear in the heart of a weak man, such as Judge Carter.

Sometimes, Byram said, people are just evil.

***

When Rigsby goaded me into my discovery of Eli in the church's cellar and I ran off down the hallway, he of course never called the cops. Rather, with Legrand dead and my brother and the judge exposed, Rigsby knew he had only one play left to make. He had to get rid of my brother, Sarah, and me. Then all he would have to do is ridicule whatever desperate claims a corrupt ex-judge might make about supposedly being extorted by the nice new preacher in town.

It was a smart play. It might have worked, and he even might have been praised as the man who stopped prison escapee Eli Andrews from his criminal partnership with the notorious Hiram Legrand, if it wasn't for Jeanne Healey.

Agent Healey was working by herself in town when I went to the church last Sunday night. Just as I was dashing down the hallway to the church's cellar, she had found LinkedIn messages between Rigsby and Eli. She sprinted to her car and raced over to the church, getting there just in time to hear Rigsby shoot my brother. She found the open cellar door and quietly slipped in as Rigsby was mocking me. She was taking aim at the back of Rigsby's head in the very moment I'd charged him, and in so doing, she saved my life.

I spent time on the phone with my congressman's staff earlier this week, asking them to support her for the FBI's highest award for valor. When she stopped by the house to thank me, she brought a printout of a strand of LinkedIn messages between Rigsby and Eli. They'd been written five months ago.

I walked up to Grandpa's cabin to read them:

LinkedIn Message

To: Elijah E. Andrews

From: Reginald Rigsby, Esq.

Did you read the essay I sent to you?

LinkedIn Message

To: Reginald Rigsby, Esq.

From: Elijah E. Andrews

Yes. Interesting.

LinkedIn Message

To: Elijah E. Andrews

From: Reginald Rigsby, Esq.

It <u>is</u> interesting, isn't it? The Christian apologists say their god can do anything. If you were all powerful, wouldn't you immediately feed the hungry? Stop all wars? Free the innocent? Make sick people healthy? But the Christian god does none of these things.

LinkedIn Message
To: Reginald Rigsby, Esq.
From: Elijah E. Andrews

That backstabber I used to call my brother once sent me a Bible verse that said we can't know the reasons why God does what he does.

LinkedIn Message
To: Elijah E. Andrews
From: Reginald Rigsby, Esq.

Christians love to say that the Christian god is a mystery. But Christians still must believe that their god would do SOMETHING to help. Yet he never does. Innocent people die. Good people are locked in jails. And the Christian god does nothing about it.

LinkedIn Message
To: Reginald Rigsby, Esq.
From: Elijah E. Andrews

All good points

LinkedIn Message
To: Elijah E. Andrews
From: Reginald Rigsby, Esq.

Yes. If you had the power, would you have allowed your parents to die in a horrible car accident, leaving you exposed to abandonment by
your brother? No, you would never have let that
happen. You would have saved your parents,
and yourself. But if the Christian god exists,
then the Christian god let those things happen
to you.

"Oh, Eli," I said to the wind blowing across the overgrown field at Grandpa's cabin after I finished reading. Then I tore those plain sheets of white paper into small bits and threw them up to be scattered by the wind. In the coming seasons, they would be rained on, then dried by the sun, then rained on and dried again, the cycle repeating over and over until eventually the little pieces of paper broke down and disintegrated, becoming part of the dirt underfoot.

I had stayed up there on the mountain a long time that late afternoon, saying goodbye to my brother in my own way.

***

Sunday morning

In the morning before church, Sarah and I had held hands and walked outside with Emma and Henry. Yellow buttercups were popping up in the lawn around the house, flecking the thick green grass with their buttery-yellow petals. I would cut the grass when we got home from church. We were going to have a cookout at our place later in the afternoon for all the searchers and volunteers who helped us, and I wanted the place to look sharp.

When we got to the church, we found Rev. Crosley seated on the chair next to the pulpit in front of the congregation. He had stopped the chemotherapy, though he still gratefully accepted the pain meds I gave him. He told me he wanted to live comfortably and well for what remained of his life, and that was all.

Sarah and I sat in one of the middle pews with Henry and Emma between us. Sarah's hair was pulled up on one side with a barrette. The weather this first Sunday in May was warm, and she was wearing a springtime dress that went a bit below her knee. When she crossed her legs and rolled one foot around on its ankle, I took in her pretty calves. Then she saw me looking and reached over the kids to give me a little nudge.

"You're a sinner, Luke Andrews, looking at me like that in church," she whispered with a smile on her face.

"I don't think Rev. Crosley would mind too much."

"Better throw an extra ten bucks in the plate when they pass it around, just to be safe."

"I will."

When Rev. Crosley rose to speak at the pulpit, the eyes of the whole congregation were on him. His voice was neither deep nor strong, but none of us missed a word he said.

When I was young, my father wanted me to grow up to be a scientist. So he always made sure I was taking the right science classes at school, and over summer breaks he often brought home books for me to read.

One day he brought home some books by chess grandmasters. He had heard that some of the best scientists in the world kept their minds sharp with chess, and we had an old chess set around the house.

I tried to understand the books he gave me, but I couldn't. I'd stare at the pages, but I could not follow their intricate strategies or see ten moves down the road, like the grandmasters could. I was just nowhere near up to their level.

Later, my father gave me a book about Albert Einstein's discoveries. This was high-end stuff. Using just a pencil and paper, Einstein figured out how gravity equaled time, and time was really energy, and gravity and time could bend light. Or something like that. Even now I can't say it right. Einstein's work was so far beyond me that I couldn't begin to understand it. Again, just like with the chess grandmasters, I was nowhere near up to Einstein's level. I couldn't begin to understand what he was saying.

Now, the answers were there. There were complex strategies that would win the game for the chess grandmasters. And Einstein had solved some of the great puzzles of physics, if you could follow him. Those answers were there. I just couldn't see them.

Did my inability to see those answers that grandmasters saw in chess, or that Einstein saw in theoretic physics, mean that there were no answers?

351

No, of course not. My inability to see those answers didn't mean there weren't any. I couldn't understand them, couldn't see the answers, but they were there.

Why then should our inability to understand God's reasoning be any different? Why should we think that we are up to the level of God's understanding in all the mysteries of life? Why should we believe that there are no answers to why He does what He does, simply because we as ordinary people are not able to see those answers?

Those words hung in the air as Rev. Crosley gingerly got out from behind the pulpit and stepped down from the altar. Once he was down to the level of the congregation, he stood in the center aisle in our midst and finished his sermon.

On Palm Sunday, Jesus came into Jerusalem riding a donkey with adoring crowds laying palm branches in his path and saying "Hosanna!," the ancient Aramaic word meaning, "Save us." It was nothing less than a call to Jesus for divine help.

But before that week was done, Jesus was betrayed by his own disciple in exchange for just 30 silver pieces. Another disciple abandoned Jesus, swore he didn't even know Jesus, rather stand up for him. And the crowds of people that had adored him at the start of the week allowed him to be crucified, and killed, just a few days later.

Yet after that week was over, on the first Easter Sunday, Jesus arose from the dead to save us. All of us. Even those who had persecuted him so terribly.

This is the message of faith, hope, and love we have in the midst of a world of doubt and pain. We can be angry at Jesus. We can deny Jesus and abandon him. We can even allow him to be whipped, crucified, and killed. But God will never stop loving us. God follows us wherever we go, with boundless love. And when He does, He walks to us on feet that once were crucified and now are healed, and he comforts us with hands that once were crucified and now are whole.

This is why we celebrate the great love of God. It is not always understood by us, sometimes even rejected by us, but always is there for us.

And that is why we sing.

As Rev. Crosley made his way back up the steps of the altar, the choir burst into a hymn. It was not a somber hymn, but instead a bright and sunny one, a song of hope and joy, of bursting spring-time, of a new dawning. As the congregation joined in, the words in response to their verse came unbidden to my lips.

"Amen, pastor," I said. "Amen."

THE END

Albemarle County, Virginia
April 7, 2015

Closing Note

I hope you liked *Virginia Dawning*, although I realize that it may have been a little hard to read at times. Even in fiction, and even when you expect a happy ending, the thought of children being kidnapped away from their loved ones is not a pleasant one.

But evil must be confronted, for it exists. Yes, I know there are some who say that there is no evil, that there is no right or wrong, and that everything is relative. But I don't buy it. Take war alone. Those who have seen the atrocities of war, heard the anguish of its victims, smelled its smoldering ruins so strongly that they could taste it in their mouths – they do not deny that evil exists. It does exist. The real question, for all of us, is how to deal with it.

I don't claim to know the answer, but surely the right answer about what to do about evil has a lot to do with love.

English speakers only have one word for love, but the ancient Greeks had many. There is *pragma*, the warm and deep love of a married couple for each other, which you see between Sarah and Luke Andrews in this novel. (There also is some *eros* between these two, but this is not *that* kind of novel.) Then there is *storge*, the natural love and attachment of parents to their children, as Luke and Sarah feel for their two little ones. There also is *philia*, a brotherly love, such as the strong bond between comrades-at-arms, which you hopefully saw between Luke and his best friend, Stumps Dixon.

And finally there is *agape*, the charitable love shown not just to friends or offspring or husbands and wives, but to everyone. It is love given even when it is not reciprocated. It is love given even when it comes at a sacrifice. *Agape* is the hardest one for people to show.

If evil is the absence of good, just as darkness is simply the absence of light, then maybe the best way to overcome evil is to spread as much good as we can, for as long as we can, wherever we can.

And what is good? Well, Paul once wrote to a group of people in the ancient Greek city of Corinth that at the end of it all, when it's time to count what really matters, all that is left is faith, hope, and love, and the greatest of these is love.

The greatest of these is love.

Maybe that's the answer to the question. When we look at the suffering we see in the world, and we ask God why He doesn't do something about it, perhaps His gentle reply is, "I already did. I created you."

So go love as much as you can. Love of all kinds, wherever you can, whenever you can, for as long as you can. It'll do some good.

-John Davidson

Acknowledgements

So many people helped me with this book. To all of you, I am grateful.

A big thanks go to Matthew Bowen, Sean Gibbons, Anne Hadley, Nancy Healey, Jean Hudson, John Kitzmann, Beth McMahon, Steve Emmert, Sarah Santos, Terry Tereskerz, and Jeremy Tor for patiently reading early drafts of this novel and offering invaluable suggestions for improvement.

I owe a major debt of gratitude to my parents and the family that came before them. On both sides, they were dirt-poor immigrants to the United States. They had enormous courage to shake a leg and get on over here. If it weren't for them, I wouldn't be me.

I'd like to thank FBI Agent Jane Collins for her helpful insights into the crucial work of the FBI. She is a credit to the Bureau. I'd also like to thank my buddy and fellow wrestling fan, Dr. Mark Lepsch, M.D., for helping me with some of the medicine in this novel. Any errors in this novel are entirely my own, and were made despite the efforts of these and other kind people to save me from myself.

I must also thank the great lawyers of the Virginia Trial Lawyers Association. The kind comments and encouragement of so many of you kept nudging me along to completion. Your clients know, just as I do, of the tremendous work you do on behalf of justice. Keep it up, and ignore the snarky naysayers.

I cannot thank John Grisham enough. For reasons that escape me, he picked both of my short stories, the only two I have ever written, out of stacks of submissions in a fiction-writing contest held during the Virginia Festival of the Book. When *The Hook's* stellar editor-in-chief, Hawes Spencer, called me to tell me I'd won, the two of them unknowingly gave me the boot in the tail I needed to write this novel. I am eternally grateful for Mr. Grisham's kind comments and advice.

Finally but most importantly, I thank my wonderful wife, Gail. A teacher of English with a heart of gold and the pen of a poet, you are my first, last, and greatest editor. Hands down, you are the best choice I have ever made in my life. In this moment of completion, I just wanted to say, I love you.